The Tokyo Bicycle Bakery

Su Young Lee

ISBN: 9798677593451

WORKS BY SU YOUNG LEE

The Tokyo Bicycle Bakery

For Mike, Linc and Church

1. Cheesecake with a mirror glaze cherry on top

Tokyo's Narita Airport was as lively as a sunny sea town in the peak summer season. Hana walked along the main concourse dragging her suitcase and staring wide-eyed at all the crowds. It seemed lots of people were coming back from or going away on holiday. She walked past one group of tourists holding surf boards and wearing aloha t-shirts, past another bunch of businessmen in dandy suits carrying briefcases, then stopped in front of a red telephone box.

She felt scared and excited at the same time. She closed her eyes and thought about the last time she'd seen Jin. It was on a night ferry from Korea to Japan over a year ago, before he'd started his studies in Tokyo. Hana remembered dim moonlight on the East Sea, winding narrow roads in the backstreets of Osaka, a watercolor purple sunset and Jin's soft and warm hands.

Someone brushed past her, dragging her back to the present. She looked at the phone box and counted to five slowly and thoroughly in her mind. It was an old habit of hers, to count to five whenever she felt nervous.

"Why five?" Jin had asked her once. "Why can't it be three or four?"

"Isn't five a perfect number?" she'd answered. "A hand has four fingers and a thumb and a foot has five toes. It makes me calm and relaxed."

Jin had just smiled.

After counting to five, Hana took a deep breath and picked up the phone. She took a notebook out of her bag and read the number, pushing the small square buttons on the phone pad carefully. 080-333...

"Hi, I can't answer the phone right now. Please leave a message."

It was Jin's low and husky voice.

Hana's heart sank. It was over two months since he'd answered his phone. He'd warned her this might happen; he was busy preparing for his classes and dissertation before the summer holiday started, but he hadn't answered the phone or replied to her emails once since then. It was so strange, because they'd been planning to move in together once she finished university, and that was only one term away now.

They'd both been excited about the plan: Hana had started studying Japanese, saving money from part-time jobs, and even gotten her working holiday visa. Then Jin had simply stopped contacting her.

"It's me, Hana," she said into the receiver. "I've just arrived in Tokyo. Surprise! I couldn't wait to hear from you, so I've come anyway." She took a breath and continued. "Are you in school? I'll come to your place and wait there. Good luck with your class and see you soon."

As soon as she hung up the phone, her mind cleared a little. She was here to meet Jin, so that's what she would do. Whatever happened, at least she'd get some answers. She nodded firmly to herself, clutched the suitcase handle tightly and strode to the Limousine Bus station on the opposite side of the airport lobby.

The huge Departures blackboard stopped her dead. It was filled up with lots of different destinations and departure times. Shinjuku, Shibuya, Yokohama... Hana blinked her tired dry eyes and read the Japanese characters one by one.

"Where are you headed?"

Hana turned. A young salesgirl with red lipstick and a perfect sleek ponytail was looking at her.

"One ticket to Shinjuku please," Hana replied in slow but clear Japanese.

"Single or return?"

Hana had to think for a few seconds. "Single."

The girl printed a ticket, put it on the desk and circled the exit gate and departure time with a red pen. "Exit 2. The bus will leave in ten minutes so you can head over now."

As soon as she stepped outside of the Arrivals lounge, a steamy hot wind blew strands of her hair across her face, sticking it to her clammy cheeks. She brushed the strands away and tied them back with a hair band. In moments a Limousine Bus stopped in front of her and the bus driver came over. He checked her ticket and quickly put her suitcase in the luggage compartment under the bus. His every movement was smooth and efficient, like a ballet dancer. Hana climbed up the steep steps into the bus. The cool, dry air-conditioned air was a welcome relief. She sat in a window seat at the back of the bus.

"This bus is leaving soon. Please fasten your seat belt."

The Limousine Bus departed after the driver's announcement. Soon hills, small trees and rice farms appeared through the windows, but the green slowly changed into gray as buildings and houses sprang up. Hana leaned her head against the window frame and fell asleep. She had a dream of eating a twisted red popsicle with Jin, sitting next to each other on a balcony with a sea view. Her lips and tongue became rhubarb-red and a sweet and sour strawberry taste filled her mouth. The sunshine on her cheeks was beautifully warm.

"This is Shinjuku. Shinjuku station. Please don't leave any belongings."

Hana abruptly opened her eyes at the driver's announcement, banging her head on the window. She frowned and rubbed her forehead with her palm, then fixed her tangled hair and got off the bus, blinking in the light. Her mouth was still full of the fake strawberry taste.

Out of the bus station, she walked along a busy road past the Keio department store and into Shinjuku train station. It was a giant maze of complicated train lines and platforms, where thousands of people were walking here and there and hopping on and off different trains. Hana tightened the strap of her bag, rolled the suitcase forward and walked into the crowd like a surfer getting swept away by a big human wave. She bought a green travel card with a penguin on it from a vending machine near the platform and held it tightly; this card would take her to Jin's place. Something about that felt surreal.

Jin had told her his one-room flat was located in a quiet residential area near Gokokuji shrine, just walking distance from his university, Waseda. He'd said he usually woke up to the sound of the monk in the shrine singing his morning sutra, and steadily beating two wooden blocks together in prayer.

Hana imagined Jin's sleeping face, next to a big bright window full of sunshine. Jin sometimes looked like a monk or a priest; he had a different kind of aura from normal young guys in their early twenties, which Hana loved.

She read the tube map very carefully and double-checked Jin's address. She was planning to take the Tozai Line to Waseda from Shinjuku, then ring him again near Waseda university.

She got off at Waseda station and walked past a Kendo club, ringing with the sound of students hitting each other's plastic armor with wooden swords. At a crossing there was a weirdly shaped and colorful Gaudi-style building. She stopped in front of a telephone box on Waseda main road and called Jin again, but he didn't pick up. She now felt extremely tired, so she sat down on the steps of the tall Waseda clock tower building.

Her feet felt like they were burning in her thin trainers. She stretched her legs, moved her toes and watched students practicing a play in the clock tower courtyard. People strolled in the Japanese gardens of a nearby hotel. The sun was going down little by little, and she watched it sink with her mind empty. Soon it became completely dark, and she was on her own on the steps.

She found another phone box and called Jin one more time, but there was still no answer. She lifted her bag; it felt even heavier than before. She clutched the handle of her suitcase tightly and started walking; past a narrow bridge, past a park with a pond full of frogs and narrow saplings, past countless tall buildings and shops.

Finally, Hana found the hill where Jin lived, lined with thin wooden houses. It was not so late yet, but still there was nobody around and silence filled the air. She walked to the top of the hill and went into a nearby convenience store. The doorbell rang and the welcoming call of the staff made a cheerful and echoey harmony.

She imagined Jin picking up an onigiri seaweed rice ball and a can of chilled beer here, on the way home after finishing his classes at night. She felt weird to stand in the same place that he would usually stand. It made her excited and anxious at the same time.

She bought a bottle of sparkling wine and two slices of cheesecake. Mirror glaze red cherries sat on top of the smooth and shiny cakes. She thought of Jin's thin lips drinking the sparkling wine, and his long fingers cutting a piece of cheesecake and picking up the slice. His lips would taste like sweet cherries and his arms would be soft and warm like freshly baked genoise.

Hana left the convenience store and took out the hand-drawn map Jin had sent her several months ago. She knew his flat was nearby. She crossed another pedestrian crossing and walked into a small, steep alleyway. There was a dry cleaner's with an old and tatty sign, a ramen noodle restaurant with two red round lamps on each side, a gray concrete two-floor building which seemed like it might collapse any minute, and at the end of the alley there was a long and thin white building.

Hana stopped, let go of the suitcase handle and put the plastic bag of sparkling wine and cheesecake down on the street. She fastened her shoelaces and tied her hair back precisely. She took a tube of lip balm out of her bag and ran it over her dry lips several times. She splashed green tea perfume on her wrists and neck, then took a long, deep breath. She gripped the suitcase handle in one hand, the plastic bag in the other and entered the building.

Up the dark and narrow steps she went, her footsteps making loud echoes in the empty hallway. 201, 202, 203, 204. She stopped in front of room 205 at the end of the corridor. There was a tiny stained-glass window in the center of the sky-blue metal door, shaped like a ladybird. There was a small doorbell on the side, and she reached out to touch it. Her fingertips were trembling.

'Will he have got my messages by now?' she wondered. 'Will he be in the apartment? Will he be in the school still? Should I call him again and wait in a café nearby?' She became restless and her chest hurt. She closed her eyes and counted to five very thoughtfully, then opened her eyes and rang the doorbell. There was no answer. Hana waited for five seconds and rang the bell one more time.

Ding-dong.

The sound echoed in the dark and empty corridor. She put her eye to the tiny ladybird window. She could see a warm glow from inside. Hana pushed the bell a bit longer this time.

Ding-dong. Then footsteps were coming over. The heavy metal door opened slowly. Hana's heart started bouncing like a mad hummingbird.

The door half-opened, and then there was a girl leaning on the doorframe, half-asleep. She had long straight velvety hair and wore a short see-through slip. One of the shoulder straps had slid down off her shoulder and her big round breasts were showing clearly through the powder pink lace. Hana was so shocked she almost fell to the floor.

"Hello?" the girl said.

Hana didn't know what to say. "Isn't this Ji- Jin's apartment?" she stammered. The thin handle of her suitcase barely supported her.

The girl's eyes narrowed slightly. "Who's that?"

"Jin. His name is J-Jin Kim."

The girl frowned and shook her head. "I have no idea what you're talking about."

Hana felt confused and desperate. "It should be right here. I've got the address." She took the crumpled paper out of her pocket.

"Who's that, hon?"

Now there was a man's low voice from behind the door. Hana's mind went completely blank. The door opened wider to reveal a big, muscular guy in a black t-shirt, standing there and staring at Hana.

"Ah... I came for my boyfriend, Jin. He's studying International Business in Waseda University." Hana's eyes were full of tears and her voice felt like it was fading away in the air.

"I've never heard that name before," the guy said. "We don't buy stuff from strangers, so don't come back, and don't ring the bell again."

Even before Hana could open her mouth to reply, he shut the door. Her ears went numb from the slamming sound and everything went dark. The plastic bag dropped on the floor and the sparkling wine and the cheesecake boxes made a sharp clattering sound.

2. Monaka with tears

Hana first met Jin through a classic guitar group at Busan University in Korea. They drank cheap wine, played guitar and sang songs together on the Beauty Bench on campus. It was beautiful to watch white magnolia flowers falling from the trees while sitting on the bench. Anybody walking by when the magnolias were in bloom looked beautiful, like magic.

Hana and Jin used to sit there together and rank the people walking past. Six, seven, eight, nine. They would get tipsy and give people random numbers. One time Hana stood up and started walking and posing exaggeratedly, like a model. Jin grinned amiably and raised both hands.

"Ten. Absolute ten out of ten."

Hana fell asleep under the flickering fluorescent light in the corner of a 24-hour Internet café. 'Ten out of ten'. She had a dream of Jin giving her a big smile with his arms wide open under the moonlight, surrounded by white magnolia flowers in full bloom. His smile was beautiful, but somewhat sad and lonely.

She woke up in the early morning, and her whole body ached. She stretched her arms, went to the café's bathroom and was shocked by her face in the mirror. Her eyes were red and swollen from crying, her hair was messed up, her arm was scratched and her knee had a big bruise on it from bumping against the heavy suitcase as she walked yesterday.

She washed her face and arms with cold water, then combed her hair and tied it back with a rubber band. Her throat was burning like magma. She took a Monaka ice cream sandwich out of the fridge in the café shop and tried to pay 100 yen to the guy at the counter, a teenager with bright green hair. He just looked at Hana and rubbed the piercing through his upper lip instead of taking her money.

"That Monaka is ancient yo. It's been sitting there for years. It must be a fossil by now."

He talked like a rapper, half singing, half talking. Hana put the money down on the counter, went back to her desk and opened the Monaka without saying a word. It was rock hard and covered with lots of small bits of ice. Hana picked the ice away, then wiped a tear from her eye.

She took a bite from the crispy Monaka wafer, revealing the layers inside: vanilla ice cream and sweet bean curd. The fossil didn't taste so bad. She finished it completely and licked her fingers. Her throat felt better and her belly was slightly full. She logged into a computer, opened up her emails and started to write.

'Where are you, Jin? I'm near your apartment now. I've come to see you at the address you gave me before, but there were other people living there. Maybe I've got the wrong address. Is everything OK? Let me know as soon as you read this email. I'll wait around here.'

Hana felt emotional but forced herself not to cry. She sent the email and walked down the long and narrow steps from the Internet café, into an alley near the Waseda clock tower. A hot wind was blowing and it was hard to breathe. Cicadas were chirring loudly and the sky was clear blue with no clouds. It was a hot and humid morning and the narrow street was totally quiet.

Hana wandered along without any sense of direction or purpose, feeling lost. On a balcony overhead someone was beating dust out of a futon with a wooden bat, like a drummer practicing in a clumsily soundproofed room. On the right sat a row of old dwarf apartments and thin three-floor wooden houses with steep triangular roofs. In front of them were small cars parked perfectly like Lego blocks in each parking space, with all their side mirrors folded neatly in. There was only a tiny space between the cars, and all of them were in perfect mint condition, just like they'd come out of the manufacturer yesterday.

At the end of the alley there was a telephone box. She hurried and called Jin.

"This number is unable to take your call right now."

It was an emotionless machine voice. Hana stood there holding the phone for a while. It wasn't even his voice on the answering service now. 'Where has he disappeared to?' she wondered. She'd already lied to her parents about coming to find Jin, saying she was just staying in her friend's house for a few days. Now she didn't know what to think. She knew she should call her mom, but she didn't feel like it.

Hana's parents were always busy and angry. They'd get into big fights and blame each other for whatever small mistakes they thought Hana had made. It had made for an anxious and lonely childhood, and she'd been an introverted child anyway, not confident in making friends or socializing. She'd probably become close with Jin because he was the opposite of her parents: calm, considerate and good at listening. He'd been her sanctuary for years. From time to time he'd been like a counselor. She hadn't thought that was especially strange or weird at the time, but thinking back now, she realized she didn't know much about him.

Jin didn't particularly like anything or dislike anything. He'd always been surrounded by people at university, but like her, he didn't have any close friends either. Apart from hanging out with Hana, he spent most of his time in the library, or walking around the little mountain behind the university, or sitting and reading a book on the Beauty Bench.

She wondered. Maybe he'd planned this somehow; to avoid settling down and just disappear one day like a morning fog.

Hana was pulled from these thoughts by a tiny meowing sound. She looked around, and saw two small kittens coming toward her from a backstreet. They looked dirty and hungry, so Hana took a cheese string from her canvas bag, stripped it into small pieces, then gently put her palm down to let the kittens sniff the cheese.

They sniffed each piece carefully then ate them all in a twinkling, licking her hand when they were done. Their tiny whiskers tickled her wrist, but she didn't move until they'd completely finished their afternoon snack. One kitten had a black coat with white socks and the other kitten had a white coat with black polka dots. They looked like non-identical twins.

"Where is your mummy, kitties?" Hana asked in a whisper.

The two kittens wiped their soft pink noses on her hand instead of answering, then walked back behind some trash bins in the backstreet. Hana watched until they were out of sight, then stood up and started walking slowly forward again. In front of her a delivery man in a green and yellow uniform was holding a big cardboard box. He crossed the sidewalk and approached one of the houses.

"Delivery service," he said, knocking on the door.

"Delivery service," Hana copied in a quiet voice. She thought a delivery person didn't have to talk a lot, so it could be a good job for her, though they also had to know the area well and carry big heavy parcels, so maybe not.

She considered it further as she wandered along slowly. What if she couldn't find Jin soon? It was a big question. She didn't want to go home right away, back to her parents, but her savings wouldn't last for long. Maybe she could get a job? She had a working holiday visa, but she hadn't prepared anything else for her stay in Japan. She'd only focused on seeing Jin.

She shook her head and turned off the narrow street. She passed back by the park with the trees and the little pond, past a bridge over a river framed by cherry

14

blossom trees, and walked onto a bustling market street. A lady was out watering roses and sunflowers in front of her florist's shop. She smiled at Hana when their eyes met. A nice smell of freshly baked baguettes wafted out of an old bakery with no sign, while next door was a bicycle shop displaying heavy 'mamachari' bikes out front.

'Whale ramen – limited edition, high in collagen!'

A handwritten paper sign in the window of a ramen shop drew Hana's attention. Hana's late grandmother's specialty had been thinly sliced translucent strips of steamed whale. Well-cooked whale meat fresh out of the steamer was like fine tiramisu, with beautiful gradations of black, white and brown. Hana realized she'd only had a Monaka ice cream sandwich and nothing else that day. She went into the ramen shop without thinking twice; the sliding door made a squeaky sound.

"Welcome, how many customers?" the waiter asked in a big and cheerful voice. He had a small white towel knotted on top of his head, and wore a dark navy blue cotton apron with oil stains on the front.

"It's only me."

"Come on in, and please buy a ticket from the machine." The waiter pointed at a ticket machine just inside the door.

Hana studied the machine for a moment, then pushed the button for whale ramen and the button for kimchi. The ticket machine printed out two tickets, which she handed to the waiter. Sitting at the bar, she drank iced rooibos tea and munched bean sprouts sautéed with sesame seeds and soy sauce. The bean sprouts were cooked perfectly al dente, not too soggy, not too hard, complemented by the earthy aroma of sesame oil.

"Thank you for waiting," the waiter said, and placed a square wooden tray on the bar top before her. On top sat a bowl of hot steamy ramen and a small bowl of kimchi. She swallowed a spoonful of the clear ramen broth using a wide Chinese spoon. The heat of the mild whale broth, with just a kick of sea salt, spread throughout her body, and she finished all of it in the blink of an eye. She'd heard that eating well-made, tasty food stimulated the body's endorphins just like being in love.

When Hana opened the sliding door to leave, the sunlight was weaker than before. Further down the market street there was a small bookshop with shelves of comic books and magazines out front. Hana took a free Town magazine from a rack by the door.

Next to the bookshop there was a Yakitori barbeque restaurant, then a fish shop that had steamed red octopus and soy-sauce-marinated yellowtail fish in the window. A sweet and savory smell wafted off fried potato and meat croquettes on a skillet outside a butcher's shop. Next to that a cake shop was selling 'taiyaki' donuts in the shape of fish, filled with custard, chocolate or green tea-flavored cream. On the front stall of a tired old vegetable shop, Hana found a batch of beautiful shiny red apples that could have stolen Snow White's heart, placed delicately in woven wicker baskets. She looked up at the sign.

'Kawanami Vegetable Shop.'

The sign seemed to have been there for decades; the color was faded and the corners were worn down and coming apart. The glass door was closed, and the inside of the shop was dark with no sign of an attendant. Still, the red apples in the middle of the stall seemed to glow, calling for her to choose them.

"Hello?"

Hana called through the glass several times but there was no answer. When she was about to turn around and leave, an old lady abruptly opened the sliding door and hobbled out of the shop.

" Hello, can I please have a bag of these apples?" Hana asked, pointing.

The old lady grunted and tried to put the apples in a paper bag, but it seemed she was having some difficulty, trying to open the bag at the bottom instead of the top.

"It's OK," Hana said with a smile, giving her the money. "I'll just put them in my own bag."

The old lady opened her mouth slightly without moving any other part of her face, not even an eyebrow. "Fine." Her voice sounded like a weak wind blowing.

Hana sat on a yellow seesaw in a small children's playground and ate one of the apples. It was full of sweet and sour juice from good quality sun and soil. The flesh inside was a beautiful honey gold. She thought Snow White would not feel so sad to die from eating this apple. While she ate, she started reading the Town magazine, looking at the local jobs classifieds. Supermarket clerk, restaurant waiter, karaoke staff, pizza delivery staff... She moved onto the next page.

'Part-time Studio Assistant wanted. Designing photo albums. 3 days a week. Graphic skills highly desirable.'

Hana had won a website design competition at university, so she was quite confident with graphics programs. She drew a big circle around the photo studio job. She also found some free Japanese language classes organized by the ward office, and a local guest house advertisement with a photo of smiley young people. She finished the apple, got off the seesaw and called the guest house from a nearby phone box.

There was a space in the ladies' dormitory room, so she made a booking for herself, then went back to the Internet café. She checked her email again but there was no reply from Jin. She sighed and took her bag and suitcase from the locker. It was a long walk to the guest house along narrow, steep streets, quite far away from the station, and it was tiring to drag her heavy suitcase. She walked until she was pretty exhausted, then she took a break and looked up the hilly road.

The guest house stood at the top of the hill. The whole building was painted an overwhelmingly hot pink, so nobody could walk past without noticing its existence. Hana felt a strong sense of warmth from the owner, ensuring that her customers would never feel lost in a foreign place.

After another few minutes of hiking, Hana wiped the sweat from her face with her t-shirt sleeve and walked into the hot pink guest house. Inside it was dark, chilly and surprisingly traditional looking compared to the modern exterior. Many pieces of vintage dark wood furniture lined the walls of the lobby, well-polished, with a nice shine on their surfaces. Perhaps it was a barn or old factory conversion. The ceiling was high and had a graceful curving arch at the top. Hana met eyes with a goldfish swimming inside a fish tank filled with green leaves and seaweed. She sat down at the same level as the tank and waved at the fish.

"Hi there."

The goldfish made air bubbles when it opened its mouth.

"Hello."

A low and husky woman's voice came from over Hana's shoulder. She turned and saw a petit middle-aged lady standing behind the reception desk. She had a perfectly round cabbage-shaped hairstyle, and wore a long and flowery pink dress, quite the opposite of her masculine voice.

"You're the one who just called me, right?" the woman asked.

Hana nodded. "Yes, I'm Hana. Nice to meet you."

"I'm Oyama." The woman tilted her head to the left. "Come, follow me."

The building had one long corridor dividing it into two sides: one for men and the other for women. Ms. Oyama guided Hana up the stairs to a room on the third floor of the building. There was no elevator. Every footstep along the corridor made the old wooden floor squeak, and Hana felt relieved that she wouldn't be taken by surprise by ninjas in the middle of the night.

The room was long and narrow with three metal-frame bunk beds, like a school dormitory. There was enough space for six people, but the room seemed empty for now, with no other guests. Ms. Oyama pointed at the top of a pink bunk bed with her pink fingernails.

"Use this bed. Do not listen to music with a speaker or talk loudly after 10 pm. Try to have a shower before ten if possible. Bread, jam and tea are available from 7 am to 9 am in the kitchen, and there are eggs as well which you can fry or boil for yourself. Be careful with your own belongings and put important items in the locker, as I'm not responsible for any lost items." Ms. Oyama handed over a clover-shaped locker key and left the room.

Hana took a quick shower, sat on top of her bunk bed and looked at the steep street outside the window. There was a telephone pole that looked like the Leaning Tower of Pisa, but with lots of cables attached to it in a complicated spiderweb. She was unsure if the pole was leaning because it was weighed down by the weight of the cables or if it was just sitting on a tilted road.

She watched the sun set, then climbed down from the bunk bed and stretched her arms. She walked back down to the market street and bought a bag of freshly baked fish-shaped taiyaki cakes with chocolate custard filling. She held the warm bag and stopped beside the florist's. The window was full of colorful flowers and plants, and a sign on the glass read '50% off on flower pots.'

Hana found a tiny peppermint pot nestled among the big ones on the sidewalk. Peppermint tea was Jin's all-time favorite tea, since he'd had asthma in his childhood. She kneeled down in front of the pot, watching the tiny leaves move in the wind.

"If it has plenty of sun and water, it will thrive", said the florist lady, standing over Hana. She wore a white linen dress with a big blue hydrangea painted on the middle. "It makes a good scent when you clean the leaves."

Hana carried the bag of taiyaki in one hand, the peppermint pot in the other and climbed back up the steep street. As soon as she was sitting on her bunk bed again, she put her pot in the middle of the windowsill. When she poured water on the soil, the plant drank it up with a dry and thirsty squelch. She touched the leaves with her pinky; they already had a stronger green color than before. Finally she wiped the small leaves with a clean cloth, and a refreshing minty fragrance wafted over the bed.

With the brown paper taiyaki bag on her lap, she took out the first warm fish and had a big bite of its tail. It was filled with sweet, smooth chocolate and custard cream. She licked the chocolate off her lips and watched the dark sky and the stars through the window. The stars were shining over the telephone pole and the roofs of the low shops and houses. A cool wind came through the open window and ran its fingers through her hair. She could smell rain coming.

When Hana opened her eyes in the morning, it was raining outside. She had a bad headache and a sore throat. She put a thin cardigan on top of her pajamas and went down to the ground floor, where she sat in a corner of the dark and empty kitchen and watched the rain while drinking hot green tea. The clock's ticking sound and the rainy wind sound filled up the quiet kitchen. There were no other customers in the guest house and it was completely empty.

"Today," she said quietly to herself. "Today I'm going to find Jin."

She washed her cup, went back to the room, had a quick shower and changed into a simple white t-shirt and blue jeans. She went out of the guest house and walked a long way along the steep street, passing the park and the bridge with cherry blossom trees, until she was back at Waseda University. The courtyard under the clock tower was peaceful and quiet apart from the heavy rain hitting her umbrella. Nobody was out walking on the campus on a rainy Sunday morning, not even a cat. Big leaves fell from the trees and made a pattering noise in the gutters when the rain hit them.

Hana had an uneasy feeling. She wasn't sure if this was a good idea. She stood outside one of the dark campus buildings and hesitated for a second, then walked up the concrete steps. The International Business Laboratory, a sign proclaimed. She took a deep breath and knocked on the door. The door made a heavy scraping sound when it opened.

"Yes," said a young student with short hair and thick black-framed glasses, staring at Hana. Past him she saw a huge bookshelf taking up one whole side of the room, while a big table covered with various thick books lay in the middle.

"Ah, hello," Hana said. "I'm looking for Jin Kim, he's a postgraduate student of International Business Studies. I wonder if he's here?"

"Jin Kim?" The young student touched the arm of his glasses and made a confused face. "I'm afraid I've never heard that name before."

"Oh really..." Hana couldn't hide her disappointment, and tried to add more details. "He's thin and tall. And he's a Korean student."

"Hang on a second," the young student said, and thought for a moment. "I'm an undergraduate student, so I wouldn't have met him, but I did hear about one foreign graduate student who dropped out recently."

Hana's eyes flashed wide open. "Do you know what happened to him?"

The student chewed his lip. "I heard he went to South America to travel? I think that's right. People were surprised because he only had one term left until graduation, but I don't know much more than that." The young man scratched his forehead. Hana suddenly felt deflated and exhausted. She barely managed to say thank you, and left the building feeling completely lost.

'South America...' she thought to herself. It seemed so strange. 'He went for a trip without telling me? But why? Why did he disappear like that all of a sudden?'

At a phone box around the corner of the building, Hana made a call to Jin's mother.

"Hello?" came the older lady's voice.

"Hello, Mrs. Kim, how are you doing? This is Hana."

Jin's mom sounded pleased to hear Hana's voice. "Oh, Hana. It's nice to hear from you, and I'm well, thank you. How are things with you?"

"Things are going well," Hana lied, "thank you. But have you heard from Jin recently? I haven't talked to him for a while. I heard he was busy preparing his dissertation though." Hana tried to sound light and breezy, like she was doing OK. She didn't say Jin might have taken an unexpected trip to South America, as she didn't want Mrs. Kim to worry over a rumor.

"Oh yes," Jin's mom said brightly, "he came back for a quick visit just a week ago. Did he not come see you?"

"Ah..." Hana's voice trembled. Jin had gone back to Korea? "I guess we missed each other."

"Oh," Mrs. Kim trailed off. "Well, he did say he was very busy these days, finishing up his studies. He lost a lot of weight too, but hopefully everything will get better after graduation." She paused for a moment, perhaps not sure what to say. "I'll definitely tell him to give you a call when we next speak though, and I'm sorry you haven't had a chance to catch up with him. Is there anything going on with the two of you?"

"No, no, I don't think so," Hana said quickly. "I was just wondering if he was doing all right, and about you too." Hana's voice got quieter. "I probably contacted him when he was busy, that's all."

"Come over sometime," Mrs. Kim said. Her voice sounded sweet and sympathetic. "You don't live so far, and I haven't seen you for a long time. Once Jin comes home, let's have a party together. I miss you both."

"Thank you, Mrs. Kim. I'll call you again. Have a great day."

"You too. Thank you for calling, Hana."

Once Hana hung up the phone, the pain in her chest grew so bad that she couldn't breathe well. She leaned on the damp wall of the building and closed her eyes, focusing on getting air into her lungs. Like that, her whole body got completely soaked. Raindrops landed on her white trainers and made a puddle on the floor.

3. Lonely double waffles

Hana was dripping wet by the time she arrived at the guest house. Her face was stiff with the cold. Ms. Oyama was dozing off with a newspaper in her hands at the reception desk, and there was an ashtray full of cigarette butts in front of her. Her perfectly round cabbage-shaped head moved gently back and forth as she breathed.

Hana went up to her room and changed into dry clothes. Through the window she looked at the thick gray clouds hanging in the sky, full of rain. She poured water in a big mug and used it to clean the peppermint leaves with her damp fingers, then drank the rest. Once the thirst was gone, hunger came next.

She walked down to the dark, empty kitchen and found an ancient iron waffle tray with lots of scratches and burn marks. It seemed it hadn't been used for a long time, because it had a thick layer of white dust. Hana went to the reception and gently spoke to Ms. Oyama, sitting there as stiff as an Egyptian mummy.

"Hello, Ms. Oyama, do you mind me borrowing your waffle tray?"

Ms. Oyama turned her head slowly, like a gangster in a black-and-white film, and looked up at Hana with her expressionless face. "You can use whatever you want, if you wash it and put it back."

"Thank you," Hana said, then went to buy some groceries from the nearby supermarket. She bought pancake flour, milk, sweet chestnut jelly, cheddar cheese and a mixed salad and set them all down on the kitchen table. Cold damp air seemed to fill the solitary kitchen.

She mixed the pancake flour and milk into a big bowl then sliced the sweet chestnut jelly and cheddar cheese into small cubes. She rubbed a stick of butter on each side of the waffle tray, letting it heat up over the gas stove, and when the butter was steaming, she half-filled both sides with the pancake mix, added some cubes of sweet chestnut jelly and covered them over with more batter.

When she closed the waffle tray, it made such a nice and sweet smell. As soon as it was done, she made another waffle with the cheddar cheese, and soon there was a rich savory smell alongside the sweet, accompanied by a hearty sizzling sound.

Soon the two golden-brown waffles were sitting on a plate before her. She spread icing sugar on the sweet waffle and bunched the mixed salad on top of the savory waffle, then put her hands together and gave a slight bow. It was a Japanese kitchen, after all, so it seemed important to respect Japanese traditions.

"Thank you for the meal," she said. Her voice echoed in the empty kitchen.

The waffles were crunchy on the outside and slightly chewy and soft inside. Hana finished the savory waffle with its oozing cheese then moved on to the sweet waffle with the soft chestnut jelly. She sighed with satisfaction, feeling silly and stupid that she'd been so miserable a minute ago but now felt happier just because she had a full stomach. Life was sometimes unbelievably simple. Hana cleaned the waffle tray and the plates, then sat back down and turned the TV on.

Several guys in black suits and black ties were talking fast and laughing at each other on a comedy variety show. One of the guys started shouting and hitting the other guy's head. She changed to a documentary channel, where pretty young girls in pastel-colored puff-shoulder dresses were playing with baby deer in a petting zoo. She was about to turn the TV off when she caught some footage of the Tokyo marathon on a news channel.

The clips showed an endless flow of runners passing in front of various Tokyo landmarks: Sensoji temple in Asakusa and the Waco building in the Ginza shopping district. It made her think of the marathon she'd run several years ago, with Jin and her guitar club friends.

Sok had worn a fake blonde wig and carried a guitar even though everyone in the club said it was a bad idea. When he declared he was going to give up around the twenty-mile mark, some of the group had started criticizing him.

"I told you to leave your bloody guitar at home, didn't I!"

"Why do you have to carry that stupid thing with you right now? Throw it away."

"No, I won't give up on my guitar," Sok had said, lying on the floor and panting like a dog. "It's my soul."

Hana's friends complained but they couldn't just abandon Sok on the street, so Hana, Jin and the others supported him like a wounded soldier on a battlefield. He carried his guitar like a big rifle, half-walking and half-running on a cold but sunny day in early March. The last three miles were a big stretch and everyone was exhausted. Hana felt almost like the original marathoner, Philippides in Greece, ready to die honorably for his cause. Sok started singing a Queen song while clutching his side.

Jin played the guitar and everyone sang like total mad people. Finally, they crossed the finish line together, dragging their legs like heavy logs. They all applauded, hugged and congratulated each other for their achievement. Life was not lived alone, Hana had learned. It was an important lesson. With good companions any challenges could be overcome.

She turned the TV off and went to close the kitchen window. The late night wind was chilly on her cheeks, with a hint of heavy rain and black clouds overhead. She went back to her room and logged on to the Tokyo marathon webpage. She couldn't predict what would happen in a year, but she hoped to run another marathon with Jin and cross the finish line together. She sat in the dark room alone and imagined happy marathoners running in the streets while cherry blossom trees bloomed all around.

She registered her name as well as Jin's on the Tokyo marathon page, and as soon as she sent the registration form, she received an automated confirmation email.

'Thank you for your registration. Please note that the Tokyo Marathon runs on a lottery system and we will get back to you with the result shortly.'

'Would Jin have received this email?' she wondered. 'Where is he now? Why did he disappear?'

Hana had a lot on her mind and her body felt heavy. She imagined Jin reading the confirmation email under the sun in Argentina or Cuba. She tried to imagine them running together past the Imperial Palace and Tokyo Station in a year's time, but it was difficult. She felt tired from thinking a lot and walking so much. It had been a long day.

Just as she was slumping low against the wall and beginning to drift asleep, the door opened wide with a big bang and three young blonde girls came rushing in.

"Oh my goodness me, this room is so cute. Pink everywhere!"

"Wow, look at this bunk bed! It looks like we're in a boarding school dormitory."

They chatted excitedly and put their bags down on the floor while Hana sat up and rubbed her eyes. A girl with blue eyes and freckles on her nose stretched out her hand.

"Hola! Nice to meet you. I'm Stephanie."

"My name is Mona," said another, not giving Hana a chance to speak.

"I'm Elizabeth," said the third, "you can call me Elly."

"We're from Spain," Mona went on, speaking fast with a strong accent. "We're travelling in Asia for two months for our summer vacation. We already explored Taiwan and just came over to Japan today. What about you?"

"I'm Hana. I'm from South Korea." Hana hesitated before saying any more. "I came here to see my boyfriend."

"Oh really, where is he now?" Elizabeth's eyes sparkled.

"Ah, well..." Hana's voice got smaller. "He's at a conference in South America right now, so I'm waiting until he comes back."

"We'll go to Seoul next week," Stephanie said, changing the subject easily. "Can you recommend some good places to visit?"

Hana nodded. "Sure, of course. Let me think about it."

"Yeah!" The three girls raised their voices at the same time.

The next day the four girls took a train to Chofu in the western suburbs of Tokyo. Hana didn't have anything else to do, and was tired of thinking about Jin all the time, so she decided to join them. The weather cleared up and there was a beautiful blue sky. They looked around Jindaiji Temple and followed a lovely walking trail which featured lots of street paintings from the spirit-monster anime show, GeGeGe no Kitaro. Mona kept herself busy taking photos of the streets and Elizabeth took a funny photo of herself next to a painting of Kitaro. Hana felt good to be around them; they were so lively all the time.

After a long walk, they went to a soba noodle restaurant converted from an old wooden house. They had handmade rough soba noodles and vegetable tempura mixed with burdock roots, sweet potatoes, onions and carrots, then finished off by drinking the hot soba broth.

"Wow, this soup is so warm and earthy," Elizabeth said as her cheeks turned pink. Hana picked up her bowl of hot broth and blew on it. She thought of Jin blowing on his hot drinks to cool them down. He'd always had a 'cat tongue', so he wasn't good at drinking hot tea or eating hot food.

Stephanie made a dreamy, satisfied face. "This is so tasty. I feel like the food's cleansing my whole body."

The girls had another walk after the meal, following the mysterious sound of music coming from the other side of the road. After a while they found a small orchestra playing classical music under a big oak tree in a shrine. The orchestra played 'Like the Flow of the River' by Misora Hibari, followed by Brahms' 'Hungarian Dance' and Mozart's Clarinet Concerto. People nearby were drawn in by the lovely music, forming a crowd. To Hana it seemed as if happiness was floating over the clear summer night's air like soap bubbles.

Every day that week, Hana and the Spanish girls went somewhere different together; always so busy tasting new things, talking about Japan, chattering about something and nothing. For Hana it felt like a holiday from herself. When she was with Mona, Elly and Stephanie she didn't have to think about her real life, or about Jin, or anything.

On their last night, the Spanish girls made seafood tacos with lots of chopped cilantro and lime juice in the guest house kitchen. Hana made stir-fried spicy rice cakes called topokki. She put the long, soft rice cakes in a frying pan along with parboiled fishcakes, thick-sliced onions, carrots and half-boiled whole eggs, added a spoonful of spicy gochujang red chili paste, a dash of chili flakes, caster sugar, fish sauce, plum juice and water and boiled the mixture down. When it had reduced to a rich red sauce, she sprinkled roughly chopped spring onions and Mozzarella cheese on top.

"What is this soft and chewy thing?" Mona asked, scooping up a rice cake with her fork. "I've never seen it before."

"It's called a dduk," Hana said. "It's made of steamed ground rice; I'm not sure if you'll like it." Hana rested her head in her hand and watched the girls' faces as they chewed carefully.

"It's almost like chewing gum," Stephanie said, sounding impressed. "It has a really interesting texture."

"It is spicy, sweet, salty and mixed up with all kinds of different tastes and textures in the world. It's really good." Elizabeth drank some water while chewing a dduk. Mona cut one of the boiled eggs in half with a spoon, poured the sweet chili sauce on top and put it in her mouth. They were so focused on eating that the kitchen became absolutely silent.

"Oh it was good, and I'm so full," said Mona when she was done. Hana looked at the others; they all looked satisfied, with lips that were swollen like red plums. It was their last night together and they were quieter than usual. They listened to Alejandro Sanz's music and drank Asahi beer. They talked about their schools, boyfriends, families, travels and just went on and on with no break. Mona became teary when she talked about her Ragdoll cat, Maya.

In the morning, before Elizabeth, Stephanie and Mona headed off to Kyoto, the four girls ate smoked salmon onigiri rice balls, umeboshi plums and drank hot brown wholegrain rice tea.

"Contact my friends when you're in Korea," Hana said, and gave them a piece of paper with her email address and her close friends' phone numbers.

"Hana, you should let us know if you come to Spain," Elly said brightly. "We'll host you and guide you." One-by-one the girls gave Hana long and tight hugs.

The guest room suddenly became empty and quiet after the three Spanish girls left. Hana lay still on the bunk bed and stared at the white ceiling. Every day she'd called and sent an email to Jin, but there was still no reply. It felt worse now, with the girls gone, so she wrote another email about the girls and how funny they were. She even called her parents too, to tell them that her trip to her friend's house would be longer than she'd expected, as she'd gotten an intern job at a big bank in Seoul. It was a lie, but it seemed easier than telling the truth. Her mom didn't sound convinced, and it was clear she wanted to ask a lot of questions, but Hana didn't know what to say.

What she really wanted was to ask if her parents were still fighting so much, but she didn't. It was none of her business, after all. Instead she hung up the phone, and just hoped their relationship had gotten better after she left the house. It was hard to think of home without imagining the sound of plates shattering, electronic devices breaking, her mom and dad's raised voices with Hana crying alone in her room, feeling terrified.

She was alone now too though, not afraid but feeling sad and lonely. She closed her eyes, not sure which was worse. The whole world seemed gray in front of her. She didn't want to open her eyes again. She'd thought she would be happy to leave her parents' house and meet up with Jin, but Jin wasn't here. She tried to think of his calm low voice and his wide, thin eyes, but strangely she couldn't even picture his face in her mind.

'Were we even together once?' she wondered. 'Was everything a dream?'

She felt confused. She realized life was like a winding trail you had to walk alone. There was no way to know if there was a big puddle, a huge rock or a group of cows blocking the road ahead before you started walking. She'd told the girls she was waiting for Jin, but she didn't even know if he was coming back. Maybe tomorrow he would call and things would go back to just the way they'd been before. Maybe he wouldn't ever call again. There was no way to know.

She had a long and deep sleep for the first time in a long time. She woke to the sound of cicadas singing their high-pitched songs under a strong sun. Her pillow was soaking wet and her cheeks were damp. She took off her pajamas and took a cold shower to properly wake up. While she was waiting for her laundry to be done in a nearby coin laundry place, she had a soda-flavored sky-blue ice pop for breakfast and read another free Town magazine, looking again at the jobs, the language school and the volunteer opportunities.

She had only one term left until her university graduation, but somehow she didn't want to go back. Back to her parents' house, to the shouting and broken plates. Without Jin she didn't know if she could face it. Maybe she just wouldn't go back. She could stay in the guest house and think about what to do. Perhaps it was time to move on and do something completely new.

That afternoon she went to the ward office and got her foreign registration card, which would allow her to work. Straight after that she bought a new cell phone and a bicycle. She wouldn't have to use phone boxes anymore, and she could easily go wherever she wanted, as long as it wasn't far. The bicycle was bright orange with a woven rattan basket. She felt free riding it down the narrow street outside the guest house with the wind blowing in her face.

Over the next few days she explored all the interesting little shops in back alleys around Waseda: a handmade jewelry shop with lots of silver and crystals; a small gallery with free exhibitions by local artists; a vintage store full of Bohemian-style lights and accessories. It was a joy to cycle around the small streets and find unique and pretty shops on sunny afternoons. It became her favorite hobby.

On the way out of the small gallery one day, after looking carefully at a cartoony painting of a carrot, an onion and a potato bubbling happily in a pot-au-feu, she came across the Culture Center run by Shinjuku ward office. She'd read about it in the Town magazine. She parked up her bike and went inside.

A schedule board in the lobby said they had a yoga class, a guitar class and a cross stitch class running on the ground floor, with a small tatami-mat room for tea ceremonies in the corner. On the second floor there was the free Japanese volunteer school: Sakura Japanese language school.

She stood in front of the school for a while, thinking. She hadn't set out to come here, but maybe she'd come here on purpose without realizing it. After getting the phone and the bike, her savings were already running low. If she wanted to stay and figure some things out, she had to get a job, and for that she needed to speak Japanese a lot better.

She took a deep breath and gently opened the door. The hanging door chime made a light twinkling sound, and a young round-faced guy walked out of one of the classrooms to meet her.

"Hello, I'm Takeuchi," he said, speaking slowly and clearly. "Are you here to study Japanese?"

Hana nodded. "Yes, I am."

"Great, please write your name, address, phone number, your preferred lesson date and time, your Japanese level and what you'd like to learn on this paper." He gave her a registration form and a yellow pencil with an eraser on top of it.

Hana read the questions on the paper carefully, like a patient reading a prescription in a hospital, then wrote her answers with a bit of help from a dictionary. After looking over her registration form, Takeuchi had a quick interview with her to check her level.

"Thank you for the interview," he said politely afterward. "Your Japanese is quite good already. Where did you learn it?"

"Thank you," Hana replied. "I learned it by myself, but there are lots of things that I don't know yet."

"I believe you will get much better soon. I'll give you a call once I find a volunteer teacher." He bowed politely as she left.

She got a phone call from Takeuchi two days later, asking if she was willing to come and study on Wednesdays at 11 am. She happily said yes.

Takeuchi welcomed her warmly and took some time to explain everything. The Sakura Japanese school was run by retired teachers in Shinjuku ward, to help foreign exchange students learn Japanese. It was free but the volunteer teachers were all passionate about teaching, and very willing to help their students. The other students were mostly older teenagers or in their early twenties, studying at various universities in Tokyo, but there were also some expat housewives who'd come to Japan with their husbands. All the students' nationalities were diverse, with people from China, Korea, America, England and so on.

"Students who come here for the first time are mostly shy and unsure about their Japanese skills," Takeuchi went on with a big smile. "But they become fluent in a year or so and they get comfortable living in Japan. I feel very proud of them."

Each student had their own dedicated teacher, so the teachers could make customized schedules, listening to what their students wanted and providing it. One-to-one classes were a good way to make positive relationships between teachers and students, Takeuchi explained, and also increased class effectiveness.

Hana's teacher was a retired high-school teacher of Japanese literature, Mr. Abe. He had suffered polio when he was little, so his left leg was always slightly painful, but he had a very cheerful character and was popular among both teachers and students. He played ukulele in the school and brought cut flowers from his garden to use as teaching materials.

"This is a sunflower," he said in Hana's first lesson, holding up one flower at a time, "this is a daisy, and this is called a mallow flower." He also showed Hana photos of his garden. "Look, the mallow flowers didn't bloom last year, so I didn't think they would this year, but they've bloomed beautifully, haven't they?" He talked about when the different flowers would bloom and how much water he gave them, and of course he didn't forget to teach her the different colors too: yellow, white, purple, dark blue etc.

"Yellow is also called the egg yolk color. A sunflower looks like an egg yolk from a freshly laid egg in the morning, doesn't it?" He smiled. "I cut this one this morning. When it is wilted, put a pinch of sugar in the vase or cut the edge of the stem a bit, then it'll get healthier again."

Mr. Abe gave Hana the sunflower after the class. The stem was wrapped up in wet newspaper. She put the sunflower in the basket of her orange bicycle for the ride home, then in a vase back at the guest house. She changed the water every day, adding a spoonful of sugar each time. The sunflower stayed beautifully yellow and fresh for the whole week.

Sakura Japanese school had social events sometimes. Takeuchi encouraged her to join them, saying it was a good chance to practice her Japanese. Hana went along shyly at first, but soon became friends with a lady called Nok, from Thailand. They went to drink green tea together at a nearby tea house. Nok said she'd met her husband in Bangkok where they fell in love at first sight. She talked about how sweet, caring and diligent Japanese people were. Her voice sounded like a bird singing.

"Nok means bird in Thai," she said in her sweet voice. "What does your name mean?"

"Hana means the first or something unique in Korean, and it means flower in Japanese." Hana replied.

"It is a beautiful name, just like you."

"Nok is a lovely name as well."

Nok and Hana smiled at each other.

"What brought you to Japan?" Nok asked.

Hana thought about that for a panicky moment. She didn't want to tell Nok all about Jin; how he'd gone missing, how he might be in South America and wasn't answering any of her emails. She didn't want to lie either.

"I just felt like a change," she said.

4. Matcha green tea cream Swiss roll cake from Uji, Kyoto

Every night Hana woke up several times to check her emails. In the day she felt insecure and foggy most of the time. Nok had asked the question she'd been thinking about endlessly in the back of her mind, and she couldn't come up with a good answer. She wasn't sure why she was staying in Japan without Jin, but she wasn't sure why she had to go home either. The only time she felt any connection with the real world was when she was surrounded by people in the Sakura school.

One day at the end of the summer, Nok invited Hana, Mr. Abe and Nok's teacher Mr. Mizuki to her house for lunch after class. Nok's house was located near Tama Central Park on the Keio Line; a wooden two-floor house with a small garden. It was a long bicycle ride, but Hana enjoyed it. Nok greeted her brightly at the door and led her through to the garden,

Thick white hydrangeas bloomed dramatically in the flower beds, and the green leaves from an overhanging maple tree shone beautifully in the afternoon sun. Soon these leaves would take their summer clothes off, Hana thought, and put on their velvety dark winter trench coats, saved in the wardrobe for a whole year.

Nok served a hot green curry, a pad Thai, some fresh spring rolls with tiger prawns and leeks and a green papaya salad. Everyone stopped talking and admired the handmade porcelain plates, tinted green and engraved with lotus flower patterns. The food smelled gorgeous.

Nok talked about her summer holiday in Okinawa in her birds-singing voice; about the emerald-blue sky and white sand beaches. Hana thought about the soft sand and white waves of Oryukdo island, washing over her feet as she walked along the tideline with Jin by her side. Mr. Abe gave a mini lecture about his new hobby, Shiitake mushroom cultivation. He seemed pleased about his starter culture progress, seeded in well-dried oak tree logs he'd prepared in the winter.

"It's important to keep the right temperature and humidity," he explained. "Also experts say it is good to roll the logs in the middle of the cultivation, to get even results, but I decided to leave it in God's hands." He seemed pretty excited about it all.

Mr. Mizuki talked about his recent Kyoto trip. "It was too hot, so I felt dizzy as I walked around, but it was fun to take the Shinkansen bullet train and have a special lunch box in the train." He folded up his fan up and seemed momentarily lost in thought. "It might be difficult to travel that far again, so I enjoyed every moment."

Hana savored the taste of the tender pad Thai, fresh spring rolls and spicy green curry while listening to everyone's stories.

"What about you, Hana?" Nok asked with a warm smile. "Are you doing anything fun these days? Summer holiday plans?"

Hana tried to think of something fun to tell them. Not that she woke up several times every night to check her emails in the dark. Not that she kept her shoes, clothes and a packed bag ready under the bed at all times, like someone preparing for an earthquake or a disaster. She never knew when Jin would contact her and ask for her help. She couldn't make any plans to be far away from his school or his old apartment. She sat there silently for a long moment, twirling a strand of hair behind her ear, until finally she spoke.

"I've been busy lately, so I haven't done anything special."

While everyone was having sweet, thick tapioca coconut milk for dessert, Hana nodded along without listening to them. Instead she focused on the sound of delicate skylarks chirping and high-pitched cicadas singing. The cicadas were trying their best to show their existence to the world, as if recovering from their lonely and hard seven-year hibernation spent under the dark ground. The cicadas would go back to Mother Nature in only a few weeks' time.

'Did Jin disappear to go and cry alone, or did he cry so much he disappeared without realizing it?' Hana puzzled over the question but found no answer.

After the luncheon, Mr. Mizuki gave everyone a small paper box of Matcha green tea, which he'd bought in Uji, Kyoto.

Mr. Abe tapped Hana's shoulder gently with a somewhat sad face as she unlocked her bicycle. "I don't know what's going on, but good luck, Hana."

Back at the guest house, she opened the round Matcha box. Once she opened the lid, she could smell the delicate, bitter sweetness from the bright olive-green, grainy Matcha powder. She thought for a while and decided to use it for fresh cream swiss roll cakes. She added a teaspoon of corn starch to a genoise sponge batter to make a light and spongy texture, then baked it in one of Ms. Oyama's shallow cake trays.

Once the flat green genoise sponge was out of the oven and cooling on a non-stick rack, Hana made a stiff whipping cream from Hokkaido fresh double cream mixed with Matcha powder and icing sugar. She boiled some red beans, rubbed off the skins and ground them with caster sugar in a handmill, then spread generous layers of olive-green whipping cream and sweet red bean paste over the sponge. She carefully made a few long slices at one edge to make the sponge easier to roll, then gently rolled the whole cake.

The combination of bittersweet Matcha cream and earthy sweet red bean paste made a powerful, refreshing aroma. She wrapped the rolled cake in a parchment paper, twisted the edges to keep it moist and put it in a plastic tub in the fridge.

The next morning Hana went down to the reception desk with two nicely-cut pieces of Matcha cream swiss roll cake on a plate, but there was no sign of Ms. Oyama other than an empty teacup and the morning newspaper. Hana left the plate next to them with a handwritten note.

'Good morning, Ms. Oyama. Please try some Matcha cream swiss roll cake slices that I made last night. Have a good day.'

Hana put the cake box in the basket of the bicycle and rode carefully to Sakura Japanese school. After class, all the teachers and students sat down together in the tatami-mat tea room, drinking hot Hoji tea and eating her cake.

"This is amazing," Takeuchi said, after taking a big bite. His eyes widened. "I've never had such soft and tender swiss roll cakes before. It has a great balance between bitterness and sweetness too. I'm surprised."

"I'm glad you like it," Hana replied bashfully.

"Really, this is so good, Hana," Nok agreed. "So sweet but refreshing at the same time. Did you carry it all the way from your house?"

Hana blushed. "I carried it on my bicycle."

Nok stared at her for a moment. "Wait, you carried this delicate cake in that tiny bicycle basket?"

Hana nodded.

"How did you stop it from getting smushed?"

Hana blushed a little more. "Well, I padded it a lot, and walked some of the way. I was quite worried about it smushing."

Mr. Abe laughed. "Well, you needn't have worried, Hana! It would be delicious even if it was smushed!"

Everybody laughed.

"Cake bicycle delivery," Nok said wonderingly. "Like Kiki's Delivery Service. Wait, I've got it; you're the bicycle bakery! Who needs a broom when you have a cute orange bicycle with a basket?" Nok gave her a big smile.

Hana's cheeks burned, and she was relieved when the conversation moved on from talking about her bicycle and cake. Mr. Abe played a sad love song by Rimi Natsukawa on his ukulele, 'Nada Sou Sou (Full of Tears)'. It somehow made Hana think of one white seagull flying over the deep blue ocean, all on its own.

"Hana, have you been to a fireworks festival before?" Nok asked Hana.

Hana shook her head. "No, I haven't yet."

Nok made a dreamy face. "Oh, it's so magical. I feel like princess Jasmine from Aladdin when I wear a yukata." Hana frowned at the new word, so Nok explained. "A yukata's like a simple, casual cotton version of a kimono. Japanese people always wear them to watch fireworks. I love watching the fireworks over a chilled beer while wearing a yukata. You can forget all your worries." She smiled and nudged Hana. "Hakuna Matata! You just feel free and totally be yourself. The fireworks season starts soon so let's definitely go together." Nok smiled and took a bite of the swiss roll cake.

"Sure, let's do it." Hana nodded.

The firework festival was in Chofu city a week later, half an hour west of Shinjuku station on the Keio line. There were lots of people dressed in yukata all along the Tama River. Hana borrowed an extra yukata from Nok and wore it for the first time in her life. Nok burst into laughter when she saw Hana.

"Hana, come this way. Let me fix your collar. If the right collar is on top of the left collar, it means the person is dead, so we don't want that." She winked. "You should show your left collar on top of the right collar, as you're beautifully alive." Nok fixed Hana's collar and Mr. Abe smiled at them.

Nok had gone to the park early and secured good seats for everyone with a large picnic mat, so the Sakura school people could sit down comfortably, enjoy boiled edamame soybeans and drink chilled beer while waiting for the fireworks to start. A hot, steamy wind blew down the Tama River, but nobody seemed to mind because they were excited for the fireworks.

When the sun finally set the fireworks festival began, and people raised their voices in excitement. Flowers, cartoon characters, smiley faces, love Cupid signs and lots of different images burst across the dark summer sky, chased by loud explosions. The Sakura school people were chatting, laughing, taking photos, eating food and drinking beer. Looking at them made Hana somehow feel lonely and solitary.

Mr. Abe played more Okinawan music on his ukulele. Hana sat down quietly at the corner of the mat and drank Ramune fizzy soda and ate a soy sauce-marinated sweet chicken meatball stick. Nok sang a beautiful Thai love song and Takeuchi and some other students cheered along, giddy and tipsy.

Sooner or later Hana felt a cool breeze coming off the river. While everyone was happily watching the fireworks, she could only think about Jin, her parents and her school friends. The summer vacation was going to end soon, and she still didn't know what to do. The one thing she was certain of was that she didn't want to go home. She would have to explain everything to her parents, and she didn't know how they would react.

'Is Jin looking at the same sky as I am now?' she wondered. She raised her finger and pointed at one of the long twinkly fireworks as it draped down the sky. It fizzled and disappeared against the pitch black night. She kept watching until the last grand firework burst like the last shooting star in the universe; there was a big bang then it disappeared slowly and completely from everyone's sight. There was total silence for a second. Hana almost felt relieved for the moment of stillness and solitude.

The evening of intense brightness and excitement was over. The sound of her round paper fan rubbing against the ribbon of the yukata echoed around the dark, empty alleyway to the guest house, along with the clop of her thick wooden sandals touching the cold asphalt ground.

5. Kimura photo studio and Snow White apples

Hana tried to be careful not to spend too much money, but soon her savings ran very low. She circled several job advertisements in the free Town magazine, and practiced making phone calls with Mr. Abe so she could do it smoothly without getting nervous. A waitress job from a Korean restaurant, a clerk of a convenience store, and a photographic assistant in the photo studio. She recognized the last job; it had been in the Town magazine on her first day in Tokyo. Maybe it was hard for them to find good assistants.

The three interviews were lined up. The Korean restaurant provided free Korean lunches, which was a bonus, but it was full of barbeque smoke, and she didn't like that. The convenience store job seemed relatively easy, but she was not very confident in dealing with money. The last interview was with the photo studio. The place was small, old, and the sign was mostly faded by the sun.

'Kimura photo studio.'

Hana opened the glass sliding door. There was a large rustic wooden table with six chairs in the middle of the room, some stools for photo shoots in one corner and a brown leather sofa for three to four people in another, with several big cameras on tripods scattered around. Portrait photos hung on the while walls, alongside several ceiling-heigh shelves and cabinets for storing photo albums. Hana looked closer; the photo albums were alphabetized by customer name.

The owner Mr. Kimura was a beardy guy wearing thick brown glasses, and his wife Yoko was the shop manager. They worked as a team and ran the small business together.

Mr. Kimura explained her tasks and showed some photos he was editing for his clients. The job involved checking printed photos to make sure they looked correct and pointing any errors to be fixed. If there were no photo-related tasks, she would organize folders of old photos and check the inventory lists of albums and frames. The Kimuras offered only minimum wage, but the job looked interesting and her graphics skills would be helpful.

"Could you start working from tomorrow?" Mr. Kimura asked at the end of their interview, adjusting his glasses slightly. "I know it's short notice, but there really is a lot of work to do."

Hana was surprised to have the job offer straightaway, but happy. "Sure, I can. Thank you for the offer."

After the interview she felt extremely tired, as it was her first time to have such a long and formal conversation in Japanese. On the bicycle ride home, she thought that studying more Japanese would help. Having a job and a stable lifestyle would definitely help too, for both her physical and mental health. She pedaled and thought about Jin contacting her. If she settled down a little, then maybe she could help him more when he called. In her head she'd developed this image of him lost in South America, running out of money, looking for a familiar face.

As she rode, she grew more excited about the possibility of Jin contacting her than about getting a job. She felt light as a feather as she pedaled her bicycle up a steep hill. The wind had a cool edge and she knew summer was fading.

That night she couldn't sleep well; she was too excited about the new job, and the money that she'd use to help Jin. Sometime early in the morning she gave up trying to sleep and baked a fresh peach tart instead. She put the still warm tart tin carefully in the basket of her orange bicycle and cycled to the studio a little after dawn.

"Hello," she said, as she opened the door and gingerly stepped inside, holding the tart tin before her.

"Good morning, Hana!" Yoko said brightly. She was sitting at the big worktable. "Please come on in. And what are you holding there?"

Hana smiled. "Oh, I baked a peach tart this morning." She held the tin out to "I had some peaches spare."

Yoko took it with a smile. "Wow, it's still warm. Thank you for this, though of course you didn't have to."

Hana bobbed a little bow. "It's fine, I like baking, and..." she trailed off. "Um, is it OK if I park my bicycle in front of the shop?"

Yoko peered out through the window to Hana's bike. "Is that your orange bike? It's so cute! And yes, of course you can park it, right there on the corner is fine. And you carried this tart in that little basket?"

Hana reddened a little more. Yoko was the second person to point out her bike's small basket.

"It fit OK," she said shyly. "I'm pretty sure it isn't smushed."

Yoko laughed. "I'm sure it isn't. I bet you're an expert on that bike. OK, well, first day!" She turned. "Honey! Shall we have a cup of tea and a slice of this tart?"

Mr. Kimura appeared from behind a stack of albums on the cashier's desk, smiling. "Sounds good. I'll get the tea."

Hana stood awkwardly while Yoko popped up and busied herself setting out plates and cutlery on the table.

"Have a seat, please, Hana," Mr. Kimura said, and pulled out a chair for Hana at the worktable. The electric kettle started making a boiling sound with warm steam, and he hurried back over.

"Thank you." Hana sat at the edge of the table. There were some photos of children in colorful kimonos scattered across the surface, and she studied them.

Mr. Kimura appeared by her elbow, holding a cup of hot tea. "As it's your first day, we'll mostly show how we work here, and get you started gradually. Our main customers are children for the Shichi-Go-San festival. Have you heard of it before?"

Hana shook her head.

"It's a Japanese traditional celebration for seven, five, and three-year-old kids on their birthdays. They dress up with their parents and pray for health and well-being. These are the photos that we're working on now." He pointed at the photos on the table. "We also have customers for weddings and some other traditional birthday celebrations, like twenty and sixty." He picked up one of the larger photos. "Your job will be checking these deluxe photographs, finding imperfections and fixing them on the computer. When that's done, we print and gloss them, then you'll check one more time. If they're good to go, we'll frame them or put them in a photo album for the customer. If they're not ready, we go through the process again. Does all that sound clear?"

Hana nodded sincerely. "Yes, it sounds clear to me."

"Great, then let's eat," Yoko said, bringing the tart over; now sliced and sitting on a pretty ceramic cake stand.

"Thanks for making this," Mr. Kimura said, and poured hot green tea into mugs while Yoko placed three tart slices onto plates and handed them round.

Yoko had a bite of the tart first, then opened her eyes wide and turned to Hana. "Oh my! Are you a professional baker? It's so moist and the bottom of the crust is so flaky. How did you do that?"

Hana felt embarrassed. "Thank you for saying that. I didn't really do anything special."

"Seriously, you could sell this." Yoko had a bigger bite and a sip of green tea.

"Yes, it's a really a good cake." Mr. Kimura agreed.

Hana smiled. "I'm glad you like it."

For a few minutes they all enjoyed their tart and tea, making small conversation about the weather and Hana's travels with the Spanish girls, then Mr. Kimura put both hands on the table.

"All right, shall we get to work?"

He brought several newly developed photos and put them on the table, alongside a pair of thin white gloves. "Firstly, we check if there any imperfections or color fade." He patted the gloves. "These prevent fingerprints on the photos. It can be tricky, so just do your best. When you've looked at these, we'll go through them together. You'll get the idea quickly enough."

Hana nodded, slid on the gloves and started studying the photos of cute children in various colors of kimono carefully.

"Remember, it's your first day, so don't work too hard, OK?" Yoko winked at Hana and Hana smiled back.

After a few hours of checking, taking Mr. Kimura's corrections, then checking again, Hana had decided it was an ideal kind of job for her. She enjoyed sitting at the big rustic worktable, working on her photos. Mr. Kimura was mostly quiet, but he seemed a warm-hearted guy. Yoko was obviously a sweet and caring person. Hana thought they were a perfect match, and she enjoyed being around them. She knew it wasn't a long-term job, but it felt good to be earning money, and to have a place to go.

A week passed like that; working at the Kimura photo studio in the days, going to the Sakura school in the afternoon and evenings. Summer was nearly over, and Hana watched the calendar as the days went by. Her final school term would be starting soon, and still she'd heard nothing from Jin. She wondered what the right thing to do was. She knew she had to talk to her parents, so after a morning shift at the photo studio she called home.

Her mom sounded surprised to hear from her. "Hana, what's going on?" she asked. "Are you OK? I called you several times but I couldn't reach you. I thought I would have to call the police or something."

Hana felt guilty to hear her mom's worried voice. "Mom, I'm actually in Japan right now. the other job fell through, and I felt like a change. I got a new job in a photo studio in Tokyo." She paused, but her mom didn't say anything. "I should have told you earlier. Sorry." Still her mom said nothing. The awkward silence felt uncomfortable, so she tried to change the subject. "Are you there? How's Dad doing?"

Her mom took a deep breath. "I suppose you're an adult now, so you should live your own life, but why did you lie to us? Are you with Jin?" She sounded surprisingly calm. She'd probably already guessed Hana was not at her friend's house. "The summer holiday is almost over and your next school term will start soon. What are you going to do about that?"

Hana took a deep breath too. "I am sorry for lying. It was only supposed to be for a few days, but..." She trailed off. "I wasn't sure what I was doing, so I didn't know how to explain it to you. I came out here to see Jin, but he's not here." She could feel the tears creeping up on her, and pushed on quickly. "Now I want to try out a new life in Japan, so I'm going to take a year off from the school."

Her mom didn't speak for a long moment. Even Hana was surprised. She hadn't planned that at all. When her mom did speak, Hana thought she was going to shout and get angry like the old days, but instead she got even calmer and quieter than before.

"Oh dear. Why did you make such an impulsive decision without any plans? You've got only one term to finish your university. I know you won't listen to whatever I say, and I know I can't change your mind, but you're not a child anymore, Hana. You should be responsible for your own decisions. You're just like your dad." She raised her voice a little. "To be honest, your dad is unwell these days. He's got some issues with his lungs and some high blood pressure. He drinks and smokes a lot and it just gets worse, but he won't stop. He's like a big stubborn baby and never listens to anyone even his doctor."

She gave a big sigh then went on. "You should take care of yourself too. You're out there on your own with no one to help you. Do you know that?" Her voice got louder suddenly, and turned sharper. "Don't give me a headache anymore, Hana. I just want to be alone and not have to deal with this useless family business. I don't want a husband or a kid anymore. I want to die on my own without any human contact."

It was the kind of thing her mom sometimes said. Hana doubted she could live a peaceful life even if she lived alone. She would find something to complain about and shout at anyone nearby if she was unhappy.

'Happiness is in your mind, Mom' Hana thought, but she didn't say it. "Mom, stay well and be nice to Dad."

"I don't know anymore. Do whatever you want to do. I'm busy so I'd better go." Before Hana could answer, her mom hung up the phone.

Hana felt lost, but it was not a bad feeling. She walked along the road, watching her feet. She put her head down and walked and walked while thinking nothing; past the alley with the cats, past the park with the frogs, past Jin's old apartment. When she looked up, there was a small old lady in front of her, carrying two heavy bags and walking slowly like a tired turtle, almost falling off the pavement. Hana ran over to her.

"Can I help you?"

The old lady turned around slowly. "No, it's OK, I'm old but I can do my own stuff." She sounded like she was a little annoyed.

"I'm going this way anyway," Hana protested. "Let me help you until the end of this road at least." With a little convincing, the old lady let her take the bags. She had cleaning liquid, toilet paper, green tea, mackerel, seaweed, tofu and lots of other small household items. It seemed she was living on her own and did her own grocery shopping without anyone's help.

"It's lovely weather today, isn't it?" Hana said brightly, looking at the side of the old lady's wrinkled face.

"Yes, clothes will dry nicely today," said the old lady. She looked more relaxed than before. They walked onto the market street and the old lady pointed at a small vegetable shop with her old spotted fingers.

"Here we are."

She pushed a small red button on the wall and the half-rusted metal shutter lifted up with a big squeaky sound.

On a big table inside the shop there were horse radishes, shiitake mushrooms, onions, potatoes and red apples in wooden baskets. They all looked fresh and shiny, but the apples shone most of all.

It took Hana a moment to remember; was this the Snow White apple shop, the place she'd found on her very first day?

"Excuse me," she said politely, "I think I came here a few months ago. I bought some of those apples."

The old lady looked at the apples, looked at Hana, then snorted. "You want some apples, huh? I knew there'd be something."

Hana felt horrified. "No, I'm sorry, I didn't mean-"

"It's fine," the old lady said, putting some of the beautiful red apples in a brown paper bag. Hana noticed she'd mastered the bags better than before. "Young people these days, everything comes at a price," she muttered to herself. "Here." She handed it to Hana. "Take this and go ahead."

"No, really, it's all right," Hana said, waving her hands, but the old lady kept holding the bag out.

"Listen. I don't believe in free stuff. Nothing is free in this world." She was stubborn and serious looking, with such sharp eyes. She was like a totally different person from the lady who had almost fallen on the street a few minutes ago.

"Well, thank you," said Hana " They are delicious, and I'll take them, then." She took the bag, bowed at the old lady with respect and left the shop.

Hana took one apple out of the bag and had a big bite while she was waiting for the green light at a crossing. A rush of sweet and sour juice spread in her mouth. The skin was thin and the apple itself was hard with a great texture. It was just as delicious as the Snow White apple she'd had that first day. It had an honest and sincere taste, as if the farmer had grown it with great attention and affection. She kept on eating the apple in great cheerful crunches.

She walked for quite a while after that, arriving back in the guest house to realize she'd eaten all the apples, so there were only apple stems left in the empty bag.

6. Lemon drizzle crêpe with royal icing sugar

As Hana worked at the Kimura photo studio, she gave out prizes in her mind to the children in the photographs. She awarded one for the best facial expression, one for the best Shichi-Go-San costume, and so on. Sometimes the children wore traditional outfits from their own countries and sometimes they wore kimono. She didn't get involved in taking the photos or meeting customers, until a few weeks in when Mr. Kimura asked her to help.

"There'll be a Korean boy and girl next week for their Shichi-Go-San photos," he said. "Can you help with the photo shoot?"

"Of course, I can," Hana said with a smile. "I'm happy to help."

On the day of the photo shoot she was nervous and couldn't eat properly. She put on light pearl purple eyeshadow, black mascara, coral-colored blusher and light orange lipstick. She wore a well-ironed white shirt and a beige H-line skirt, splashed on some of her favorite Issey Miyake perfume, then went to the studio earlier than usual.

The Tokyo Bicycle Bakery

The Korean family arrived twenty minutes before their reservation time: Mom, Dad and two little kids.

"Nice to meet you," Hana said in polite Korean, standing beside Yoko and Mr. Kimura to welcome them in. "My name is Hana and I will be your photo assistant today. Mr. Kimura will take photos and Yoko will be in charge of the photo editing and general matters."

The mother smiled to hear a Korean voice. "Hello, Hana. I'm Sumi, this is my husband Gon and here are our two kids, Jun and Bomi." The two kids beamed up at Hana. "I'm glad you have a Korean staff-member today. I was a bit worried about my Japanese skills."

Hana translated this, while Yoko and Mr. Kimura nodded warmly.

"You're very welcome," Yoko said, and Hana translated. "Your outfits are so beautiful,"

"Thank you," Sumi replied happily. "This is called a hanbok, the traditional Korean costume. My younger sister is a hanbok designer, so she made them specially for the ceremony."

Yoko smiled, looking very impressed.

"How old are you, young lady and gentleman?" Hana asked the children.

"I'm Jun," the bigger boy replied. "I'm five years old and this is my little sister Bomi." He was wearing a sky blue top and light pink trousers. "Bomi is only three years old."

"I am going to be a big sister soon," Bomi said, smiling up at Hana with no front teeth. Bomi was wearing a colorful top, a yellow skirt and a small silk flower hair band.

The photo shoot went very smoothly after that. Mr. Kimura took the photos speedily so Jun and Bomi wouldn't get tired out, and Yoko used toys to attract the children's attention. Mr. Kimura asked Hana to request poses or certain expressions from the children, and she kept on checking that their clothes and hair were still looking good.

Jun and Bomi had individual photos taken, then duet photos, then with the whole family. It took over two hours, and at the end Jun and Bomi fell asleep on the sofa.

"I'm sorry that the kids fell asleep," Sumi said with an apologetic face. "I'll wake them up and we'll head off."

"No problem," Yoko said with no hesitation, this time catching Sumi's meaning in Korean. "A lot of kids fall asleep after a photo shoot. It's tiring even for adults. It was good that they didn't start crying in the middle!"

Hana translated, and Sumi smiled. "My husband likes to take photos, so our kids are used to it."

Yoko nodded. "Shall we have a cup of tea while we wait for the young lady and gentleman to wake up?" She made hot royal milk tea and laid a big banana pound cake in the middle of the table. "Some kids cry and get fussy over photo shoots," she went on. "Once they're in a bad mood, it's difficult to pull things around, and the shoot gets delayed. Then we take a break and I bring warm milk and a banana pound cake. Kids always stop crying over sweets."

Everyone had a good laugh at that, and enjoyed the cake and the tea. It was a soft and sweet cake that anyone would stop crying for. Yoko wrapped up a big piece of the cake and handed it to Sumi.

"For the kids, with warm milk later."

"Thank you so much," Sumi said with a small bow.

Sumi and Gon took the half-asleep Jun and Bomi to the car. In the street Sumi handed Hana a piece of paper with her number on it. "You were a great help for us today, thank you. We came here recently for my husband's work, and a lot of things are still new for us. Would you come to our house for dinner sometime? I'd really appreciate it. Let me know when you're free."

Hana took the paper and smiled. "Thank you. I'll call." She waved at the family until their car was out of sight.

It got darker, and the sky became reddish purple on the bottom and a warm glowing orange on top. It was getting pretty chilly at night now, and fall was coming.

Back in the shop, she mopped the floor, wiped the worktable and left the studio after saying goodbye to Mr. Kimura and Yoko. She pedaled her orange bicycle and thought about getting another part-time job. With some more money, maybe she could afford to move out of the guest house and rent a small studio apartment nearby. She thought about how impressed Jin would be, when he saw her settled lifestyle.

Back in the guest house, Hana took a long shower, dried her hair with a towel and had some warm milk with a splash of Kahlua alongside another slice of Yoko's banana pound cake. The rich, sweet tastes made her whole body feel warmer. She laid on her bunk bed and stroked the leaves of her peppermint pot with her pinky. The plant had grown taller by several inches already, and gave off a strong, refreshing fragrance as she touched it. On the radio, Yo Yo Ma's cello suite and Priscilla Ahn's song Lullaby were playing. Her body felt like a whiskey-soaked sponge. She hoped to have sweet dreams.

After the Korean family came by, the number of foreign customers to the photo studio increased. Hana got more photo-shooting jobs, along with a small salary increase. As she spent more time at the studio, Yoko started treating her almost like a younger sister, often sharing homemade cookies or Japanese-style snacks and finger foods with her.

In the early fall, Nok became pregnant. She took a break from the school, but Hana still had a catch up over tea with her sometimes, talking about her baby plans and Hana's customers in the photo studio.

"Are you going to settle down in Japan and raise your baby here?" Hana asked, while drinking thick sweet mango juice in Nok's lovely hydrangea-filled garden.

"Well, my husband has a business here so I think we will live in Japan for a while." Nok touched her belly in a gentle, loving way. The baby's foot made a small leafy pattern on her skin. "I'll miss my hometown and my family but I can visit them, and they can come stay with us anytime."

It was a lovely visit, but on the bicycle ride home Hana felt herself getting sad, as if a dark gray sky was falling around her. Her life in Japan was quite comfortable now, and she had some nice friends and a job to pay for her food and bills, but still she didn't feel happy. It seemed like the more she settled down, the emptier she felt.

Since the three Spanish girls had gone, she'd met several people in the guest house, but they always went off for other adventures, and Hana always stayed behind.

It was like sitting on a busy train watching people get on and off, but she didn't have the courage to get off with them. Instead she just kept on riding, with no idea where she was headed. She woke up in the morning and went to bed at night, then did the same the next day. She didn't know what would come next, but she couldn't plan anything solid either.

She opened her eyes before dawn the next morning, with a sore throat and a headache. She sat on the bunk bed's edge and tied her hair back with a rubber band, then opened the window. There was a low wooden thunking sound ringing through the complicated spider web of black electric wires, followed by the low sound of a monk praying. His calm voice resonated across the dark morning sky.

Hana got changed quickly, went outside and walked toward the sound. There was a funeral ceremony in a small shrine on the other side of the hill. People in black suits, black ties and black dresses were watching the funeral service. The monk sang and hit a small wooden drum in front of a tomb. There was a round bamboo vase with long and thin wooden sticks inside, each carved with the names of the dead. Incense was burning, and there were small flowers in a stone vase. Nobody was crying or making a noise; they attended the ceremony silently and sincerely.

Hana wondered what they were feeling. How would she react if her parents died? What if Jin was dead, and she never received a message from him at all? She wondered that life and death might not be so far apart.

She took a long walk in the park and sat on a bench in front of the fish pond for hours, feeling empty-headed. When she returned to the guest house, it was already dark outside. She was hungry and decided to make gimbap; rice wrapped in seaweed paper. Into the rice she added sweet and sour horseradish, boiled spinach, thinly sliced fried carrots, burdock, eggs and seafood sticks. She put sesame oil and sesame seeds on the surface of the gimbap and cut it into inch-thick slices with a sharp sushi knife. The inside of the gimbap looked like a colorful flower.

She placed some of the best-looking gimbap pieces on a plate on a wooden tray, along with a bowl of hot miso soup with tofu and seaweed, then went to the reception desk. Ms. Oyama was there, watering her plant pots. She had a big bandage on her right arm and her cabbage hair didn't look as neat as usual.

"Is everything alright?" Hana asked.

Ms. Oyama looked up. "I slipped on the steps yesterday and I sprained my elbow."

"Oh, I'm sorry to hear that," Hana said, studying her pale face. "Have you been to the hospital?"

Ms. Oyama shook her head. "It's not a big deal. It'll get better soon."

Hana set the tray gently on the desk. "Let me know if there is anything I can help with. I just made gimbap and miso soup. I'll just leave this here."

"How kind," Ms. Oyama said. Her eyes were red and she looked exhausted. "But I don't have any appetite now."

"Then what about a cup of tea?" Hana pressed gently. "I made hot corn silk tea in the kitchen. I think you should at least drink something."

Ms. Oyama and Hana sat down opposite each other at the long kitchen table. It was the first time they sat together in the guest house. Hana poured hot corn silk tea into the porcelain cup.

"Please try this tea."

"Thank you," Ms. Oyama said, then touched her hair with her left hand. "I haven't been able to do a good job on my hair since I hurt my elbow. Doesn't it look messy?" She turned so Hana could see the back of her head. It wasn't as perfect as her previous hairstyle; some hair had fallen out of the cabbage shape and looked slightly fluffy.

"Ah, it looks great," Hana said nervously. "It's just as good as your previous hairstyle. I don't see any difference."

Ms. Oyama gave a small grin, and Hana was surprised to see that she could smile. It was the first time she saw Ms. Oyama's face light up. "You really aren't good at lying." She picked up the porcelain cup to take a careful sip. "Though it is nice to hear even if it is a white lie." She paused for a moment, and her face looked a lot more relaxed already. "You're different from other young people these days. Can I ask why you came to stay here, if you don't mind?"

Hana squeezed her hands together. Her palms began to feel damp with sweat. It was the same question Nok had asked, but Hana didn't feel like she could lie again.

"I came to Japan to see my boyfriend," she began, speaking slowly. "It may sound strange, but he was more than a boyfriend to me. He was the most important person in my life, like my family, my best friend." She paused, but Ms. Oyama was looking at her expectantly, so she went on. "I didn't have siblings, so I grew up alone. I didn't have many friends either. He was the only person I felt comfortable to be around and I could be myself with. He knew what I thought without me telling him, but then he came to Japan, and he just stopped contacting me." She took a breath. " I felt like I was left alone in a dark and empty room." Hana took a gulp of the tea and fiddled with her hair. "So I came out here to look for him, but there were other people living at his apartment when I knocked on the door. I'm not sure if he ever lived there, or if he lied to me, or if he just disappeared like a fog." She thought maybe she should stop there, but Ms. Oyama had closed her eyes now to focus on the story, so she kept on.

"I looked everywhere. I called his family and all our friends, but no one knew anything. Someone said he'd gone to South America. I thought about getting a flight and looking for him, but I didn't know where to start. I couldn't understand why he wouldn't tell me about something like that. That really hurt."

She caught a tear before it could run down her cheek. She was glad Ms. Oyama's eyes were closed. "After that I just decided to stay. I don't know why. I thought he might call me, but he hasn't." More tears fell, and she caught them all silently. "That's when I found this guest house. I was lucky. Thank you." Hana gave a small bow.

Ms. Oyama opened her eyes. "You're welcome, but I've done nothing."

Hana smiled. "I keep thinking he'll call me, but he doesn't. Maybe I'm a fool to keep waiting. I don't know what I should do now, but I miss him so much. I want to see him again, so I suppose I'll just keep trying my best, and wait." Hana took a deep breath. Ms. Oyama was watching her carefully. "It makes me feel so light to tell you this. I haven't spoken to anyone about this apart from you. I felt guilty to keep it a secret, even from his mother too."

Ms. Oyama was silent for a long moment, then slowly opened her mouth. "What do you want to do if you do see him again?"

"I don't know," Hana replied, feeling calmer now. "But I want to know he's OK. Also I'll ask him why he disappeared without telling me."

Ms. Oyama nodded thoughtfully. "The reason why he disappeared may not be important, though."

It took Hana a moment to understand that. It didn't seem to make sense. The older woman just cleared her throat and continued on in her husky voice. "It's been twenty years since my husband left me and our house. We had a baby boy. One day while my husband was away for work, my son and I went to the market. My husband was working as a gardener in the Imperial Palace, and he always started his work early, even before the sun rose. It was his birthday, so my son and I were planning his party with the theme of a Japanese summer garden." Ms. Oyama closed her eyes again, like she was back in the memory. "From first thing in the morning, my son was very excited about it. He was an active boy who loved walking. He was wearing yellow chicken-shaped shoes that made a bright, cheerful sound whenever he took a step. They were a Christmas present and he loved them so much he even wanted to wear them inside the house. He was such a cute boy." She gave a light sigh. "Well, I was in the market choosing a big and fresh sea bream for my husband's birthday dinner. After I bought it and turned around, my boy was gone." Ms. Oyama opened her eyes slowly. "Do you mind if I smoke?"

Hana nodded. Ms. Oyama lit a cigarette and smoked it deeply. Her hand holding the cigarette shook. "I ran around looking for him like a crazy person. I went insane." She stopped talking and inhaled the cigarette again. "It turned out my little boy fell into a manhole in a nearby construction site. He was found three days later. His small yellow chicken shoes were dyed black. His tiny body was completely wet and cold." She held her head in her hand. "My husband left the house that day and never came back. If my son was alive, he would have been around the same age as you." She tapped the ash in the ashtray and cleared her throat, then went on in a shaky voice.

"After my boy's funeral, I demolished the house we'd lived in together and rebuilt this guest house. I wanted to make it stand out and be visible, so my husband could come back and find me anytime he wanted. I haven't gone anywhere in the last twenty years. I didn't take a trip once. I was only living to see my husband again, but now I think it was better that we got separated that way, and never saw each other again. I probably couldn't have handled the guilt if we'd been together." Ms. Oyama fell silent, thinking deeply. After a long silence, she went on.

"No matter what happens, live the life that you wish. Everyone deserves a happy life." Her cigarette was now just a stick of ash. Hana reached out to Ms. Oyama and held her hands. They were surprisingly thin and cold.

"Can I ask you for a favor?" Ms. Oyama said, pulling her hands awkwardly from Hana's and touching her big bandage instead.

"Yes, of course."

"My arm isn't quite right yet. Could you help me with cleaning the floors and the fish tank? I'll pay you about the same amount as a convenience-store wage."

"No problem," Hana replied cheerfully. "I helped my parents a lot, because they were both working. Also, I don't need money. I have a part-time job now."

"It would be good if you could help me for a month," Ms. Oyama went on. "I don't want to ask for free so please take it as a side job. Thank you for the tea." She pulled the chair out and stood up with a pained expression. Hana watched as she walked slowly out of the kitchen.

Hana was left at the table alone. After a while she microwaved the cold gimbap and miso soup, then with the TV on. The speakers made a dull machine noise, and the pale blue color from the dead screen poured into the empty kitchen.

Jin 1

Jin opened his eyes in the morning and noticed his left hand had disappeared.

He often had strange dreams, so he didn't take it seriously at first. He thought it was just another dream, but when he went to the bathroom and looked in the mirror, he realized something weird was going on. His left hand was completely gone, like it had been rubbed out by a sharp eraser, or it had never been there at all.

He rubbed his eyes and gazed at himself vacantly. There was a guy with thin and long eyes looking back at him in the mirror. The guy looked familiar and unfamiliar at the same time. Jin couldn't take his eye off him. The clock pointed at five. It was before dawn and it was still dark outside.

'If I go back to sleep and wake up again,' he thought to himself, 'everything will go back to normal. I've been stressed by my dissertation and busy with my part-time job recently. I need to sleep more.' He yawned and went back to sleep again.

He opened his eyes to the sound of birds chirping and the thunking sound of the monk smacking wooden blocks together in the shrine next door. Sunshine poured through the gray blackout curtain onto the bed. He took a deep breath and raised his left arm slowly. There was still only empty air in the place that his hand was supposed to be.

He was completely speechless. He didn't even make a sound. His whole arm shivered. He didn't feel any pain or discomfort though. For a long time he just stared, trying to figure out why his hand wasn't there. It 'felt' like it was still there, but frozen in some kind of invisible cast.

He reached over to the bedside table and tried to pick up a mug with his missing hand. He was stunned when the mug moved. He couldn't feel anything. He squeezed harder, and the mug hovered a little. When he tensed his whole elbow and arm, the mug actually lifted into the air slowly.

It felt totally abnormal.

He turned on his computer and started searching the Internet for answers, using only his right hand. 'Symptom of a body part disappearing,' he tried. 'Is it possible to have an arm disappear?' He also searched for 'Paranoia' and 'Schizophrenia,' but couldn't find the answers he was looking for. In fact, he didn't know what he was looking for. His laptop screen showed the search results for mental hospitals and therapists. He sat on the chair like a blank canvas. Dizziness hit him, and he blacked out.

When he became conscious, the clock was pointing at five again, though it was getting dark outside. He was totally exhausted. He thought all this must be because of stress or fatigue, but he didn't know for sure.

He thought about not going to his part-time job, then he remembered there was a wedding party at the restaurant that night. He had a long shower and got dressed, then climbed on his bicycle, squeezed the handlebar very tightly with his invisible left hand, and started pedaling awkwardly. It was difficult to balance, especially while cycling uphill toward the French restaurant near the Kanda River.

He had started working as a part-time pâtissier at the restaurant a few months earlier. He was a student of the Business School in Tokyo, but he'd been influenced by his girlfriend back in Korea, who loved to make desserts. After that he'd naturally become a big fan of baking. He enjoyed making creative things that made people happy. In fact, he liked making desserts more than studying for his business degree.

The more he worked in the French restaurant, the more he wanted to be a full-time pâtissier. The summer vacation was starting soon but he didn't feel like going back for the next term. He hadn't told anyone yet, but he knew his girlfriend would support him for sure.

He parked his bicycle in the alley behind the restaurant and walked through the kitchen door.

"Good evening," he said politely to the chefs. Everyone was busy preparing ingredients for the big party tonight.

"Hey there," the chefs replied cheerfully. It seemed that nobody noticed his hand had disappeared, they were just focusing on their own work. Jin felt somewhat relieved. Maybe it was all in his head.

It was a Friday night at the start of a long weekend, so the restaurant was busy, but Jin managed to complete all his work, though it was difficult using a knife. The bride and the groom seemed to enjoy their wedding party with friends and family. Jin watched with relief as the waiter took his chocolate soufflés out for the last course, then headed home sometime after midnight.

He cycled fast downhill from the restaurant, past the small cemetery next to the shrine. It was a pitch dark, dry night without a breath of wind. The blue fluorescent light in the corridor of his building flickered with a loud clicking noise. He opened the sky-blue metal door of his apartment, filled a pint glass with water at the sink and drank it all in one go, then fell on the bed without even changing his work clothes.

Through the window he saw a red crescent moon in the black sky. Dogs were barking outside. The sound of it came to him like repeat signs in a musical score, echoing again and again in the darkness. He fell asleep slowly.

In the middle of the night, he opened his eyes and his body felt strange. He couldn't move and he couldn't even close his eyes. He was lying in the dark and looking up at the ceiling. There was nothing else he could do. His body felt like it was shrinking down to a piece of thin origami paper, slowly dissolving in a big dark ocean. He wept though he didn't know why.

The next morning the sun rose as normal, the birds were chirping and the monk in the nearby shrine was reciting his sutras and hitting his wooden blocks gently. It was a perfectly normal morning, but Jin still couldn't move his body at all. He just lay on the bed and looked up at the ceiling.

It was only around midday that he could finally get up and walk around the house. After that he didn't remember how he spent the day, how he went to work, what desserts he made, what he ate for lunch, or how he came home again. Nothing. He remembered nothing for the entire day. The next thing he knew it was night again, and he was floating above the floor by two inches.

He tried to push his feet down to stand on the floor, but the more he tried, the more resistance he felt, like he was pushing two negative magnets against each other. He bit his lips nervously and floated around the apartment by holding onto the walls, like a little boy trying out skateboarding for the first time.

His mouth was as dry as the Sahara Desert in the middle of summer. He poured water in a pint glass, drank it all then drank another pint of water straightaway. Extreme hunger stabbed at his belly. He took a green apple from the fridge and had a big bite. He could feel the sour apple juice as it went down his throat and reached his empty stomach, causing a sharp pain. He threw the apple away on the floor and gave a big sigh. He leaned on the chair next to the window. The red crescent moon was shining again in the black sky. A cool wind came through the open window and dried the sweat from his forehead. His whole body was shivering badly. The clock made a loud, consistent ticking sound through the empty apartment.

He turned the TV on. A lion was sprinting through long golden grass under a bright sun. A deer was running with its long thin legs desperately kicking. Soon it was snatched by the lion. The camera zoomed in so that the lion's red eyes filled the big screen. Jin turned the TV off and closed his eyes, cleared his dry throat and tried to calm himself down. He fell asleep on the chair.

After a while, he woke to a dull vibration in his left hand. He opened his eyes. There was the smell of rain on the wind. His feet were icy cold and he felt a weird electric tingling where his hand should be. Water dropped on his toes. Now rain was pouring through the open window. A sudden roll of thunder and flash of lightning broke the silence of the black sky. He tried to close the window but he couldn't move. All he could do was blink, but even that was painful. His eyelids felt extremely heavy, like heavy rocks in a deep ocean that had never been discovered by humans.

The next morning Jin sent a text message to the French restaurant's executive chef, took sick leave and went to a psychiatric hospital near his apartment. A doctor in a white gown looked into his eyes calmly.

"What can I help you with?" he asked.

Jin didn't know where to begin, so blurted it out. "I feel totally weird and something is going on with my body." He raised his left arm for the doctor to see. The doctor looked at his arm and his face then smiled back at him. He didn't see anything unusual.

"Have you had any extra stress recently?"

Jin shook his head with despair.

"Do you sleep well at night?"

"No, I don't sleep well at all. Not since the incident happened."

The doctor leaned in. "What kind of incident do you mean?"

"Well, a few days ago I woke up in the middle of night with some pain in my left hand, and I couldn't move, and my eyelids felt heavy. I tried to move my body but I couldn't move even a fingertip. That morning my left hand was missing." Jin sighed again. "I know it sounds strange, but it happens every day now."

"You're having nightmares," the doctor said kindly. "Some people have such deep unconscious stress that it causes a strange feeling. It's a symptom that a lot of people have these days in the modern world. It could be a symptom of insomnia as well. But if you treat it in the early stages, you'll get better. I'll write you a prescription for a sedative to help you sleep. If you don't get better after a week, please come back." He typed the information into his computer while he was talking to Jin.

"Umm... what is the correlation between stress and a body part disappearing?" Jin asked.

The doctor turned to him and spoke in a voice that was like calm classical music. "I think you need to take a break from what you're doing and take it easy for a while. Being exposed to nature, like on a beach or on a mountain, is a good way to relax. Exercise is another way to relax. Meditation too; if you have difficulties doing it alone, I recommend you join our group therapy which has music and yoga."

Jin left the hospital holding his prescription and a leaflet for the hospital's yoga therapy class. He suddenly felt a deep hunger. He went to a vegan restaurant and had a vegetable- and mushroom-mixed rice bowl with tofu pancakes for lunch. After that he walked over to the park, sat down on the bench and watched leaves falling in the frog pond while drinking sweet and sour plum juice from a convenience store.

He sat there for almost half a day and only left the park in the late afternoon. In his apartment he listened to meditation music and read 'The Art of Happiness' by the Dalai Lama. He thought about the purpose of his life and wise selfishness vs. foolish selfishness. He closed the book and looked out through the window. A purple sunset dyed the buildings, cars and people who were walking on the street. He finished the book and listened to his music twice more, then had a shower, changed to a clean and ironed pair of pajamas and laid down on the bed. He swallowed one of the pills from the hospital too. He thought about his girlfriend, his family and friends, about the Okinawan beach where he was planning to take his girlfriend with the savings from his part-time job. He thought about his half-finished dissertation and the Royal Banquet cookbook for 18th-century French cuisine that he'd ordered online. He was tired but couldn't easily sleep. He started counting sheep jumping on green grass, and slowly drifted off.

The next day he lost both his hands. He shivered from the cold even though it was early summer.

"The weather forecast says it will be hotter this summer compared to last year. Global warming is becoming a big issue, isn't it?"

He was in the French restaurant. One of the chefs was gently boiling custard cream and wiping sweat from his forehead with a towel.

"Yes, you're right. It's already hot." Jin agreed with the chef cautiously, but both his legs were shivering badly under the sink. Since he'd lost both his hands, it was getting more difficult to balance his body. He had to grit his teeth and focus so hard to squeeze the icing onto his red velvet cakes. In the shiny steel worktop his eyes looked very tired, with many strange dark circles dappling his face like age spots. While he was putting coffee syrup on the ladyfingers, the executive chef came over.

"You're quite serious at work these days, aren't you?"

Jin was shocked. "Pardon me?"

"It's good that you take it very seriously, but don't work too hard. OK?" The executive chef gently patted Jin's shoulder, smiled and left the kitchen. The sous chef glared at Jin fiercely.

Jin felt lost for words. He went quiet and tried to work on his own. When the other chefs made snacks on their break and had a nice chat, he just stared at his face in the shiny stainless worktop, and looked through the kitchen window at the trains passing by outside.

"What are you thinking of?" a young chef asked him.

"I have no idea," he said. "I don't know what I'm going to be."

The young chef laughed. "What are you talking about? You just got a compliment from the executive chef. He rarely does that." He paused for a second. "Is something going on at your school?"

Jin blinked his eyes slowly. "My body is going weird."

"What about it?"

"It... it's disappearing."

The chef looked confused. "What? Are you catching a cold?"

"Don't I look strange?" Jin pulled away from the chair. The young chef had a quick look at him while chewing a thinly sliced omelet.

"Hmm... you do seem a bit tired. It's better to eat well and stay healthy in this kind of weather."

"Yes, you're right," Jin said, feeling his face flush hot. "Thank you."

He didn't have any strength to pedal his bicycle up the hill anymore. He left it in the back alley by the kitchen door and decided to walk home. He tried his best to stand on the floor of his apartment but the more he tried the more his feet bounced off the floor. He tried to jump and force his feet down but that just caused a sharp pain in both his hands and made his knees shake harder. The floor looked a million miles away from his two floaty feet.

The next day he cancelled his apartment contract. He got rid of all his furniture and left his textbooks in the school department office.

"I'm going to take a break from school and travel around South America for a while," he said to his professor, in the middle of a group seminar. The professor was leading a lively discussion of global business accounting practices, but he went quiet when Jin spoke. His classmates all seemed surprised too.

"Really?" the professor asked, looking confused. "Summer vacation starts soon and you only have one term left until graduation. What's going on?"

Jin stood up, nodded at his professor and left the seminar without giving a clear answer. He didn't even know why he chose South America. It just popped into his head and he simply made a decision by saying it.

He transported his clothes, shoes, toiletries and his bicycle to an Internet café, where he slept and had his meals; mainly pot noodles and onigiri rice balls bought from a convenience store nearby. It was like a homeless person's lifestyle, but at least he didn't have to be a burden to other people or ask them for favors. He decided not to go back to his school again, though he didn't want to quit his part-time job yet. He had to think about what to do next, but before that he needed to see his mom. He didn't want to see his girlfriend because he didn't know what to say, and he wasn't confident he could deal with her disappointment at his new condition.

He opened his laptop for the first time in weeks and opened his email box. 250 unread emails. He clicked the first email.

'Hi. It's me. How are you doing? I worry about you since I haven't heard from you for a while. I know you're busy with your dissertation, but let me know once you read this email. I'll hunt you down if you don't come back to me! Summer vacation is coming and I look forward to seeing you soon.'

Jin closed the email and thought he couldn't continue living like this. He had to end it by saying goodbye to his current life and going somewhere very far away. He sent a text message to the executive chef in the French restaurant instead of to his girlfriend.

'I'm sorry for the late notice, but I'll take a few days off and go home to see my mom. It's urgent family business. I'll come back in two days.'

He had a reply from the chef in an hour.

'Sure, I hope everything goes well. Say hi to your mother and see you soon.'

Jin left his bicycle in front of the Internet café and headed to Narita Airport. He fell asleep leaning against the small oval window of the airplane, and had a dream of sharing a strawberry popsicle with his girlfriend. The sunshine was warm and her lips were bright and shiny red.

"Our flight is landing in Busan International Airport in 15 minutes. Passengers, please fasten your seat belts." Jin opened his eyes to the pilot's announcement.

He arrived in Busan, took two long distance buses then walked along the unpaved hills in the forest until he stood in front of a green orchard. A middle-aged lady was checking the leaves of the apple trees and pruning branches in a professional manner. He stood in the middle of the road and gave a big dry cough. The lady looked around. Her eyes opened wide and she ran over to him.

"Gosh, who is this?" she called excitedly. "Why did you not tell me you were coming home?"

Jin smiled at her awkwardly and walked over. "Mom, how have you been?"

She smiled broadly and took his hand. "I'm fine, but it's so good to see you! You've lost a lot of weight, though. It's hard to live on your own in a foreign country, isn't' it? Come on in." He pulled his invisible hand out of her hands and took a step back. He was so nervous that she might notice something was wrong.

"Why is your hand so cold?" she asked. "It's freezing cold. You're not eating well, are you?"

Jin sighed. He wasn't sure if the sigh was from relief or resignation. "I'm fine. Shall we go in?"

In the kitchen, his mom turned the classic FM radio on and hummed along while she cooked; making rice in a cast iron pot, stirring miso soup with diced zucchini and tofu, pouring soy and honey-glaze sauce over a beef and glass noodle stew, grilling seaweed brushed with perilla oil and mixing sliced cucumber and onion with apple vinegar, red chili pepper flakes, soy sauce and sesame seeds.

Jin sat at the kitchen table and sipped hot Hoji tea, watching his mom's back as she cooked. He used to think she was like the genie from Aladdin when she was cooking. She was like a magician. Within what seemed like moments only, she laid freshly cooked green beans and rice on the table, along with zucchini and tofu miso soup, honey soy sauce-marinated beef and glass noodle stew, perilla oil-grilled seaweed and the cucumber and onion salad with sour fermented kimchi.

"If you'd told me earlier, I could have prepared more," she said with a sorrowful face. "But anyway, how's your school? Only one term until graduation! Are you excited?"

"This is a feast," Jin said, changing the subject and putting a big spoonful of rice and kimchi in his mouth.

"Eat slowly. There's a lot more food here." She looked at Jin warmly. The wrinkle lines on her eyes had gotten a bit deeper. All the time he was slurping the miso soup, chewing the sweet and spicy cucumber salad and eating the rice and beef stew, she didn't take her eyes off him. After dinner, they pruned the apple trees and burned dead branches in a fire pit together. She put sweet potatoes wrapped in foil on top of the fire.

In his old room, Jin checked out his school photo albums, along with old handwritten letters from his girlfriend, old poems, and a black and white photo of his mom and dad from when they were young. Time had stopped in his room, it seemed, and nothing had changed since he'd left the house. He sat on his small chair, organizing his belongings and gathering his various photos in one box. At the top of the pile lay a shot of their family, smiling happily under a cherry tree: his mom and dad with no wrinkles, Jin in the middle with no front teeth. It was one of the few photos he had with his dad. He didn't have many memories of his dad, so it was like a faded dream to see him in the photo.

He fell asleep at the desk and opened his eyes to a deep vibration sound. His body was still falling into the endlessly deep ocean. He couldn't breathe. He couldn't think properly. He felt so sad and lonely.

As soon as the sun rose, Jin had a quick shower then put his favorite poems and the cherry-tree family photo in his Boston bag. His mom was busy cooking breakfast for him.

"Mom, I can't come home for quite a while," he said, pouring freshly brewed hot black coffee in a big mug.

"Why, what's going on?"

"I'm busy with my dissertation and I have a part-time job now." He didn't meet her eyes on purpose, only looked down on his feet.

His mom put a soft hand on his elbow. "You have your own life now, son. I respect your decisions, and I want to support you. I can't do much for you now we live so far away, but let me know if you need any help, OK? Call me regularly, too."

"Sure, will do." His voice trembled.

When he opened his Boston bag at the airport, he found lots of well-ripened small apples and a couple of grilled sweet potatoes, as well as a handwritten postcard.

'My darling son. I know it is hard to study and live alone. Your mom feels sad to see that you lost weight. I wish I was living nearby and cooking nice meals for you. It's unfortunate to be far way, but I always pray for you and support you with all my heart. Good luck with your studies and be safe until we see each other again. Lots of kisses and hugs. Mom xx'

Jin closed his teary eyes and thought about his mom for a while. He turned on his mobile phone, which he'd kept turned off for weeks. Five missed calls and two messages.

"It's me again. Where are you now? I'm coming to find you. Call me back."

He turned his phone off again and got on the airplane. As soon as he arrived in Narita Airport, he took a Limousine Bus to Shinjuku station, changed to a train and headed to the French restaurant on the Kanda riverside. It felt weird to hear so much noise suddenly; cars honking, people walking and talking, loud music and white noise from electrical goods shops. He felt drained but he squeezed enough energy out of his brain to open the kitchen door.

"Hey, how's your mother?" the executive chef asked, tapping his shoulder gently. "Did you have a good time at home?"

"Yes, it was good. Thank you." Jin put the bag of apples on the kitchen table. Both the beautifully fresh olive-green apples and his tired face with its dark circles were reflected on the shiny stainless steel worktop.

"Oh, these look tasty," the chef said.

Jin made a cinnamon apple crumble and vanilla ice cream for the kitchen staff's dessert, before the main dinner service. While they were eating it all their faces looked like shiny apples. Afterward they said how refreshing and scrumptious it was.

"This is worth dying for," one of the young apprentice chefs said.

The executive chef raised his empty plate. "How about serving this dessert tomorrow, a special on the four-course lunch menu for ten tables only?"

"OK," Jin said.

Soon after that, dinner orders poured into the kitchen. The chefs moved like well-trained soldiers. Jin simmered nicely cut white peaches with syrup to make peach tarts in a well-baked short crust pastry, then caramelized golden brown sugar on top of crème brûlées with a sea salt crust.

The tarts and the crème brûlées disappeared into the customers' happy mouths. Jin stopped working and looked around at what the other chefs were doing. They all wore clean black chef outfits, each focused on their own work. Shallots were frying with butter, béchamel sauce was boiling slowly, rosemary and thyme-seasoned thick lamb steaks were grilling on a cast-iron skillet. He felt a great energy rising from the smells, sounds and heat of the kitchen. It reminded him of watching his mother's back in her cozy farm kitchen.

Jin took a deep breath and focused on his baking. He made petite-sized meringue cookies for coffee and tea, boiled whole chestnuts with syrup and piped fresh chestnut crème on top of the Mont Blanc cakes. Of course, he also made the cinnamon apple crumble with fresh vanilla ice cream, for ten tables only. His body felt like a big flame burning on a small candle, but he ignored it and kept on going.

When he was having a break over hot chamomile tea, the executive chef called him.

"The customers want to talk to you, is it OK?"

"Pardon?" Jin asked. He was shocked, but nodded in agreement after several seconds.

The dining room was full, with customers talking in low voices, delicate wine glasses clinking and calm classical music playing softly in the silences. A middle-aged well-dressed couple looked up at Jin. The lady had pink cheeks and a thoughtful expression.

"It was one of the best desserts I ever had in my life," she said. "The taste was extraordinary. It sounds strange, but I felt as if I was floating above the ground while I was eating it."

The gray-haired guy smiled at Jin and shook his hand. "It was a good gift for our thirty-year wedding anniversary."

Jin cleared his throat. "Ah, thank you."

That night in the Internet café, Jin's entire body felt like it was slowly melting, like a snowman in April. He couldn't properly stand up or move his body well anymore. He couldn't remember how the time had passed or how he'd come back from the restaurant. A colorless, transparent moon shone down from the sky. Jin sat in an armchair next to a window and looked at his family photo, all together under the cherry tree. The moon in the photo was perfectly round and white. It felt like maybe he could reach back in time when his invisible fingers touched the moon. He tried to stand up but he couldn't move his body. Warm tears soaked his white t-shirt.

The next morning, his body was completely gone. His face looked like a totally different person's face in the mirror, hanging in the air. He sat in a corner of the dim Internet café under a flickering fluorescent blue light and bought a ticket to Buenos Aires for that afternoon. He spent the money that he'd saved for the Okinawa trip with his girlfriend, because he knew it could never happen now.

He wrote a simple note to say he was quitting and left it in the basket of his bicycle behind the restaurant. He believed the executive chef would find it and take care of the bicycle as well. He also wrote a postcard for his mom.

'Mom, I'll be very busy with my studies for a while, so you might not be able to reach me, but there is nothing to worry about. Take care.'

His girlfriend would be sad to hear he was gone, but she would forget about it and start a new life. Jin felt guilty but couldn't think of any other way to deal with it. He was devastated and exhausted. He closed his eyes. He didn't know what to do and couldn't possibly guess what would happen next. The only thing he knew was he had to disappear far, far away.

"Passengers, we will soon close the gate for the flight to Buenos Aires. Passengers who haven't boarded yet, please go to gate A15." The announcement rang through the airport.

Jin stood up and moved slowly to the gate, holding his black Boston bag and dragging his feet in their tatty white trainers.

7. Mille-feuille with fresh whipped cream and strawberries and the cats

On the way back home from the photo studio one evening, Hana heard a rustling sound coming from an empty alley. She stopped walking and tried to figure out where the sound was coming from. She was holding her bag tightly with both hands, ready to run to the other side of the road, when a sound came from the darkness.

"Meow."

Hana kept her eyes wide open and looked deeper into the shadows.

"Meeooowww," came the sound again. She moved toward the tiny pathetic voice slowly and carefully. Two filthy and terrified-looking young cats were sitting on top of each other in the corner of the dark alleyway. One was black with white socks and the other was white with black spots.

"Ah," she said happily, "you're the cats that I saw several months ago in front of Jin's old apartment!" They'd grown bigger, but they looked so thin, as if they hadn't eaten well for a long time. The cat with white socks didn't even have enough energy to groom itself, so its white socks had become gray. Hana felt heartbroken to see it.

"Don't go anywhere. I'll be back soon." She ran to a convenience store around the corner and bought a can of wet cat food, a bottle of water and a paper plate. She managed to get a pair of disposable wooden chopsticks too. When she ran back to the alleyway, the two cats were hugging close to each other, so they wouldn't lose any warmth from their tiny bodies.

Hana poured a bit of water on the paper plate and mixed it well with the wet food, smashing the bigger pieces with the wooden chopsticks. The cats came over and ate all the food without even chewing it, then licked up the liquid in such a big hurry. Hana felt like she understood how the two young cats felt.

"You're Jiyo, and you're Miyo," she said, pointing at the cats as they groomed themselves happily after their big dinner. "You're my boys from now on."

Since Hana had named the cats, she fed them every day, in their secret spot in the alleyway. Whenever she passed by, she always looked for the cats first. Sometimes they turned up with gritty eyes and scratches on their noses, or only one of them showed up, so Hana got worried, but each time they ran over and showed her their bellies like they were seeing their mom for the first time in a long time.

Probably it was just because they were hungry, but Hana was so happy that someone was waiting for her and appreciated her existence in this alien place. She felt warm and special to be around the cats. Every living thing needed a little help and affection, after all. When

Hana gave the cats delicacies such as boiled chicken breast or cod fillets on her pay day, and the cats kneaded her hand or foot after eating the food, Hana felt like she had her own little family.

"Jiyo and Miyo, I'll adopt you boys once I have a place to live on my own," she told them often. "I promise you." It gave her a deeper motivation to work hard and settle down. Jin would be happy about that too.

Jiyo and Miyo sometimes left Hana unwanted presents in their food bowls. A half-cut cockroach or a tail of a rat made her freak out, but she didn't show her emotions to the cats, and thanked them instead. One day, a blue glass bead and a scallop shell were lying in the food bowls. She washed them, put the glass bead inside the scallop shell and set them as decorations on the windowsill next to her bunk bed. The glass bead had a lot of small air bubbles in it. She sat on the windowsill and put her eyes close to it. She could see a beautiful Milky Way through the tiny surface of the glass bead.

She opened the window wide open. The air was fresh and the wind was cool and sharp, blowing through the window so hard that it knocked her canvas bag off the end of the bed. Hana picked it up, but a name card had fallen out. There was a phone number and a pretty handwritten name on it, 'Sumi Kim'.

"Who is this..." Hana mumbled to herself, turning the card over. "Ah, the Korean family from the photo studio!" Sumi had asked Hana to call, but she'd completely forgotten about it. She wasn't sure if Sumi had given her the number to be generous or if she actually wanted Hana to call, but she was curious how the two kids were doing, Bomi and Jun, so she decided to call.

"Oh, it's lovely to hear from you," Sumi said brightly. She sounded pleased to be called. "I was thinking about calling the photo studio and checking how you are doing, so this is good timing."

"Sorry I forgot to call you earlier," Hana replied. "How're Bomi and Jun doing?"

"They're doing good! Jun disliked his kindergarten in the beginning but now he's made some friends and he's getting used to the new environment. Bomi asked me several times how the photo studio girl was doing." She gave a little laugh. "Do you have any plans this Sunday? What about coming over for lunch?"

Hana flushed a little. "Yes, that sounds nice. Thank you for inviting me."

"Great, the kids will be very excited. We look forward to it."

Hana took note of the address and hung up the phone. It was the first time she'd been invited to someone's home since Nok, so she felt excited and nervous at the same time. She was thinking about what to bake for them, and remembered there was a puff pastry in the fridge. A mille-feuille would be perfect, but with whipped double crème and strawberries instead of mascarpone cheese, for the kids.

Early on Sunday morning she took the puff pastry out of the fridge and left it to reach room temperature. While the pastry was defrosting, she had a shower, changed her clothes and put on light make-up. She placed a sheet of parchment paper on a long, thin metal tray and put the puff pastry on it, then spread caster sugar evenly on top, prepared another pastry in a separate tray, and put the two trays in the preheated oven.

She checked the address while the pastries were baking, then made whipped cream out of fresh double cream with added vanilla beans and caster sugar. The freshly baked, golden puff pastries looked light and crunchy on the cooling rack. Hana cut the pastries carefully so as not to break them, then added the whipped cream and thinly sliced strawberries in several layers, with more caster sugar and honey-glazed mint on top.

She boxed up the bigger mille-feuille, and cut a slice of the smaller one and put it on a plate. Ms. Oyama was not at her desk, so Hana left the plate with a note on the reception desk.

Hana carefully placed the cake box in the basket of her orange bicycle and added some padding to protect the box, then started cycling slowly, enjoying the morning sun and the nice breeze. Sumi's place was located in the middle of the hustle and bustle of Shinjuku; a new tall apartment building with a big lobby and a brand-new auto lock system. Hana checked the door number and rang the bell at the entrance. The door opened automatically and the concierge guided her to take the second lift to the 20th floor.

Sumi opened the door as soon as Hana popped out of the lift. She was wearing a white cotton dress and a purple hair band.

"Welcome," she said, smiling widely. "Was it OK to find the place?"

Hana smiled back. "Yes, it was easy to find it. Thank you for inviting me."

"Hello!" Bomi and Jun greeted her enthusiastically at the same time.

"I saw you parked your bicycle," Bomi said with a mischievous smile, showing off her missing front teeth. "You carried that box like it was a baby girl!" She leaned closer and whispered. "What have you got in it?"

Hana ducked down and answered in a loud whisper. "Oh, I'm a bicycle cake delivery service, and today I've brought you a big cake! Here you go, young lady.' Hana made a big show of handing the cake box to Bomi.

"Yeah, Daddy, look at me, I've got a present!" Bomi held the box up high. Sumi's husband Gon stood behind them and waved, wearing a pink kiddy apron and holding a big salad bowl.

"Oh, thank you, Hana. That's so kind! Please, come on in."

Sumi led her down a narrow hallway into a big open kitchen-diner living space, with a high ceiling and tall, wide windows. It was so bright and airy. Paintings on the walls and two colorful sofas lifted up the space and made it cozier.

While Bomi and Jun led Hana on a tour around the house, Sumi and Gon loaded down the dining table with soy sauce-marinated beef stew with whole chestnuts, stir-fried glass noodles with bright bell pepper strips, balsamic vinegar and honey dressing rocket salad, seaweed soup with clams and black steamed rice.

"Oh my goodness," Hana exclaimed when she saw it all. "When did you cook all this food? It's like a birthday party."

"It's not a big deal," Sumi said, squeezing Bomi and Jun with a smile. "We haven't cooked much recently because we were busy dealing with these two little monsters. It's been a long time since we invited someone over, so we're very glad you're here with us today."

For some reason Hana thought of her parents back home. Her mom and dad ran a small interior shop; they always came home very late and very tired every evening. When they were at home, they argued loudly and blamed each other for the smallest things. Whenever it happened, Hana would just go to her room, put her headset on and raise the volume of the radio. She'd promised herself she would leave the house as soon as she graduated university.

Now she was here, in the home of this loving, happy Korean family, and it almost made her want to cry. The thought struck her that maybe she'd come looking for Jin just as an excuse. Of course she was worried that he hadn't answered her calls or emails, but also she'd needed a reason to leave the house. She'd always thought she wouldn't miss her parents once she left them, but now, well...

"Hana, are you alright?" Sumi asked. Both she and Gon seemed a little concerned.

"Of course," Hana replied quickly, feeling flustered. "I just haven't had Korean food for a long time, so I was thinking about what to eat first."

"Oh, we've got a lot here so please help yourself to as much as you want." Sumi smiled warmly and moved the plates closer to Hana.

"Hana, enjoy!" said Bomi.

Every dish was cooked beautifully, with a great balance of flavors, not too salty, not too greasy, not too sweet or spicy.

"These glass noodles are so good," Hana said, enjoying the delicate dish with its vivid colors. "The texture is amazing."

"Thank you. I added homemade soy sauce from Korea. I made a lot so I'll pack you some later."

"Mom, I'll try it too!" Jun and Bomi tried hard to hold the slippery glass noodles with their kids' chopsticks, but it wasn't easy. Gon put the noodles in a small bowl, chopped them with scissors, fed the kids and wiped up the mess all at the same time.

After lunch Bomi and Jun got some boardgames out and the adults cleared the table, then everyone sat around the sofa and had Hana's mille-feuille cake while drinking green tea.

"I want another piece," Jun said excitedly.

"Me too!" Bomi cheered.

They played board games all together and had a fun time. Hana finally stood up from the sofa when it started getting dark outside, putting her bag on her shoulder.

"Thank you so much. It was a really fun day."

"Are you leaving?" Bomi asked, about to cry.

"I'll come back soon," Hana said, and hugged Bomi. Bomi only let Hana go after promising she would come back after seven days.

"The biggest number that she knows is seven," Sumi whispered to Hana. "Please do come again soon." She handed Hana a paper bag with stir-fried glass noodles in a plastic tub. "Put it in the fridge and fry it with a bit of water and sesame oil. Then it'll be like it's freshly made again."

Sumi's family waved at Hana until she couldn't see them anymore. Hana held the paper bag like a baby and took a train, leaning her bike up against a pole. On the train, a dog sitting on a girl's lap next to Hana sniffed at the food in her bag desperately. Hana got off the train, rode past the market street and went along the street toward the guest house. The area had a homey smell now, and she felt relaxed and comfortable to be there. When a gentle rain began to fall, she hurried along.

Jiyo and Miyo meowed as soon as they heard her coming. They were just like her childhood dog, who'd known each person just by their footsteps. That thought made her smile.

"Where are you boys, you must be hungry," Hana called softly toward the dark alleyway. Jiyo and Miyo pricked up their ears in the darkness. Hana opened her bag and took out a can of cat food. She always carried cat food with her now, as she didn't know when she would meet the boys.

She knelt at the corner to prepare their food, then there was a sharp banging noise from the alley. Hana looked up to see a car stopping in a screech of brakes. The door opened and a young driver shouted into the dark.

"What the... this stupid cat ran under my car! How unlucky." The young guy noticed Hana was looking at him, then put his black hoodie back on and drove quickly out of the alley.

Hana dashed into the shadows. Her heart was pounding so hard.

"Boy, look at me," she called, "open your eyes!"

Jiyo was lying on the cold concrete like he was in a deep sleep. Hana held his little body and tried to wake him up. The white and black mix of fur on his forehead had a sharp blood mark across it. His white socks were filthy with mud. He was unbelievably warm and unbelievably small.

"Pussy cat. I brought your favorite food. Open your eyes. Please."

Hana's tears dropped on Jiyo's small head.

8. Kawanami vegetable shop

That night Hana had a severe fever and migraine. She threw up whatever she ate, and only managed to drink a sip of water before she fell into a deep, bottomless sleep. The next day she called the photo studio and said she needed to take some time off. Yoko seemed worried about her and wished her to get better soon.

After sleeping for two full days, Hana could still barely get out of bed. She looked at herself in the mirror. Her face and hair looked dried-out and there were blisters on her lips. She opened the curtains and cleaned up the room.

In the fridge there was leftover double cream and strawberries. She poured the half-rotten strawberries and double cream into the blender along with some sugar and lemon juice. Her throat was burning. She added a handful of ice cubes and watched them blend with the strawberries until the color became light pink. She poured the strawberry sherbet into a tall glass and drank a little. The strawberries, lemon and ice slowly refreshed her head and mind. She washed the glass and had a long shower.

The cat funeral was scheduled for that afternoon, and it went smoothly, with Mr. Abe's help. He'd called the funeral service company, so when she arrived in the shrine with a small box of Jiyo's body, the staff handled everything without Hana having to do anything. Jiyo lay inside the box with his eyes calmly closed. When she saw his pink paws, she burst into tears again.

He was cremated and his ashes were buried in the shrine. Hana spent all her savings on his funeral, but she didn't feel it was a waste of money. Jiyo would be safe there and would not need to worry about food, cold weather, danger or pain ever again. He would be in eternal peace.

After the funeral, Hana left the shrine and walked with no purpose. She looked down at the concrete pavement and her feet. It was about to rain. The sky was full of thick gray clouds and it was cold. She pulled up her hoodie. She walked until it was late at night and all the shops were closed, but she could smell butter chicken curry somewhere. It made her hungry, and she realized she hadn't eaten anything other than strawberry sherbet.

As she was walking down the dark and empty market street, looking for the shop selling butter chicken curry, a crashing torrent of rain suddenly fell from the sky. She'd forgotten to bring an umbrella, so she just ignored the rain and continued walking. The rain beat down harder until soon she was completely wet and cold. She stood under the edge of an old blue plastic awning. She rubbed her hands and blew warm air on them. Her breath steamed like cigarette smoke.

Her nose and hands felt raw and numb. She put her palms against her head and sighed deeply, then heard a faint noise at the edge of the street.

"Meow."

Hana lifted her head at once.

"Meooowww."

It was a cat's voice. Soon after, a small, soaking wet cat with white fur and black polka dots came over to Hana and sat behind her legs.

Hana squatted down to stroke his head. "It's you, Miyo. I thought you were gone too."

She'd only ever seen them together before. Now Miyo was alone.

"I'm sorry," Hana said. "I should have looked after you better." The cat licked her cold hand. She took her jacket off, dried the cat and fed him dry cat biscuits from her pocket. He was warm underneath his soft white fur coat.

"Thank you for coming back again," she said, then started to cry. She tried to stop but couldn't, and ended up sobbing loudly in the rain. It wasn't fair that Jiyo had died. It wasn't fair that Miyo would have to live the rest of his life and never see his brother again. Hana tried to control her sobbing but she couldn't.

"Who is that?" came a sudden shout. "Who is making that loud noise at night?"

It was a sharp old lady's angry voice. Hana looked up from the wet concrete floor, abruptly silent, protecting the cat with her arms.

"Is that a thief?" came the voice again, then somebody raised a big broom over Hana's head in the dark.

"Wait, please, I'm not a thief, I don't have a weapon!" Hana waved her empty hands. Miyo ran away into a dark side alleyway. Then there was a bright flashlight on Hana's face. She narrowed her eyes against the light and raised her arms in the air.

"Who is this? Your face is familiar." The angry voice grew slightly calmer than before. Hana squinted against the flashlight, picking out the crooked old silhouette on the other side.

"You're the girl who carried my grocery bags without my permission," said the old woman, and now Hana recognized her, the old lady with heavy bags who'd looked like she was going to fall off the road. She was frowning at Hana from a face already full of wrinkles.

Hana recognized the half-faded sign on the old tatty blue awning too. 'Kawanami vegetable shop.' She remembered the delicious Snow White-red apples. She rubbed her eyes and cleared her throat.

"Are you feeding cats?" the old lady asked, raising her voice. "There are a lot of street cats digging in my trash bins these days, and you're the one inviting them all to stay?"

Hana tried to reply but she didn't have any energy left. She wanted to say, 'If I don't feed them, they may die,' but she was too cold and exhausted.

"Why don't you answer a simple question?" the old lady demanded, raising her voice even louder.

"I'm cold and hungry," Hana said. The words blurted out before she could stop them, though she covered her mouth immediately after. She couldn't believe she'd just said that to a stranger.

The old woman's wrinkles smoothed out a little as the frown faded, and when she spoke again it was quieter, though puzzled. "Why would a grown-up girl be crying on the street at night in the rain, instead of going home?"

That just made Hana start crying harder. She didn't know why she was suddenly so emotional. She felt pathetic. Her hair stuck to her damp cheeks like seaweed in the rain.

"Come on in," the old lady said.

"Pardon?" Hana managed, though she was panting now from crying so hard.

"Stop crying and come on inside. People in the whole town can hear you." The old lady shooed her along, and Hana went into the building. She dripped water on the shop's dark wooden floor and up the stairs to the second floor of the narrow building. There was a warm gas stove in the middle of a kitchen-diner. Hana was shivering from the cold but soon she warmed up.

"Dry your hair and don't drip water on the floor," the old lady complained, handing Hana a thin face towel.

While Hana took her jumper off and dried her hair, the old lady prepared dinner; wholegrain brown rice, Teriyaki sauce-boiled yellowtail with horseradish, Chinese cabbage and burdock miso soup, seasoned horse bean with sesame seeds. She laid each dish out on the old, dark wooden dining table, making no unnecessary movements as she prepared dinner. Her eyes were sparkling sharp as she tasted the miso soup.

She looked completely different from the old lady Hana had seen on the street. Back then she'd had no liveliness in her at all. What was happening now? It was all very surprising, but the most surprising thing was that Hana started eating the old lady's food without being given permission or even having it offered.

She ate so fast she almost drank the food. She couldn't stop moving her chopsticks. It was like she was a Hobbit who'd fallen under a spell. She drank miso soup then took a big spoonful of seasoned horse bean with well-cooked rice. The Chinese cabbage and the burdock were crunchy and had a strong earthy taste, like they'd just been pulled out of the soil. The horseradish was soft, sweet and melted in her mouth without needing to be chewed.

"I'm starving right now," she managed to say between mouthfuls, with her eyes wide open, "but even so I've never had such tasty vegetables in my life."

"And I've never seen a girl eat this enthusiastically. Nobody will steal your food. You can slow down." The old lady's pale face had a bit of coral color in it now.

"Sure." Hana shoveled even more rice into her mouth. After having another bowl of rice and miso soup, and finishing almost all the food on the table, Hana finally felt civilized again. The old lady drank barley tea and watched Hana finish her dinner.

"All right," the old lady said, putting her teacup down and looking at Hana sternly. "Now tell me why you were crying so hard in the middle of a rainy street."

Hana started by talking about Miyo and the cat funeral, but soon found everything spilling out of her again, about Jin and the guest house and her jobs. She cried and got emotional, so she had to stop several times while talking.

"I want to stay in Japan longer, but I spent all my savings for the cat's funeral, so I probably need to move out of the guest house soon. I may stay in the Internet café again and try to get one more part-time job until I have some savings. Then I'll get a proper place and think about what to do next." At the end, Hana sighed. All her tears had dried up and she felt quite calm.

The old lady looked at her with a curious expression. "Do you not have some family? Why don't you just go back home?"

Hana gently spun her small teacup on the table. "It's a long story, but I don't have a good relationship with my parents. Basically, I have nowhere to go back to. I need to sort out my life by myself, anyway. My boyfriend could come back at any time, and I want to be here when he does. Plus I like this area now, and I'm getting used to it more and more, so I don't want to leave."

"Young people these days have no plans and are so impulsive," the old lady muttered. "Spending your savings on a funeral for a random street cat, and crying and making noise in front of someone's house at night? It's so troublesome. When I was your age, I had to work to eat and live. I had to focus on surviving and making a living for my young brothers and sisters, so I couldn't think about waiting for my boyfriend or having a street cat funeral. What a luxury!"

Hana felt a little embarrassed. What the old lady was saying was true. She felt like she would crawl into a rabbit hole and disappear right then if there was a 'Drink Me' bottle in front of her.

"You're right," she said firmly. "I know it's pathetic. But thank you so much for your hospitality tonight. The dinner was great and thank you for listening to my story too. I'm sorry for making noise and bothering you." She apologized and stood up from the table awkwardly. The old lady seemed to be deep in thought.

"Hold on a moment," she said.

Hana bowed. "I'm very sorry, again. I really should be going, and-"

"Just sit down and listen!" the old lady commanded. "There's something I want to say."

Hana froze for a moment, then, very slowly, sat down again. She didn't know what was going to happen now. It was true, she'd eaten the old lady's food. In the fairytales, that often meant you were in their power. She thought if she sat very still and very politely, maybe there'd be a chance to escape later.

"My son is in Hokkaido and his room is empty now," said the old lady, which surprised Hana. "You could use his room until he comes back. But there is one condition." Hana knew there had to be a condition. "I can't carry heavy stuff anymore as my back and legs hurt. You need to help with the vegetable shop, and put out the vegetables in the early morning and clean the shop after it is closed." She paused and made a serious face. "Can you do that? If you're not good at it, you will be kicked out."

Hana didn't know what to say. If it was a trick, she couldn't see the bad side. "Can I really? Thank you, I..." Hana couldn't finish her sentence, and instead she showed her appreciation by hugging the old lady. She smelled like sweet soy sauce. Maybe things were going to be OK.

The rain finally stopped around midnight. When Hana got back to the guest house, Ms. Oyama was cleaning the fish tank in a long sleeveless dress with big bold red roses on it. Her arm seemed to be fully recovered and her hair had become its perfect cabbage shape as well. Hana explained the whole incident and the vegetable shop story to Ms. Oyama, and told her she would move to the shop by the end of the weekend. She felt sad, but Ms. Oyama just opened her newspaper with a blank expression.

"I've been a regular customer of that vegetable shop for decades now," she said. "Chieko Kawanami is well-known in the whole market street for being diligent and trustworthy. Now the perfect Ms. Kawanami needs someone's help after all? Life is transient, isn't it? Well, please say hi to Ms. Kawanami, and tell her I'll visit the shop sometime soon."

Hana bowed. "Thank you so much for the time being. I'll come visit you often."

Ms. Oyama lit another cigarette. "You act like you're going for an expedition to the North Pole. It's just around the corner, so it's not a big deal, is it?" She put the cigarette in her mouth slowly.

Hana knew it was her own way of showing affection. She hugged Ms. Oyama, who screwed up her face but allowed it, holding her cabbage head high.

9. Mont Blanc cake with a rum-candied chestnut

Ms. Kawanami's son's room had a somewhat nostalgic smell. Hana thought it was the scent of tatami. Soft tatami floors made of woven straw had a distinctive smell, similar to the aroma of late evening grass from her granny's backyard. It made Hana feel cozy and slightly homesick at the same time.

The room was simple and undecorated, with an old desk in front of a window overlooking the market street. The desk's worktop was a dark and shiny cocoa color, and Hana felt comfortable when she sat on the small chair in front of it. She placed her favorite peppermint pot on the desk in front of the windowsill so it could face the sun. It had grown several inches taller since she'd bought it, and the leaves shone a beautiful light green color.

She tried the narrow single bed. The old mattress squeaked, but even the squeaks made her feel somehow nostalgic. There was a light brown Martin guitar sitting in the corner, strings coated in a thick layer of white dust, as if it hadn't been used for a long time.

"Your son plays the guitar?" Hana asked Ms. Kawanami later day, but she didn't answer. In fact, she never shared any stories about her son in Hokkaido.

Ms. Kawanami was a perfectionist, and always punctual about work and time management. Her memory was extremely accurate, much better than Hana's, as if she was secretly carrying a watch and a voice recorder at all times to keep track of everything perfectly. Hana adjusted herself to be an early bird after starting to live with Ms. Kawanami.

Ms. Kawanami woke up at 4:30 every morning and swept the market street in front of her shop. She told Hana she'd never skipped a day since she'd started the vegetable shop thirty years ago, but she was feeling down these days because it was getting difficult to keep up the routine. She couldn't bend her back well from the pain.

"I can do it for you," Hana promised. "Don't worry."

Ms. Kawanami shook her head. "You barely wake up by 6 in the morning. It's easy to say the words, isn't it?"

After cleaning the market street, Ms. Kawanami's day started properly with a breakfast of hot rice and sticky natto fermented beans while reading the morning newspaper. At 5am she received a daily delivery of freshly picked vegetables and fruits from her sole supplier, the Kato family farm in Chiba prefecture. Ms. Kawanami's business rule was to sell only fresh local ingredients which were delivered on the same day.

On the first day of living together, she handed Hana a full to-do list of her daily shop chores:

'Check the condition of vegetables and fruits and get rid of dirt or unnecessary leaves. If they are small, slightly damaged or not attractive enough to sell to customers, put them in a separate box; they will be used as give-away items or for cooking dinner later on. Put harder items such as onions, carrots, potatoes and apples in durable baskets with little holes in the bottoms. Place fragile items such as strawberries and peaches in soft bamboo baskets. Ms. Kawanami will check the condition and size of the items and decide prices on a daily basis. Hana will write the price tags on pieces of paper and display the items on the stall. Leftover items are boxed with a note of their delivery date in the back of the shop and donated to local volunteer centers. Empty boxes are flattened and saved in the back of the shop and cleared on the recycling day once a week.'

At 6am, once Hana had finished her daily to-do list, everything was ready for the shop to open and welcome in customers.

One of the first things Hana did, after moving in and learning about her chores, was make a cat house for Miyo at the side door of the shop, using a recycling box and some cardboard. She put old cushions and blankets in the bottom of the box and covered the top with a durable waterproof vinyl sheet. The cat house was tucked in safely and looked cozy. She prepared some food and water bowls nearby, and every day after that she swept the cat area with a long willow brush and filled up the food and water bowls.

As the days passed and Hana settled into waking up early to do her chores, she was surprised by how many customers visited the vegetable shop at such an early time. These customers were usually housewives, chefs who worked in restaurants nearby or early-bird elderly people. They came to the market street to buy fresh ingredients to start their day. Ms. Oyama also usually stopped by in the morning to buy potatoes, onions or something. Sometimes she had a chat with Ms. Kawanami or Hana, but usually she did her shopping speedily then hurried back to her guest house.

One day, while Hana was cleaning dirt off a round, healthy looking cabbage, she found herself thinking about the time she'd cooked tomato cabbage rolls with Jin in his old apartment near their university, back in Korea. She remembered Jin's calm face and the soft and sweet cabbage rolls they'd eaten together.

'What if he sees me right now?' she wondered. 'Would he be disappointed in me? Would he think my life is like a boring carrot?' The thought made Hana feel sad. She realized she was holding a bunch of dirty carrots, just looking at them like she was completely lost in the thick and bushy vegetable maze.

"What are you doing now?" came Ms. Kawanami's scolding voice. "You cut all these healthy looking leaves. The carrots still have a lot of dirt on them. You should clean them properly." She held up a dirty carrot. "Every food has a spirit in it. Good vegetables have healthy spirits in them, and those spirits get dissolved in the food." She wagged the carrot in Hana's face. "You are what you eat, and my vegetables give healthy energy to people. That's why I don't have any intention of selling wilted, dirty, low-spirit vegetables or fruits to my customers. Do you understand?"

"Yes, I do." Hana made her most serious face and nodded like a soldier. She felt guilty about the filthy carrots, celery sticks and spinach. She stopped daydreaming about Jin, apologized to the vegetables and cleaned them nicely.

That morning she finished her morning chores a bit early. It was a day off from the photo studio, so she had some free time. She thought for a while and decided to go over to Jin's apartment. It wasn't far away, but she hadn't visited it again since that first day. She wasn't sure if Jin had ever lived there, but she wanted to check it out somehow.

She cycled to the place and felt quite nostalgic when it stood in front of her, at the end of the alley with the ramen shop and the coin laundry. The building looked worn down, with paint peeling off the walls here and there.

Hana walked up the narrow steps to the second floor of the building and stood again in front of apartment 205. She put her cheek and ear against the sky-blue door. The cold metal made her brain freeze. She waited for a while but didn't hear any sounds. She put one eye to the ladybird window and closed the other, imagining someone else was doing the same thing on the other side of the door. She blinked several times but couldn't see any light or sign of movement inside.

She turned around and looked back along the long exterior corridor. From nearby there came the sound of someone walking in high-heeled shoes, of a thick duvet being hung and beaten for dust, of the revving engine of a motorcycle. Hana looked up at the sky. It was a perfect bright blue without a single cloud. She thought she would never forget this perfect blue sky and the cold feel of the sky-blue metal door on her face, even if she forgot what Jin looked like in the future.

She walked down from the empty apartment and called Jin's number on the way back.

"This phone is either turned off or in a place with no signal."

It was a monotonous electric voice. Hana hung up the phone and sighed. She looked at the phone, and at that moment it started ringing. There was no number on the screen. Could it be Jin? She immediately felt nervous and emotional. Her heart started pounding, and she answered the call quickly.

"Hello?"

"Hey, Hana?"

Hana's heart sank. It was one of their university classmates, Sok, who ran a marathon with her and Jin. "I heard you broke up with Jin. What happened?"

She was surprised to hear that. She hadn't talked to anyone back home about Jin. "What are you talking about? Who told you that?"

"Oh, I contacted him a while ago, but he didn't reply. Later on someone told me that he went for a round-the-world trip and broke up with you. Is that true?" Sok paused for a moment. "Really, what's going on with you guys? I thought you were going to marry him after graduation."

Hana didn't have much to say to that. "He's in South America," she said, somewhat defensively. "It's for his dissertation."

"For his dissertation? Why?"

Hana didn't have any more lies. "It's complicated. I don't really understand it."

"Oh," said Sok. "Well, say hi to him when you next talk."

"I will," said Hana. "How are you? How's university?"

"Oh, that's my big news!" Sok said happily. "I graduated one term early and got a job at a local bank!" He sounded rather excited, but Hana sighed. Now she felt bad for lying at all.

"Well, I think maybe it was a mistake that I followed him to Japan. I couldn't even see him before he went to South America, but I thought he'd be back soon. Now I wish I'd just come back home and got a job like you." Hana regretted saying it as soon as the words were out. It sounded useless and pathetic.

"Don't say that," Sok protested. "Everyone was envious of you going to meet Jin starting a life together in Japan." He paused for a moment. "Even if he's not there now, he will be soon, right? You'll have a great time."

"Right," said Hana half-heartedly.

"Right," mused Sok. "So, what are you doing there now?"

"Hmm... I'm actually staying with an old lady and helping her with her vegetable shop."

Sok was silent for a moment. "Vegetable shop? What vegetable shop? Aren't you going to graduate from university?"

Hana sighed and cleared her throat. "It's a complicated story. I'll tell you everything once it's settled at some point."

"OK," he said, though he didn't sound convinced. "But let me know if you need any help. Don't hold things in, and call if you want to talk about anything. If it's tough, just come back home, all right? We're all worried about you."

"Sure, thanks for calling. Say hi to everyone."

Hana hung up the phone and felt strangely relieved. She'd forgotten there might be other people thinking of her and worrying about her in some other part of the universe. It felt strange to lie, but Sok was right, she couldn't simply give up on herself. It was true that she'd followed Jin with no special plan for herself, but if she'd gone back home straight after that, she would have felt like an even bigger loser. Now she needed to do something practical and realistic, but also enjoy herself. She was still young, after all. She wasn't dead, like poor Jiyo.

Hana stared at her white trainers and the spinning round black wheels while cycling back to the vegetable shop. They reminded her of soft and crunchy cream puffs filled with custard cream and fresh vanilla beans. Nok's words played in her head like a happy song.

"Look, here's the Tokyo Bicycle Bakery!"

Baking was one thing she was good at, and enjoyed doing at the same time. As she cycled, she thought back over all the notes she'd taken for the cakes, pies and cookies she'd made for Jin over the years. Her recipe book had become her little treasure box, filled with different recipes taken from books or magazines or the Internet, all things she wanted to experiment with in the future.

The frog pond was passing on her left, and she pulled sharply in, parked then hurriedly took out her camera. There were lots of photos of the matcha green tea cream swiss rolls and the lemon and sugar crêpes she'd made, as well as the chocolate taiyaki cakes and the shiny cherry cheesecakes that she'd tasted on her first teary day in Tokyo. She studied the photos one by one, and memories floated out of her head like she was blowing bubbles.

Jin wasn't here now, but she could still bake for other people. Everyone seemed to enjoy her cakes. Looking through the photos, she realized she'd already baked lots of things for other people without even thinking about it; the Spanish girls, the Sakura school people, Nok in her garden, Sumi, Gon, Bomi and Jun at their house, Kimura and Yoko at the photo studio, Ms. Oyama and even the cats.

Her mind starting racing with ideas of what to bake next, and for who. Sweet plans mixed up like stretchy pink gelato in her head. She realized she hadn't made any desserts in Ms. Kawanami's house yet, and she'd already been there for over a week.

She cycled fast to the vegetable shop and ran up to the second floor. There were boiled whole chestnuts heaped in a wooden basket on the kitchen table. She peeled one of the chestnuts and put the whole thing in her mouth. It was light, fluffy, sweet and had a fresh and earthy, leafy taste. As Ms. Kawanami had pointed out before, it definitely had a good spirit in it.

She peeled the rest of the chestnuts quickly and carefully, hands shaking with excitement. She put the pretty-looking ones in a bowl of rum syrup, then made a purée with the small and crushed chestnuts using a hand blender, adding oat milk and rice syrup. She sliced thin, round pastry bases from soft cornbread using a cookie cutter, then spread chestnut purée on each base and placed a single shiny rum-candied chestnut in the middle. After that she squeezed more purée over the top using a silicon icing tube. The sweet and sticky fragrance of rum wafted through the kitchen.

She made a dozen Mont Blanc cakes and took photos, then placed the best-looking ones on a tray and went down to the vegetable shop, where Ms. Kawanami was having a chat with two old lady customers.

"Please have a cake," Hana said, holding out the tray. "I made them with Kato farm chestnuts."

The three old ladies stopped talking and looked up at Hana with curious expressions.

"Ms. Kawanami, I haven't seen this young lady before," one of them said. "Who is she?"

Ms. Kawanami answered with a blank facial expression. "She's been helping me with the shop lately, as my rheumatism is getting worse in my back and legs."

Hana put the tray down on the table and bowed low. "Hello, I'm Hana. Nice to meet you."

The two ladies studied the Mont Blanc cakes closely. "My, these do look beautiful," one of them said. "Did you really make these by yourself? Ms. Kawanami, how lucky you are."

They each took a plate and a cake, smelled it first like experienced sommeliers, then slowly tasted it. The shop was completely silent while all three ladies finished their cakes. Hana got nervous just standing their silently.

"Oh my goodness," one of the old ladies whispered to the others. "I haven't had such a tasty Mont Blanc cake in all my life. Isn't it scrumptious?"

"Thank you." Hana bowed. "The chestnuts were fresh today from the Kato farm. I'm glad you enjoyed it."

"Did you use the chestnuts on the kitchen table?" Ms. Kawanami asked. Her plate was also completely empty.

"Yes, they looked fresh so I made cakes with them." Hana suddenly realized that Ms. Kawanami might have been saving them for something. "I'm sorry that I didn't ask you first."

Ms. Kawanami's wrinkles deepened. "I thought you were just an immature young girl, but now it seems you have a great talent." The other two old ladies nodded and smiled at Hana.

Hana opened up her old blog that night. 'Hana & Jin', it was called. She hadn't written anything for almost a year, not since she'd made a lot of efforts to record all her dates with Jin. She looked at a few old entries, then selected them all and marked them as Private. No one could see them now. Next she opened the settings and changed the blog's name to 'The Tokyo Bicycle Bakery.'

It made her smile to see the new title pop up in pink letters. She thought Nok would approve. Next she changed her biography, deleting Jin and writing that she was a Korean girl who lived in Japan and loved baking. The first recipe she shared was the Mont Blanc cake. She wrote out the ingredients and directions, then added photos of the Mont Blancs taken that afternoon. At the end she wrote a short message.

'If there's someone you like or someone who doesn't like you yet, bake this Mont Blanc cake for them. It may do the job.'

Hana pushed the button to publish the article on her newly refurbished blog. She closed her laptop and opened the window behind the desk, then shivered gently as a chilly wind blew through. There was a full moon over the roofs of the houses and shops on the market street.

10. Sweet pumpkin chiffon cake with maple syrup

Hana bought a mini white convection oven for a thousand yen from a sayonara goodbye sale, the kind of sale foreigners did when they were leaving the country and going back home. It was small but she could bake cakes in it with no problem. The oven had hardly been used so it was in mint condition; a simple design with a white dial and red temperature scale. It was an American brand using Fahrenheit rather than Celsius, but that was not a big deal for Hana. Just looking at it made her excited. Now she could bake and post anything she wanted.

She cycled home from the sayonara sale with the oven in the basket of her orange bicycle, thinking hard about what to bake next. The excitement made her hum and pedal faster, so her red and green patchwork hat flapped loudly and when the wind blew it felt like she was drinking cold coke fast.

As soon as she got back to the vegetable shop, she turned her new oven on and checked it worked. She studied the oven while having a peanut-butter and jam sandwich with orange juice for lunch. Her brain was full of cakes and sweets.

The winter vacation would start soon, and that was off-season in the photo studio. Mr. Kimura took family photos occasionally, but there were fewer customers than before. Yoko spent her time preparing new flyers for graduations, Shichi-Go-San ceremonies and weddings in the next spring season.

Hana had less work to do too, so she filled the hours trying out traditional photo editing techniques using paints and brushes, instead of computer graphics. It required more time and effort, but she could check the photos more precisely. She liked the results of the old-school style, as she thought it gave extra warmth to the photos. She focused on mixing the right colors and painting them on faded or missing parts of the photos. Her palette in the middle of work looked like an unfinished painting by Jackson Pollock.

"Hana, you seem a bit down," Yoko said one day, while they sat at the rustic table drinking hot tea and working. "You don't talk much either. Is anything going on these days?" Hana looked up. Yoko was knitting a colorful wool lap-blanket at the same time as checking her flyers.

"I think it's because of the weather," Hana said. She'd never told Yoko about Jin, Jiyo's death, or her new part-time job in the vegetable shop. She thought unnecessary worries might ruin their relationship. "I always feel like I'm shrinking in the winter."

Yoko yawned and stretched like a cat. "It will be good when spring comes, that's true."

Hana finished her photo-editing work and left in the late afternoon. She pedaled her bicycle hard, so she was panting when she arrived at the vegetable shop. A middle-aged, chubby-looking lady was putting Chinese cabbages and horseradish in her basket while chatting with Ms. Kawanami.

"Hi, Ms. Kawanami," Hana called, "I'm back!" She rushed up to the second floor to open her recipe book and bake something new and fun in her oven.

Ms. Kawanami came into the kitchen just as she was opening the oven door. "Hana, could you bring some hot Hoji tea down to the shop?" Her eyes settled on the oven. "And what's that?"

Hana grinned. "It's my new oven! I bought it a week ago from a sayonara goodbye sale. It was a great bargain for only a thousand yen. I thought you'd have noticed it by now"

Ms. Kawanami frowned. "You cook so much now, I hardly need to come in here. And what's a sayonara sale?"

"Ah, it's a website for foreigners when they leave Japan; they sell their belongings very cheaply."

Ms. Kawanami shook her head. "These days kids don't save money. I have a gas stove, why do you need an oven?"

Hana smiled awkwardly. "I guess I thought it would be nice to bake some cakes." The real reason was that she wanted the cakes to be completely hers, not made using Ms. Kawanami's gas oven. Of course, she couldn't say that, and Ms. Kawanami didn't seem convinced.

"Does the gas oven not cook cakes?"

Hana tried to think of something to change the subject. Her gaze caught on the Martin guitar in her half-open room, across the corridor. "By the way, I like your son's guitar. I want to buy one sometime, too. Could I practice on his a little?"

Ms. Kawanami's face got serious suddenly, and Hana realized it was a sensitive subject. She'd still heard nothing about Ms. Kawanami's son in Hokkaido.

"I need to go down to the shop," Ms. Kawanami said, ignoring the question and turning to leave. "Customers are waiting. Please make the tea."

Hana boiled the kettle, poured hot water in the thermos bottle and added Hoji tea leaves. The tea leaves made the water a gentle greenish-brown. She put the bottle and oven-heated cups on a tray and took them downstairs. Ms. Kawanami and the chubby middle-aged lady were having a chat.

"Winter Chinese cabbages are especially sweet and have a strong texture," the lady was saying. "My husband doesn't like vegetables but he loves these cabbages in hot chanko nabe stew."

Ms. Kawanami took some small cabbages out of a cardboard box in the back of the shop. "Ah well, then I will give you some more. These are small ones but taste just as good as the big ones."

The lady blushed. "Oh, thank you. I always feel bad when you give me free items."

"Please have a cup of tea," Hana said, putting the tray on the table. She poured hot tea in the teacups.

"Is she your granddaughter?" The lady asked, watching Hana. Ms. Kawanami shook her head.

"No, she's just helping with the shop for a while."

Hana nodded and went back up to the second floor. She looked at her recipe book and her oven, but somehow the Martin guitar now had her attention. She went into her room and took the guitar off its stand carefully. White dust drifted off the strings. Hana cleaned them with a dry cloth, careful to get rid of the dust between the strings too. She tuned the guitar slowly and played C, D and E chords quietly. It had a nice, deep sound.

She remembered one dim night when she and Jin drank cheap wine, played guitar and sang pop songs on the Beauty Bench on their old university campus. The memory felt sweet and sorrowful. She also thought about the rough, cold feel of her suitcase handle as it rolled over the hard concrete floor leading to Jin's apartment, that first night in Japan.

She strummed the guitar slowly and thoughtfully, playing Nora Jones' 'Don't Know Why'. It was Jin's favorite song. She missed him. She missed the night they'd sat down and watched the magnolia flowers falling on the bench like snow from the sky. Now it felt like those days would never come back again.

"Hana, please come down here."

Ms. Kawanami's voice came from the downstairs. Hana worried she might have heard the guitar, so she put it back and wiped her tears away quickly.

"Yes, I'm coming down."

When she went down to the shop, there was a young guy there, wearing a dark blue t-shirt with shiny silver letters in the middle. 'UK', they said. He had short hair and big eyes. Hana thought he must be a big fan of the United Kingdom. She looked at him and his face went red like a Snow White apple.

"Say hello," Ms. Kawanami said sharply. "This is Hikaru, Mr. Kato's son, from the Kato farm. They grow all the vegetables and fruits that we sell in the shop. His dad is unwell these days, so Hikaru will come deliver the items every morning from now. You will need to check them with him and sign the invoice. Check every item carefully OK?" Ms. Kawanami made a stern face.

Hana nodded. "Yes, I'll do that."

"Nice to meet you," the young guy said. "I'm Hikaru. I'm new at this so I'll have to learn from you."

"Hello, pleased to meet you," Hana said, shaking his hand. "I'm Hana. I'm also new, so let's learn together." She noticed his forehead was sweating and he looked nervous.

"Hikaru, you did a good job today," Ms. Kawanami said. "Say hi to Mr. Kato for me."

"Thank you," Hikaru said, hesitated for a couple of seconds like something else was going to happen, then went to his truck. He soon came back with two dark green sweet pumpkins, one in each hand.

"My father gave these to you. They've been after-ripened for a month, and taste rather nice and mellow."

"How kind. Please say thank you to your father. Take good care of your dad and tell him not to work so hard." Ms. Kawanami patted Hikaru's shoulder gently, treating him like a grandson.

"Yes, I will." Hikaru bowed deeply to Ms. Kawanami and Hana.

"Have a safe journey back," Hana said. Hikaru bowed at her again and left the shop.

"Can I make something out of these sweet pumpkins?" Hana asked Ms. Kawanami, while watching Hikaru's white truck disappear down the street.

Ms. Kawanami nodded with a blank expression. "Sure."

"I'll prepare dinner with them then."

Hana carried the two pumpkins to the upstairs kitchen, where she put them on the kitchen table and had a deep think about what to make.

After studying them thoroughly, she picked up a knife and cut them in half, then scraped out the seeds. She left one big piece for a salad and put the other big pieces in a pre-heated bamboo steamer. When they had softened enough, she took them out, let them cool slightly, skinned them and put them in the food processor with some single cream and a pinch of salt. The deep yellow pumpkin and the white cream mixed together into an uplifting chick-yellow color, which she poured evenly into three separate portions.

She boiled one portion gently in a deep saucepan, adding extra cream to make soup. It would be even sweeter than sweet potato soup. While the soup was boiling, Hana separated some egg yolks and whites and made a stiff meringue with caster sugar. She carefully folded in some corn oil and self-rising flour into the second portion of purée, then poured the mixture into a cake tray and put it in the pre-heated oven.

While the cake was baking, Hana added tomato paste to the last batch of purée to make a sauce. She mixed minced beef, eggs, finely chopped onions, thyme and a bit of salt in a big bowl and made meatballs, which she grilled then cooked slowly in the sweet pumpkin tomato sauce. She tossed fresh arugula with virgin olive oil and salt then added some thin slices of raw sweet pumpkin for a salad.

Finally, she served the chick-yellow soup in soup bowls alongside a rattan basket of crunchy warm baguettes. She spooned the soft meatballs onto a large oval plate and poured the extra sweet pumpkin tomato sauce on top. She placed the lightly baked chiffon cake on a plate with a small jug of maple syrup next to it. Last of all, she lit a tealight candle floating in a glass bowl.

Hana went down to the vegetable shop and let Ms. Kawanami know dinner was ready. She was checking invoices and bills from the sales that day. Her eyes opened wide when she entered the kitchen.

"When did you prepare all this?"

"While you were closing the shop," Hana said, pulling a chair out like an experienced waitress. "Please have a seat."

Hana poured hot corn tea in a cherry blossom-shaped porcelain cup as soon as Ms. Kawanami sat down.

"It's cold outside, isn't it?" she asked, making small talk.

"Yes, this winter is colder than the previous ones," Ms. Kawanami said, then coughed. Hana pushed her tea closer, and Ms. Kawanami sipped it. "It's nice. What kind of tea is it?"

"It's corn silk tea. It's good for bladder and joints. Tonight, I've made dinner and dessert with Hikaru's sweet pumpkins. Please help yourself." Hana moved the plates closer to Ms. Kawanami.

Ms. Kawanami tore a small portion off the baguette and dipped it in the sweet pumpkin soup. She smelled it and put it in her mouth. Then she had a bite of the arugula salad, and sliced the meatball in the sweet pumpkin tomato sauce and ate it slowly. She was quiet while she had the soup, salad and the meatballs. Hana also ate the dinner silently. The dim candlelight glowed on the table. Hana's attention was focused on Ms. Kawanami like an amateur chef in front of Gordon Ramsay; she finished eating her food rather quickly, but said nothing.

Hana cleared the empty plates and brought out the sweet pumpkin chiffon cake and the maple syrup. She also heaped Earl Grey tea leaves in a new teapot. Ms. Kawanami cut a slice of the cake and drizzled the maple syrup on top. The cake disappeared softly in her mouth. Her eyes were sparkling.

"Where did you learn how to bake cakes like this?" Ms. Kawanami asked as she cut herself a bigger slice.

"My parents had a shop since I was born, so they didn't cook or bake much at all," Hana explained. "My dinner was usually a ready-made meal from a supermarket or a pot noodle, and my mom thought desserts were bad for my teeth so she never bought me any cakes." She sighed softly. "I was always envious of my classmates saying they had cassis macarons or Victoria sponge cake for their birthdays or such, so I used to imagine the tastes and dream of eating as many desserts as I wanted. Since then I made my own recipe book and wrote down what I wanted to eat or bake in the future. I made my own imaginary recipes from my head too." She smiled, and Ms. Kawanami smiled back.

"I used to cut good-looking cake photos from newspapers or magazines and glued them in my recipe book too. When I went to university, I could finally start baking properly, in my boyfriend's one-room apartment near the school." She closed her eyes briefly, remembering those heady days. "Honestly, it was like heaven. I couldn't believe I'd lived without baking before that. I was so happy when my boyfriend ate my desserts." Hana's smile felt like bittersweet chocolate on her lips.

Ms. Kawanami wiped her mouth with a napkin. Her cheeks were light pink and looked much healthier than before dinner. "Well, it's hard to say for sure, but your baking definitely has something special which is hard to explain. Thank you for the dinner. It was tasty." She left the kitchen and went down to the shop slowly, without making any sound.

Hana washed the plates and whispered softly to herself, repeating what Ms. Kawanami had said. "Something which is hard to explain." She wasn't sure what it meant, but it didn't sound bad.

When the kitchen was all cleaned up, she cut a piece of the leftover cake and poured maple syrup on top. It was soft, light and enjoyably sweet. She'd forgotten to take a photo of the whole cake before slicing it, so she pretended to take one by making a frame with her fingers and thumbs. She would never forget this photo taken in her heart; no need to worry about losing a memory card or having a virus on her laptop.

The next morning, Hana was woken up by the sound of a truck stopping in front of the vegetable shop. She opened her window and peered down, still in her pajamas with half-opened eyes and frizzy hair. It was Hikaru's clean white truck, and he was moving boxes of fruits and vegetables from the back. She looked at the clock. It was half an hour earlier than usual, 5:30 am. Ms. Kawanami was already up as well, out brushing the street.

"Shoot!" Hana cursed and jumped out of bed, changed her clothes, had a quick wash of her face like Miyo would do and combed her hair. By the time she'd hurried down to the shop, Hikaru had already finished delivering all the boxes neatly inside.

"Ah, sorry. I should've come down earlier... I overslept." Hana scratched her eyebrows, then realized she hadn't put any makeup on her half-bald, plucked eyebrows. She felt her face get as hot as tomato soup.

"Oh, no worries," said Hikaru, reddening too. "I was nervous in case I would be late today, so I left an hour early. I didn't mean to wake you up so early though. I'm sorry." As Hana watched, his face kept getting redder, like a hot chilli.

"It's fine," Hana said, trying to settle him down before his head exploded. "I've got a lot to do anyway, and it's a good habit to get up early."

Hikaru opened his mouth to say something, but just then Ms. Kawanami opened the glass door of the vegetable shop and poked her head inside. "Why are you two staring at each other like that so early in the morning? Are you fighting over something? Is there something wrong? Hikaru, are you ill? Your face is so red."

"No, not at all, we're all good," Hikaru mumbled.

"Oh, yes, Hikaru did a great job," Hana said, jumping on it too. "Everything looks perfect here. I'll check quickly and sign the invoice, yes."

Ms. Kawanami looked doubtful. "Well, OK, I'll leave it to you. Do you want some tea, Hikaru?" She shuffled in, headed to the teapot on the counter.

"I'm perfectly fine, thank you." Hikaru wiped his forehead with a white towel from his back pocket and stood in the middle of the shop awkwardly.

"All the boxes are here and they're in perfect condition," Hana proclaimed, then signed the invoice and handed it over to Hikaru with one hand, while casually trying to cover up her eyebrows with the other.

"Thank you. I'm heading off now." Hikaru took the invoice and opened the door. Ms. Kawanami sat on her chair while sipping tea and watched them suspiciously.

"Ah, hang on a second," Hana said, before Hikaru could leave. "I forgot something. One second please." She ran upstairs and put half of the sweet pumpkin chiffon cake into a plastic tub, then put that into a paper bag along with a bottle of maple syrup and ran back down to the shop.

Ms. Kawanami was holding her teacup sternly and stared at Hana as she came back in. "I thought an elephant was making an earthquake in my house."

Hana bobbed a quick bow. "Oh, sorry. I thought Hikaru was busy so I rushed." She handed the bag to Hikaru. "It's a chiffon cake that I made with your sweet pumpkins last night. There's maple syrup inside as well. Please have it with your father and say thank you. The pumpkins were very tasty." Hana smiled, and Hikaru's face got even redder.

"I didn't expect this at all," he said, taking the bag and offering a deep bow. "Thank you."

"It's my pleasure, have a safe drive back."

"Good job, Hikaru," Ms. Kawanami called after him. "The pumpkins were good, say hello to your father."

Hikaru nodded awkwardly. "Yes, Ms. Kawanami, thank you. I'll see you tomorrow then."

Hana watched him drive away down the road, as the morning sun rose slowly over the market street. After that she went about her morning chores, thinking about how funny Hikaru's face had looked when it got so red, about ready to explode. Then she remembered how funny her face must have looked, and rushed upstairs to stencil in her eyebrows.

When she came back down, Ms. Kawanami took one look at her and laughed. "I thought you were never going to fix those eyebrows. You looked so surprised."

Hana frowned. "I have to work."

"I'm not stopping you working," Ms. Kawanami said, and mumbled something about poor Hikaru, having to see that.

At last, when she was finished with everything, Hana opened the back door of the shop to throw away some cardboard boxes. To her surprise, Miyo was there, waiting for her politely.

Hana felt her heart melt. "Oh honey," she said gently. "I was worried about you, since you didn't show your face for several days." One of Miyo' ears was cut slightly, and he'd lost some weight. Hana remembered hearing that sometimes stray cats just disappeared for a while. Apparently, the ward office took them away to neuter them.

She knelt down to pet him. He leaned into her hand and purred noisily. "Miyo," she murmured. "It was hard, wasn't it? Here, let me prepare a special meal for you."

In the kitchen she put tuna and soft pumpkin slices in the cat bowl and smashed them carefully. Miyo finished the food without blinking an eye. He was satisfied after the feast and rolled over to show his belly to Hana. Hana stroked his little head and watched him groom himself on a sunny spot on the street. After a while Miyo stretched and yawned happily, then left the street. Hana walked up to the second floor of the vegetable shop. Once she opened her laptop, she saw a comment on the Mont Blanc cakes on her Tokyo Bicycle Bakery blog.

'It looks easy to make, and tasty as well. I'll try it.'

Hana felt weird that somebody had read her blog and given her a comment. It was also pretty motivating, and she started thinking about what to bake next. It was a very productive and great start to the day, if a little embarrassing. She started humming a song opened her emails. She deleted some spam emails and was about to focus on her recipe box when an important notice email from the Tokyo Marathon drew her attention. She opened the email with a bit of excitement.

'Dear Hana Lee,

We are delighted to announce that you have won the ballot for the Tokyo Marathon.

Congratulations.'

For a moment Hana just stared. She had completely forgotten about applying for the Tokyo Marathon, but now it came back to her. She'd applied for both herself and Jin, hoping they would run it together.

With her excitement mounting, she opened Jin's university email box. They'd always shared the passwords of their school emails, so as not to lose any importance notices from the school. Jin's password was still the same as before. She checked through some emails about free public talks, book launches and donation requests, then found the email from the Tokyo Marathon. Her fingers trembled over the open button, thinking about the time they'd run together with Sok and their schoolmates. Sok had always talked about becoming a rock and roll star, but now he was a banker in a dandy suit. She wondered what Jin was doing right now.

'Dear Jin Kim,

We are sorry to say that you have lost the ballot for the Tokyo Marathon. Please try again next time.

Thank you.'

She read the words many times. It felt like her last hope was blowing away.

The rest of the day passed in a daze. She walked some, then cycled, then ended up at the Sakura school before her lesson, talking to Takeuchi about the marathon.

When she mentioned that she'd won the lottery, he looked at her like she'd won a million-dollar jumbo lottery. "Wow, that's amazing!" he said. "I've never seen someone win the ballot before. My friend, a huge marathon fan, applied five times in a row but he never got it once."

Mr. Abe was sitting in the school foyer and raised his thumb. "Hana, it's a great opportunity. Go and have fun. I'll support you."

Nok popped out of her lesson, making an exaggerated face. "Congratulations, Hana! Will you be on TV?"

Hana looked down at her hands. "I haven't decided if I'll run or not yet."

Nok ran over and grabbed Hana's hand. "What are you talking about? You can't give up! There are lots of people who'd love to run but they can't. The competition rate was twelve to one this year! Don't give up, OK?"

"Sure, I shouldn't give up," Hana said softly, still looking down at her hands. It sounded like a good thing to say.

On Mr. Abe's advice, Hana bought a pair of beginner's running shoes and some polyester toe socks from a sports shop on the way back from the Sakura school. The texture of the socks felt good on her feet.

Each day after that, she woke up early and changed to her jogging clothes before Hikaru's truck arrived in the shop, so she could jog straightaway after her morning chores. Of course she didn't forget to put on her eyebrows every morning, also. Soon both Hana and Hikaru got more efficient and faster with their work as they got used to it.

"Good luck jogging, Hana."

"Safe drive and see you tomorrow, Hikaru."

It was a nice habit. Sometimes they'd chat a little, about small things. He'd make a joke about Ms. Kawanami cleaning the street. She'd tell him about her blog. Each day, once his truck was out of the market street, she'd finish her morning chores swiftly then go for a five-mile training run.

She had to stop several times at first, as it was hard to breathe, but it was good to get fresh air and hear her heart beating hard. When she stopped at the red light of a crossing, she felt like a flying fish skimming over the waves under a red sun. Each time after she ran, there was a dull pain and heat in her feet and thighs. It was like having a new relationship, because it was always there, didn't disappear for a long time and made her keep thinking about it.

On a sunny Sunday morning, Hana was enjoying a run on the market street, waiting for a green light on the crossing opposite the vegetable shop. She wiped sweat off her face with a small towel, then noticed Hikaru behaving strangely. He was walking back and forth in front of the shop, carrying a big basket full of fruit.

She ran over and greeted him from behind. "Hi Hikaru, can I help you with anything?"

He gave a little jump when he saw her. "Oh, Hana, you startled me."

Hana hung her towel around her neck. "It's your day off on the farm, isn't it?"

"A-Ah... well," Hikaru stammered, then held the basket forward. "I've brought organic apples from my farm. They're new apples using organic methods I learned in Cuba." His face looked like the red apples in his basket. "I was there a few months ago, and I thought..." He trailed off.

"Wow, Cuba sounds exotic," Hana said enthusiastically, admiring the shiny apples. "And the apples look lovely. Would you like to come in and have a cup of tea?" She went to open the door of the vegetable shop.

"No, n-no..." Hikaru said. "I have work to do, so I'll head back. Please say hi to Ms. Kawanami."

"Ah, really? OK, well, have a good weekend and see you soon then." Hana took the heavy basket and waved as Hikaru backed away swiftly.

After watching him drive away in his truck, Hana turned around and opened the glass sliding door of the vegetable shop.

"Ms. Kawanami!"

On the dark and cold concrete floor, Ms. Kawanami was lying flat on her face.

Hikaru 1

Three months earlier, Hikaru studied earthworm soil in a government-owned farm on the outskirts of Havana. The soil was like dark cocoa powder; soft, shiny, heavy and surprisingly had no smell at all.

He was reminded of something his grandfather once said: 'Good fertilizer and soil never have a bad smell. They always smell like Mother Nature.' Hikaru picked up an organic eggplant growing in the earthworm soil, and scooped a handful of fertilizer made from vegetable and fruit skins. The fertilizer was fresh and healthy, so the fruits and vegetables would thrive in it. Hikaru put his nose to the loam. It smelled like a forest in the early morning.

'This is it,' he thought, 'this soil and fertilizer will save my farm.' He closed his eyes and imagined the young Hikaru running around the apple trees on the family farm, while the white apple flowers bloomed like popcorn.

The farm had been in his family for three generations; his grandfather, his father, Hikaru. He'd always dreamed of taking it over from his dad, so he'd studied agriculture and business at university to get ready. He'd planned to learn more about modern farming techniques after graduation then take over gradually, but his father had collapsed due to thyroid cancer before the last apple harvest season. He could still work, but was supposed to rest.

The doctor said his father should avoid chemicals and pesticides, as they might make his condition worse, so Hikaru had travelled all the way to Cuba to learn about their unique organic farming methods, hoping his father would be cured and his customers would be healthier at the same time.

The sunshine on the farm was bright and strong. Hikaru closed his eyes and opened them again. There were marigold flowers planted between long rows of green salad leaves in the fields.

"These are freshly picked tomatoes and bell peppers," the farm manager said, bringing over a big basket of vegetables. He was a healthy looking middle-aged guy with strong muscles and tanned golden skin. "Please try them."

The red tomatoes and yellow bell peppers had subtle flower smells. Hikaru picked the smallest bell pepper and had a bite. He didn't know bell peppers could be as sweet as fruit. He ate the whole thing.

"Good soil, fair weather, clean water and flowers nearby give the vegetables and fruits their distinctive taste," the manager said proudly. "Every living thing has a purpose on this farm. Our job is to find the best combinations, plant them together and grow them with love."

Hikaru studied all the different types of vegetables, fruits and flowers for the whole afternoon. It was one of the hottest and sunniest summer days in Havana. Hikaru took notes on everything he learned about soil temperature and acidity, and even sketched the vegetables, fruits and flowers that he saw in the fields.

He left the farm after dusk and went to a pub in front of the big cathedral square in the center of Havana. It was a Friday night, and the square was lively with people dancing and drinking.

He ordered a big Mojito with ice at the bar, then sat at an outside table facing the square. Many small tables were squashed right next to each other, so he had a good look at the other patrons: three guys were chatting fast in Spanish on the left; a couple were kissing and whispering to each other on the right. Hikaru had a big sip of his Mojito, then sighed and leaned back in his plastic chair. The drink was cold and refreshing and quenched his thirst from the hard work on the farm.

"Do you mind if I sit here?" came a calm and gentle voice, and Hikaru looked up. There was a young Asian guy holding a Mojito glass, looking down at him. His eyes were a sharp, bright black, with a hint of deep ocean blue.

"Of course, please have a seat," Hikaru said.

"Thank you. It's always busy on Friday nights." The guy pulled a chair up in front of Hikaru and sat down. He spoke in fluent English with a hint of a Japanese accent.

"Are you Japanese?" Hikaru asked.

"No, but I lived in Japan until a few months ago." The guy brushed his long curly hair with his long thin fingers. It seemed like he hadn't cut his hair for quite a while, so it made natural curves over his shoulders. Hikaru wondered if he'd ever seen a person with such deep and calm eyes before.

"Are you a tourist?" Hikaru asked. The young guy didn't look like a tourist but he didn't look like a local either. Hikaru couldn't think of any other topics.

"I'm learning how to let things go," the guy said in a breathy voice.

"How to let things go?" Hikaru repeated. "What do you mean?"

"I'll tell you my story, if you like," the guy said, his deep-blueish black eyes sparkling. You may not believe me, though. Either way, it's OK to hear it and forget about it."

Hikaru frowned. He didn't know what to make of this. "Sure, why not?"

The guy began. "A month ago I woke up in the middle of the night, and I couldn't move my body at all. I couldn't close my eyes, I couldn't talk, I couldn't cry. All I could do was wait until dawn came. Since then, I haven't been able to sleep well, eat well or talk to someone freely, like I'm talking to you now. After that, I started to lose my body parts, like I was wearing a transparent poncho. It started with just my hand, but soon the disappearing body parts became bigger and bigger; my arm, my leg, my waist." He stopped talking for a while and looked as if he was having a deep think. Hikaru tried to think of something to say, but nothing came to mind.

"Once I lost my arms, I couldn't hold things properly," the guy continued. "I went to a mental hospital as well, but the doctor said it was a normal symptom for people in the modern world; it could be stress or anxiety. He said it was not a big deal and it would be better to take medication and have a good rest. But it didn't get better. In fact, it got worse, and I kept on losing body parts. The worst thing was that nobody else noticed what was happening. Even my family didn't know."

Hikaru suddenly felt a strong thirst. He drank his whole Mojito in one go, then even swallowed the ice cubes as well. Again the guy went on in his calm, low voice.

"So I took a break from my university. I had only one term left until graduation, but I couldn't continue with my routine life. I told my professor, school mates and my family that I would take a year off and travel around the world. I knew I wouldn't go back, but I didn't know what else to say. I couldn't tell my girlfriend. I was confused and worried. I wasn't confident that she would believe me either. I thought if I left without telling her, she would be mad for a while but eventually she would forget about me and move on."

Hikaru found himself nodding along, like any of this made sense.

"Once I left Japan, my body parts slowly came back, as if by magic. I could feel new cells growing in my body like fresh flesh growing out of the tail of a lizard." The guy peered closely at Hikaru. "Have you ever felt cell division in your body?"

Hikaru shook his head. There was a weird energy coming off the guy, but he didn't look like a crazy person. It was a strange feeling.

"Since then, my body became extremely light, and I found I could read people's minds like small particles in the air. I don't know the reason why, but I think it happened because I gave everything up."

Hikaru looked at the guy and his head felt completely empty. He didn't know what to say.

"This is the first time I've told my story to anyone. Most people would think I'm mad if I told them this, but somehow I wanted to talk to you as soon as I saw you."

That confused Hikaru even more. "Why me?"

The guy gave a slight shrug. "Perhaps I felt a strong sense of dedication from you? You may not realize it yet, but you're a good-hearted and strong person. You'll work hard and make a success of your life. You will lose an important person soon, but don't have a broken heart. If you focus on what you do, you'll meet another special person. You'll know, if you listen to your heart carefully. All I can say is, take good care of that person."

"That person?" Hikaru repeated, feeling puzzled. The guy only smiled. It was a refreshing smile that nobody would forget after seeing it once.

"The apples will be good," he added. "You'll get great apples from great soil. Once I go back to Japan, I'd love to taste them too."

Hikaru's jaw dropped. How did this guy know about his apples? He opened his mouth to ask, but suddenly the guy was gone. Hikaru blinked. There were two empty Mojito glasses on the black plastic table; the only proof that it was not a dream.

Feeling shaken, Hikaru ordered a double gin and tonic and stared at the square under the orange dim lights. He took the large gin and tonic from the waiter and drank it straightaway. After sitting there blankly for a while, he got out his laptop and typed out his notes on the farm.

He left the pub after midnight, walking on bumpy roads alongside colorful, dilapidated buildings back to the hotel. He was extremely tired but couldn't sleep easily. He made a strong mint tea and thought about his day. It felt like his brain was swollen like cotton candy. He felt floaty and weary. He had a shower, changed to clean pajamas, laid on the double bed and looked up at the yellow ceiling light. He closed his eyes. He soon had a dream white roses were blooming one after another out of the earthworm soil, and the roses fell from the sky like rain.

Hikaru 2

The next day Hikaru checked out of his hotel early and took a bus to the international airport, ten miles out of Havana city center. He landed in Miami airport around noon.

While eating an overcooked Mahi-mahi steak and drinking a cold Wynwood beer for his lunch in the airport, he found himself thinking about the young guy he'd met the night before, and his strange prediction. 'Somebody lost, somebody gained, apples.'

It felt like a puzzle for him to solve, and he couldn't stop thinking about it. The guy might have been a crazy person, but his sharp and serious eyes were not so easy to forget, and thinking about him made Hikaru restless and nervous.

He was pretty hungry when he ordered the food, but he couldn't finish even half of the meal when it came. He left the restaurant and took his domestic flight to land in Louisville airport in the afternoon. After the customs check he walked out through security. It was quiet in the airport on a Wednesday afternoon. The weather was hot outside, the sky was beautifully blue and there were white fluffy clouds. Hikaru went to an airport diner, ordered strong-brew coffee and soft pancakes with thin crispy bacon. He was the only customer there. The waitress played Dolly Parton on the jukebox.

From a rental car company in the airport he picked up a small gray Toyota, typed the address into the navigation and set off into the Kentucky countryside. He drove on quiet highways and passed golden corn farms, until he saw a white wooden two-story house on top of a green hill. Hikaru checked the GPS and drove slowly up the hill. There were two good-looking black horses roaming and eating grass, with shiny coats like velvet. He parked on top of the green hill, in front of the house. A tall and healthy-looking old guy, with a thick white beard and a cowboy hat, stood up from the rocking chair on the porch and walked over to Hikaru.

"Welcome to Kentucky, Hikaru. I'm Jack." He took off his cowboy hat to reveal silver hair underneath, smiled and put his hand out.

Hikaru shook Jack's hand. It was a warm and firm handshake. "Nice to finally meet you, Jack. I'm Hikaru. Thank you for inviting me." He held out a sake bottle wrapped with Japanese paper, handling it carefully. "This is my father's handmade sake. He says hello. It was his idea for me to come visit you, when I told him I was going to Cuba. He said you were an expert, and he owed you a lot."

Jack laughed and took the bottle with a slight bow of his head. "This is great, thank you. In fact, I owed your grandfather. You look just like him, by the way. And expert? I hope I can help. I feel like I'm always learning, so I'd love to hear more about what you learned in Cuba." He smiled and waved a hand. "Come on in."

Hikaru followed Jack inside. The house was dark and pleasantly cool, the opposite of the hot and humid weather outside. Hikaru took a handkerchief from his cargo pants and wiped his forehead.

"Please, have a seat," Jack said, pointing at the big Shaker-style wooden table.

"Thank you." Hikaru put his bag down and sat on a bentwood chair. A blackboard hung on the white wall opposite, with lots of mathematical formulas and numbers written on it. On the table, different sized lab beakers were scattered around, filled with liquids of various colors.

Jack placed his hat on the table. "What would you like to drink?"

"I've just had dinner and coffee, thank you," Hikaru said.

Jack sat down and flashed another big smile. His deep wrinkles and tanned skin made Hikaru think he had to be an experienced farmer. "I'll be honest, I was surprised to get an email from Mr. Kato's grandson. When you told me you wanted to learn organic corn farming and Bourbon making, I wasn't surprised though. You have the same blood as your grandfather. Did he ever tell you how we met?"

Hikaru shook his head. "I don't think so."

"It was fifty years ago," Jack said, leaning back in his chair. "I was on a walking trip through the Niigata area of Japan, when I got hit by a motorcycle on a country road. Your grandfather was in a field nearby and found me. If he hadn't helped me back then, we wouldn't be able to meet like this." Jack gave a nostalgic sigh. "He took such great care of me for many months, until I was fully recovered. We talked about farming and crops through body language, and we worked together on his farm. It was a great experience."

Hikaru was surprised. He'd never known about the accident. "My grandfather just told me that his old American friend Jack helped him with farming. He was proud whenever he talked about you. My father told me that he used to receive American chocolates or colorful children's books from you at Christmas."

Jack smiled. "That's right, I kept in touch with your grandfather after I came back home. I sent him a postcard of corn fields, then he sent me new corn seeds from Hokkaido. We became really good friends." He paused and looked at the beakers on the table. "When your father sent me a letter that old Kato had died, I was shocked. I drank bourbon shots one after another, thinking about my old friend. That was over ten years ago now, though. Time flies when you get old." He smiled. "I wish I could taste his sake again. He was a genius, really. But I'm glad I've got this sake from your father." He held out the bottle. "It must be a similar taste to your grandfather's."

"I may still have some old sake my grandfather made in the shed," Hikaru said. "I'll have a look and send you some, if I find it."

Jack's eyes shone. "It's nice of you to say that. But you're not here just to catch up. Here," he gestured at the beakers, "I'm trying some new bourbon recipes now, adding more corn and making the taste deeper. It's still at the test stage, but do you want to try some?" Jack's eyes got brighter still, like a school boy full of curiosity. Hikaru smiled and nodded.

Jack led him through the kitchen and down a set of small, narrow steps to the basement. It was darker and much cooler than upstairs. Hikaru thought they would be safe there even if a hurricane swept right overhead. Jack opened the thick metal door of the basement, and the strong, deep fragrance of bourbon in smoked-oak barrels hit Hikaru's whole body. He felt like he was already drunk from the soulful bourbon, like he was floating on air.

"I'm not lying, but I've never smelled such a deep and powerful fragrance in all my whole life," Hikaru said dreamily.

"You'll taste it soon." Jack put a long thin whiskey dipper into the oak barrel and lifted some bourbon out, then decanted it into a bourbon glass. The light caramel-colored liquid swirled nicely inside the glass.

"Take a sip in your mouth, make your mouth small and round, breathe in with your nose then swallow it slowly." Jack demonstrated and Hikaru followed him; swirling the glass to make the liquor circulate, checking the color, drinking it slowly.

"It tastes like fresh-cut flowers," Hikaru said.

"Does it? It tastes different according to the ratio of ingredients and the fermentation time. Try this one too." Jack gave Hikaru a different glass. It was much darker than the first bourbon, with a rich chocolate color.

"I made it on the night I got the letter from your father. I was thinking of your grandfather while I made it."

Hikaru drank it quietly. It burned a small fire inside his throat, with a deep and sorrowful taste.

Hikaru stayed with Jack for a week, an intensive one-to-one course learning about bourbon and corn; how to grow the different varieties, the best soil conditions, Jack's secret bourbon recipes, fermentation methods and oak-barrel maintenance skills etc. It was not enough time to learn all the key skills, but Hikaru couldn't spend much longer away from his father, so he focused, took notes and photographed everything he could.

At night they sat on rocking chairs on the porch, eating pulled-pork sandwiches and enjoying Jack's handmade bourbon. Jack talked more about Hikaru's grandfather, and how much he'd enjoyed his visits to Japan.

"I'd love to host you if you visited Japan again," Hikaru said. "My father would be very happy to meet you in person."

"That would be fun, for sure," Jack said. "And I hope your father gets better soon. The earthworm technique sounds like it has real promise."

Hikaru smiled and thanked him.

The days passed by quickly in Kentucky. Hikaru occasionally thought again about the odd Asian guy who'd made his prediction, but it felt very distant from this place. There were countless stars up in the black sky, and the willow trees sang a sweet and sorrowful love song over the winds at night.

On the day Hikaru left Kentucky, Jack handed him a big bottle of bourbon.

"Give this to your father. Once he's fully recovered, have a toast with him and watch the stars together at night." Jack gave Hikaru a warm and firm hug. Hikaru took the heavy bourbon bottle, and tried to hide his tears from Jack by bowing deeply. Back in the gray Toyota, he drove slowly downhill away from the house. Jack kept waving until Hikaru couldn't see him in the mirror anymore.

He passed the golden corn farms, drove a good distance from Jack's farm until he arrived at the University of Kentucky in Lexington. He bought several books on corn farming and bourbon-making in the university bookshop. He had a large latte in the school café and bought a dark blue t-shirt with big silver letters spelling out 'UK' in the middle, as a souvenir for himself.

He left the university and drove the gray Toyota to Louisville international airport. The last several weeks away from Japan had felt like a dream. Hikaru looked down on the clouds from the plane's small round window. He leaned his head against the glass, thinking of a smiley young Hikaru with his mother and father, under the light pink flowers of the apple tree in full bloom, on the old Kato farm.

11. Apple crumble with custard ceam and a dreamcatcher

Ms. Kawanami lay motionless on the floor.

"Ms. Kawanami. Can you hear me?" Hana tapped her shoulder and shook her but there was no response. Hana called emergency services but they said it would take an hour because there was no ambulance nearby. Hana was worried that might be too late, so she lifted Ms. Kawanami onto her back and started running in the middle of the market street. She didn't have much energy left in her legs, but Ms. Kawanami was light as a feather, so Hana squeezed out her last strength and ran at a full sprint to the hospital.

Hana watched as a respirator was connected to Ms. Kawanami's pale face and she was carried to the ICU. Hana was still panting from her full sprint, but she quickly began to cool down, wearing only the thin sports shirt and jogging shorts. Once the sweat cooled, she felt extremely chilly and started shivering from cold and tiredness. She leaned back on the waiting room sofa and slowly closed her eyes.

"Are you with Ms. Kawanami?"

A young nurse was looking down at Hana.

Hana jumped up from the sofa like a popped spring. "Yes, I am."

"Please come on in." Hana followed the nurse into a small doctor's office. Her lips felt dry.

"Have a seat please," the doctor said, checking papers on the desk before looking up at Hana. "Ms. Kawanami's in a serious condition. She could have died if you'd come in several minutes later. She was lucky you thought quickly." He paused a moment, studying her. "It was a cardiac heart failure, and it seems she's been suffering from this condition for a long time. We can reduce the pain with medication, but it's difficult to predict when her heart might stop again. She must have been in enormous pain. Did she ever mention it?"

Hana shook her head. "I had no idea. She just worked hard and met customers every day." Her voice was trembling.

"Are you a family member?"

"No. I'm a part-time worker in her shop." Hana felt her face reddening. "I live with her in the house upstairs."

The doctor leaned in, seeming slightly concerned. "Does she have direct family members nearby?"

Hana bit her lip. "I'm not sure. She said she had a son living in Hokkaido, but I never heard anything about him, and it seems they don't keep in touch now. Is that a problem?"

The doctor took a slow breath. "Perhaps. She may not wake up. She may not be able to move her body even if she does wake up. In any case, she'll have to stay in the hospital for some time, so we can monitor her condition." The doctor paused a moment. "You may not be next of kin, but you did bring Ms. Kawanami in, so please do the paperwork at the counter so she can be hospitalized."

Hana felt lost. She looked around the small room. "I've never done this before, and my Japanese is not perfect. Can I invite some friends to help?"

The doctor nodded. "Yes, you can."

Hana called Hikaru and Ms. Oyama, and they came to the hospital. Hikaru came with his father, Mr. Kato. Hikaru seemed surprised to see Hana wearing the same sports clothes that he'd seen her in earlier. He took his jacket off and put it around her shoulders. It was warm, and Hana felt relieved to have them all there. Mr. Kato was a kind-faced old man who patted Hana's shoulder and encouraged her. He was thin and pale-looking, so she was worried he might collapse as well. Ms. Oyama checked the hospitalization papers, talked to several people at the counter and signed the papers for Ms. Kawanami. Hana didn't have any energy left but she bowed at them to show her appreciation.

"The hospital staff will call once there is any news on Ms. Kawanami," Mr. Kato said. "It would be better to go home and have a rest now. Hikaru, why don't you take Hana home? I'll wait here."

Ms. Oyama held Hana's cold hands. "Hana, I'll come back again tomorrow. Good luck. Ms. Kawanami is a strong lady, so she'll definitely wake up."

Hikaru helped Hana to stand. Her legs were trembling so she had to lean on him. His hands around her back were warm and soft.

"It's OK, I can go home on my own," Hana said. She was still wearing Hikaru's jacket but hadn't stopped shivering.

"I'll take you home. Don't worry." Hikaru looked at Hana with his round and big eyes. Shiny black eyes. Hana didn't know he had eyes that could make people feel relaxed and safe by just looking at them.

Hana and Hikaru walked together on the empty and dark market street. The wind was cold and the street was quiet.

"I should have paid attention, then I would have known Ms. Kawanami had collapsed on the floor," Hikaru said, looking at his feet with a guilty face. "It's my fault."

"Don't say that," Hana said softly. "It's not anyone's fault. I'm sorry that I contacted you and made you worry. I didn't know what else to do, though."

"I'm glad you called me," Hikaru said firmly, and looked like he wanted to say something more, but they were quiet after that.

He lifted the rusted metal shutter of the Kawanami vegetable shop, then opened the sliding glass door. It smelled like sweet and sour apples inside the shop. Hikaru's fruit basket lay where she'd dropped it on the floor. Hana picked up the apples.

"Thank you so much for today. I'll wash this jacket and return it." Hana said, while looking at the ground.

Hikaru smiled. "No worries at all. Return it when you don't need it anymore. Take a rest now and let me know if you need any help."

156

Hana stood outside the shop and watched Hikaru walk back down the market street. His white wool jumper shone under the moonlight.

Hana fell asleep with her sports clothes and Hikaru's jacket on, then woke up to a phone call the next morning.

"Ms. Kawanami woke up," came an impersonal voice. "Please come to the hospital."

"Of course," Hana said swiftly, "I'm on my way."

She took a quick shower, changed her clothes then ran to the hospital while her hair was still wet. Ms. Kawanami was sitting up in the hospital bed. She frowned at Hana when she came in. "What happened, where am I?"

Hana was panting and her face felt hot and red. "You're in the hospital. You collapsed on the floor in the shop. Do you remember?"

Ms. Kawanami shook her head slowly. "No, I don't."

"Well, I'm very happy you're awake," Hana said. "How do you feel?"

"Not very well. I have a bad headache." The old lady blinked and peered at Hana more closely. "What happened to your hair? It's dripping water. It's just like the first night that I met you. It looks like wet seaweed. Dry your hair, silly." Ms. Kawanami handed a thin face towel to Hana.

Hana took the towel and ran it quickly over her hair. "Oh, I'm so glad that you're conscious and can nag me again." She took Ms. Kawanami's hands. They were like dried persimmons, thin, wrinkly and cold.

A doctor appeared beside Hana then, holding a chart. "You have energy to tell people off, so it seems you can go home soon. Let me check your pulse." He moved closer and took her wrist.

"I can't die in this hospital," Ms. Kawanami said stubbornly, like this was an old argument. "I will die in my own house when I'm ready."

"Of course you'll go home," the doctor replied. "But we need to monitor your heart condition, so you'll have to stay in the hospital for a few more days."

"No, I'm perfectly fine. I need to go home. I have a business and customers to handle."

The doctor tried again to tell her to stay, then brought in a second doctor, but nobody could change Ms. Kawanami's mind. She insisted on going home and didn't listen to anybody in the hospital. "I have work to do." She was as stubborn as a rock.

After the doctors gave up, Ms. Kawanami focused her attention on Hana with a look of concern. "It seems my body doesn't work well anymore, so I'm afraid you should be helping more."

"Sure, no worries," Hana responded brightly. "Winter vacation is coming soon and my other part-time job is getting less busy. I can work more in the vegetable shop."

"I will also talk to the Kato farm. Hikaru will come and help you. Mr. Kato is also becoming healthier, so hopefully everything will go well."

"That sounds great." Hana nodded and looked at her fingertips. She thought of Hikaru's warm and soft hands on her shoulders, then shook her head and tried to think of her favorite side of Jin's face, his tall nose and thin long eyes. Hana closed her eyes but couldn't imagine Jin's face clearly. He was hiding behind a thick fog. Instead she saw a vivid image of Hikaru's smiling face and his big round eyes. It was confusing and made her feel somehow guilty.

According to Ms. Kawanami's wish, she came home that day with Hana's help. Hana made her comfortable by fixing up her bed and bringing food to her bedside table, but Ms. Kawanami didn't have any appetite. She only drank water and a bite of porridge.

The days grew shorter and the weather grew colder, while Ms. Kawanami slowly recovered. When Hana cycled to the Kimura photo shop by bicycle, her nose and ears became completely numb, like she had drunk a whole bottle of coke in one gulp.

"You look like a cute Rudolf reindeer," Yoko said, pulling down Hana's pink wool hat to cover her red ears. "It's cold outside, isn't it?" Hana took her wool gloves off and blew hot air on her frozen fingertips.

"Yes, it's really cold. We may have a white Christmas this year."

"Why don't we take a long winter holiday this year?" Mr. Kimura called over from his desk, where he was checking negatives. "We were so busy this summer, weren't we?"

"That's true," Yoko said. "Since you joined, Hana, we've gained a lot of customers. Thank you."

"Not at all. Thank you for hiring me." Hana blushed a little.

"Honey, shall we go skiing in Hokkaido and enjoy Jingisukan grilled mutton and Sapporo beer?" Yoko winked at Mr. Kimura and pretended to drink a beer.

He laughed. "That's a good idea. And what's your plan, Hana? Will you go home over Christmas?"

Several images popped into Hana's mind at the same time: the angry faces and constant arguments of her parents; the cold and windy winter sea; the pale face of Ms. Kawanami.

"I have work to do here, so I can't go home over New Year's."

"Oh," said Yoko, taking a sip of her hot cocoa while studying Hana's face. "Have you got some dates planned with your boyfriend?"

Hana felt her cheeks getting hotter. "No, not really..." she mumbled.

"Hana has a lot of secrets," Yoko said with a wink. "Ladies with secrets are attractive for sure."

The photo studio was not busy at all in winter compared to summer. Hana wore her thin white gloves and checked the photos very carefully, one by one. She spent more time and effort than before to study the photos and edit them.

"Sherlock Holmes would lose against you," Yoko teased. "Take some tea and have a break." She poured chamomile tea in a yellow Noritake vintage teapot. Steam gushed out with a sweet and flowery fragrance.

After Hana finished her work at the photo studio that day, she cycled to the guest house instead of the vegetable shop. She walked past the fish tank of golden fish, along the dark and narrow corridor until she stood in front of the reception desk. Ms. Oyama was sleeping in her chair, still holding a morning newspaper. She looked exhausted. The ash tray was full of cigarette butts. Whenever she breathed, her cabbage-shaped hair moved up and down dramatically.

Hana counted out five seconds slowly in her mind, then called her name. "Hi, Ms. Oyama." She was in a deep sleep though, and she didn't wake up. Hana took a postcard out of her bag and put it on the desk.

'Dear Ms. Oyama,' it read.

'Thank you for helping with Ms. Kawanami in the hospital. She is slowly recovering with your support. Please come visit her if you are available. We'll have a small tea ceremony on the second floor of the vegetable shop at 2 pm next Sunday.

Regards, Hana.'

Hana posted the same postcard to the Kato farm after she left the guest house. She listened out for the postcard to hit the bottom of the postbox, then she went back to the vegetable shop.

That Sunday morning, Hikaru delivered a new kind of apple. It was just one basket, and the apples were shiny olive-green, like nothing she'd seen in the Kawanami vegetable shop before.

"These are the first fertilized with earthworm soil," Hikaru said brightly. "It's really an experiment so far. I don't have many yet, but there'll be more next season."

Hana nodded, then held one of them up to her nose; it smelled like a fresh flower. She took a bite. It was a delicate taste, different from the soft, sweet Fuji apples and the sharp, sour Granny Smiths. It was a well-balanced taste with lots of different flavors and textures. It was a totally unique apple like Hana had never tasted before. Before she knew it, the whole apple was gone and only a couple of seeds were left on her hand.

"Wow," she said.

Hikaru was watching her closely. "Good wow or bad wow?"

Hana licked her lips. "Really amazing wow. This is from earthworm soil?"

Hikaru grinned and went a little red. "Yes. I'm so glad you like it."

"I think Ms. Kawanami will love them. They'll make her strong. Thank you, Hikaru!"

Hana gave Hikaru a hug, surprised she did it without even thinking. He was warm and smelled like fresh apples.

Hikaru seemed a little flustered when she pulled back, blinking furiously. He nodded once and gave a little bow. "Yes. I hope it helps. Um. Well, I better go collect my father." Hana bowed too. "I'll see you at 2. Thank you for coming over twice!"

He bowed again and stumbled out of the shop backwards.

Hana went up to Ms. Kawanami's room, feeling excited. "Ms. Kawanami, look! Hikaru gave us a brand new apple from the Kato farm. Would you like to try it? It's very tasty."

"No, I have no appetite," Ms. Kawanami said grumpily. She was as thin as chopsticks, and it worried Hana.

"You should eat something so you can get your energy back and start working again soon."

"It's hard to swallow any food," Ms. Kawanami muttered. "I wish there was a pill to replace food. It's a pain to chew anything."

In the kitchen, Hana looked hard at the new apples and tried to think of what to make for Ms. Kawanami and the guests to eat. She peeled the apples very thinly and diced them, then mixed all-purpose flour, oatmeal, brown sugar, cinnamon powder and butter to make a crumble. She put the crumble in the fridge. Cold crumble would make the texture crunchier when she baked it, striking a good balance with the softly cooked apples. Next she caramelized the apples in brown sugar and Calvados brandy over a low heat. She added the caramelized apples to a baking tray, spread the crumble evenly on top and put it in the preheated oven. Soon the smells of sweet apples and cinnamon filled up the kitchen.

"It smells nice," came Ms. Kawanami's reedy voice. Hana could just see her sitting up in bed now, through the half-opened bedroom door.

"I'm baking apple crumble with Hikaru's apples," Hana said. "And I told you yesterday, but do you remember Ms. Oyama and the Katos will come see you later on? They're keen to know how you're doing."

Ms. Kawanami's face got darker. "It's a burden for everyone. Why did you invite them?"

"No, they were happy to be invited. They'd like to see you." Hana walked over and held Ms. Kawanami's hands. They were like dry twigs, with no strength or warmth at all.

After that she finished up her chores, fed Miyo, and spent a little while cooking some more snacks. The doorbell rang while Hana was setting the table. She went down and opened the glass sliding door to let Mr. Kato and Hikaru in. Hikaru was holding a bunch of coral-colored peonies.

"Twice in one day!" Hana said, smiling at Hikaru. "Come on in, please. The flowers look lovely, Ms. Kawanami will be pleased."

Mr. Kato took his coat and hat off. He looked pale and thin. "I'm not sure if we're bothering Ms. Kawanami."

"Not at all. Let me take your coat." Hana led them upstairs, where Ms. Kawanami was reading a newspaper in bed.

"Thank you for coming," she said, nodding at them. "I owe you both for coming to the hospital."

"Hana did everything, so there was nothing for us to do." Mr. Kato looked at Ms. Kawanami like an elderly son looking at his old mother. "You look much better. You'll be recovered soon."

"Thank you. I shall." Ms. Kawanami put her wrinkled hand on Mr. Kato's thin hand. "You look thinner than before, Kato. You should look after yourself well."

Hikaru held out the flowers. "Ms. Kawanami. It's good to see you."

"These are more suitable for Hana, don't you think?" Ms. Kawanami asked, looking up at Hikaru. His cheeks grew redder, and she seemed pleased. "Could you put these in a vase, Hana?"

Hana took the flowers, cut off the bottoms and put them in a big glass vase on the dining table. The others followed her, with Hikaru assisting Ms. Kawanami.

"Shall we have a cup of tea?" Hana asked. "Please have a seat."

"Thank you," said Mr. Kato. Hana held Ms. Kawanami's shoulders and helped her to sit. Her thin legs were shivering.

Everyone sat down. Hana took the warmed apple crumble out of the oven and put it on the table. At the same moment, the glass door slid open downstairs.

"Perfect timing," Hana said with a smile, as Ms. Oyama came up the stairs. She added a warm custard boat and three teapots on the table. The warm and sweet fragrances wafted over the table.

"These are Hoji tea, chamomile and Lady Grey," Hana pointed. "The apple crumble is made from Hikaru's newest apples."

Ms. Oyama sat down and touched her perfectly round cabbage-shaped hair. "This is so you, Hana. When did you prepare all this?"

"I haven't done that much. The apples were fresh and had a lovely smell, so hopefully the crumble tastes good." Hana poured Hoji tea in Ms. Kawanami's teacup. The old lady curled her thin fingers around the teacup, blew on the surface and drank slowly. Hikaru poured Chamomile tea for his father and Hoji tea for himself. Ms. Oyama enjoyed a strong cup of Lady Grey.

"It's very nice." Mr. Kato's face looked relaxed.

While everyone was enjoying the tea, Hana cut the crumble and spooned a slice onto each plate, pouring custard cream on top. Everyone stopped talking and had their crumble quietly.

Hana's lips were dry from being so nervous. "I'm not sure how it tastes," she said cautiously.

"What kind of apples are these?" Ms. Oyama asked. Her eyes had gotten bigger. Ms. Kawanami was chewing the cake very carefully.

"I'm not sure what type of apple it is. I've never seen it before." Hana looked at Hikaru.

"Yes, it's a hybrid type," he said. "Granny Smiths have a sharp taste but they're not sweet. Fuji apples are sweet but they're less tangy. I wanted to make an apple that had both a sweet and a sour taste, with a good sharp texture, so I mixed several types of apples together." Hikaru looked serious. "I also used a very special Cuban fertilizer, which adds extra richness. Now I need to study more to make the right type of apple that I'm looking for. It will take some time." His big round eyes shone with excitement and enthusiasm. Hana thought it was marvelous that he was explaining about how he grew his apples. He was so sincere, and chose his words carefully so everyone could easily understand. It made him look like a proper, mature adult.

"Kato, your son is so passionate about farming that you don't have to worry now. How lucky you are to have a son like him." Ms. Kawanami's cheeks were slightly pink. Her plate was completely empty, with every drop of custard completely gone. It was the first food she'd finished after coming back from the hospital.

Mr. Kato looked at his son proudly. "Since Hikaru came back from his trip, he's become very serious about new farming skills." He coughed and put his hand on his chest several times while he was talking. Ms. Oyama poured him more hot tea whenever Mr. Kato coughed painfully. Hana thought he looked thinner, with a darker face, than when Hana had seen him in the hospital just a few days ago.

Hana took another bite of her crumble thoughtfully. The flavor of the apples really was incredible. It was strange to think how much work went into that. "Now I understand," she said. "The first bite is sour, then it gets sweeter in the second bite. They also have a beautiful fragrance and a great texture. I feel like it's a magic apple."

"Anybody want some more?" Ms. Oyama asked, and put a bigger slice of the crumble on her plate before anyone else could move. Ms. Kawanami lifted her plate slightly without a word. Hana laughed happily.

It was a perfect afternoon, like a clean white ironed tablecloth. Hana thought it must be the same for Ms. Kawanami. After everyone left, Hana washed the plates and cutlery. Ms. Kawanami was sleeping in bed by then, wrapped up in a soft, thick padded vest. Hana washed the sink with a sponge and wiped it with a dry cloth. She could see her face and coral cheeks in the shiny silver steel.

Out on the balcony, Hana put the washcloth on the drying rack and rested her arms on the railing. Lights were switching off one by one in the buildings on the market street. In the middle of the dark and empty street, a ginger cat with long whiskers was stretching out its arms.

"Hello, pretty." Hana waved. The cat glanced at her quickly, then turned around and scratched its ears while having a big yawn. Hana looked at the purple dusk sky and the birds sitting on the tangled telephone wires. She hoped tomorrow would be like today, and that Jin would have a day like it too. A peaceful and a beautiful calm day. She hoped it from the bottom of her heart.

The next morning, Hana went down to the shop earlier than usual. She usually woke up at 4:30am every morning without needing an alarm, but that day she woke up before 4 and went downstairs quietly, so as not to wake up Ms. Kawanami. She started the day like Ms. Kawanami used to do, cleaning the street and the vegetable shop until Hikaru's white truck arrived with fresh vegetables and fruits.

"Good morning," she said. "It looks like good weather today."

"Morning. It's cold, isn't it?" Hikaru grinned and opened the back of the truck. "Potatoes are good these days. The skins are thin and they're soft and sweet inside." He looked like a professional farmer, carrying boxes of potatoes, onions, carrots and shiny orange mandarins one by one into the shop.

"Can I help you with anything?" Hana asked, reaching out to touch the cardboard box Hikaru was carrying. Her cold hands and Hikaru's warm hands touched and gave her a static shock.

"No, it's OK," Hikaru said. "They're heavy so you just sit there and I'll carry them all in."

Hana watched him go back and forth, trying to figure out what was different about him today. He suddenly looked like a proper man, rather than a young guy. He definitely was handling his farming work with a sincere and serious attitude. His big round eyes and red cheeks from the cold weather looked lovely. She almost went to touch his cold cheeks to warm them up, then caught herself and shook her head. She was quickly reminded of Jin's calm face and his thin and long eyes. Hana got confused and felt a heaviness in her chest.

"It's all done," Hikaru said cheerfully, wiping his forehead. "Please sign this paper then I'll head back."

"Sure, will do." Hana signed the invoice and watched Hikaru's truck disappear down the street.

Hana opened the boxes and displayed the items on the shelves, trying not to think about Hikaru. Her first customer was a chef of a nearby Japanese restaurant. He bought two boxes of thick and heavy horse radishes. Hana imagined what he might cook; probably his lunch menu would be a yellowtail stew with white radish, in a sweet and sticky teriyaki soy sauce.

The morning business went on as usual. The next customer was a curry restaurant chef. He bought carrots, potatoes, cabbages and onions and put them in a box like he was playing a game of Tetris. He put the box in the basket of his bicycle and cycled away. Soon middle-aged ladies and some elderly people came in and bought sweet potatoes, apples, bell peppers and mandarins.

"The mandarins here are so sweet," said a round-faced lady who bought two buckets of them. "The skin is thin and the fruit is really juicy. My kids love these and they eat a whole bucket at once."

"They're in the right season now," Hana said, pouring the mandarins in a paper bag and adding some small mandarins from the other buckets for free. Ms.

Kawanami would definitely do that too. "Full of vitamin C to prevent colds. You can make tea out of the skin too."

The lady shook her hands. "Oh, no need to add freebies all the time."

"It's OK. Enjoy the mandarins and come again next time." Hana smiled.

After the busy morning, Hana was inside folding empty cardboard boxes when a postman opened the sliding glass door. "Excuse me. Is there a Hana Lee here?" He was holding an envelope in his hand.

"Yes, that's me." Hana turned around, still holding a vegetable box.

"I have a letter for you. Please sign here." He held out the thin white envelope. The vegetable shop's address and Hana's name were written in blue ink. The handwriting was familiar to her, and Hana's heart started pounding madly.

It was from Jin.

Hana signed the paper, hugged the envelope to her chest with both hands and ran up to the second floor. She closed her bedroom door and held the envelope in her shivering hands, looking at her name and the address. She couldn't move her body. She couldn't move her fingers. She just held the envelope, breathing in and out several times to calm herself. She closed her eye and counted slowly and thoughtfully to five, then opened the envelope. There was a post card inside. She took it out and started to read.

'Hana, it's been a while.

'I'm sorry that I left and I didn't talk to you face-to-face. You must have been hurt when I left without telling you. I didn't mean to do that, but I didn't know what else to do.'

Hana's hands shook harder. Her mouth was dry and she couldn't breathe well. Jin's handwriting was so calm and peaceful, as if it was written by a monk. She'd never received a letter from a monk before, but she imagined it would look just like this. Hana took a deep breath and continued reading.

'Leaving like that was selfish, and I'm sorry, but please believe I didn't do it to hurt you. It was something inside me, something I had to manage and overcome by myself. I may have always known in the back of my head that this would happen at some point. Please don't wait for me anymore. I'm still looking for my answers. One day, I hope I can explain everything to you, but I'm not sure when that will be.'

A warm tear dropped from her eyes and landed on the postcard.

'Hana, I only want the best for you. I think you're going to lose someone special soon. It will be hard and sad, but I know you're strong enough to face it. I'm sending a dreamcatcher that I made from a willow twig. I hope you don't have any bad dreams from now on. Ah, a rich chocolate cake with good quality liquor would be perfect. It will suit you.

'Bye for now. Jin.'

Hana felt lost for words. For so long she'd believed she would meet Jin and start a new life with him in Japan. She'd wanted to believe it, even when he wasn't there.

Now he was saying it wouldn't happen. 'Please don't wait for me anymore.'

Her head was pitch black. Losing a special person. She'd never thought anybody had a special place in her heart, apart from Jin. And a chocolate liquor cake? She was puzzled by that and everything. She'd never told Jin the vegetable shop's address. The last time she'd sent him an email was when she was staying in the guest house. She hadn't known she would live in the vegetable shop back then, and she could never had guessed it.

Hana shook the envelope, and out slid a small dreamcatcher. Thin willow twigs were tangled like a spider's web into a tight circle. A thin brown thread weaved round and round the inside, holding the dreamcatcher together.

Hana put the dream catcher on her palm. She studied it carefully and smelled it. It had a light woody, salty sea smell. She read the postcard several times from the beginning to the end. She turned the postcard around to look at the picture. It was a photo of an avocado cut in half, lying on a golden beach under a beautiful blue sky. Hana stroked the dream catcher and looked at the perfect shape of the sliced green avocado.

12. Corn bread with fresh corn on the cob and the Kato farm

Christmas was coming. The Christmas lights on the market street were bright and cheerful, and calm Christmas carols were playing on the radio. Ms. Kawanami's condition was getting better, so she came down to the shop sometimes, to have a chat with the customers or check the conditions of her vegetables and fruits.

At the same time, Hana lost weight and became quieter. She spent a lot of time looking out of windows, watching people walking by or birds sitting on telephone wires.

The Kimura photo shop was closed for the holidays until the new year, and the Sakura Japanese school had also started their month-long winter holiday, so Hana spent most of her time at the vegetable shop. She made the cat house behind the shop warmer by adding more padding and soft blankets. She also regularly checked if there was plenty of cat food left, and the water bowl was not frozen over. She thought the long winter would be harsh for street cats, and she wanted them to be well-prepared.

Miyo visited Hana every day. He sat in the cat house and cleaned his velvety white and black polka dot fur coat, or fell asleep sweetly on the blankets, showing his pink paws. Sometimes other cats came by and ate the cat food too. Hana liked to hear the cats making crunching sounds when they ate the dry food. Cats with full bellies had satisfied, comfortable-looking faces. Hana loved to look at those faces, they made her feel safe too.

One morning after feeding the cats, Hana made a teapot of hot Hoji tea and some warm ginger cookies using fresh ginger from the Kato farm. In the vegetable shop, Ms. Kawanami was talking to some customers. Hana left the tea and the biscuits on the table, as she didn't want to bother them. Ms. Kawanami would share them with the customers once she turned around and noticed them on the table.

Hana walked up to the second floor quietly. There was nothing in particular for her to do. In her room she looked at the vintage Martin guitar sitting in the corner, then closed the door and sat down on the tatami floor with the guitar in her lap, handling it carefully, like a piece of antique pottery. She began playing 'Lullaby' by Priscilla Ahn. Hana played it whenever she had a chance, sometimes changing the tempo, melody, or chords.

She'd often listened to the song on the radio with Jin, eating tomato and pork stew with potatoes in his apartment on cold winter nights. She hoped Jin was having good dreams somewhere. Even if they couldn't go back to their old relationship, she still hoped to see him; to sit in front of each other again and talk about what was going on in their lives, over a pork stew with soft music on the radio.

They'd shared a lot of things. She'd always felt she could talk to him about anything and everything, with no shame or embarrassment. He'd been more than a boyfriend to her. He was her soulmate, and she missed him still.

She closed her eyes and played 'Lullaby' again and again, like a musical score with indefinite repeat signs. She hoped she wouldn't have bad dreams ever again. She hoped she could see Jin tonight in her dreams. The light and airy sound from the vintage guitar echoed in the room. She felt the guitar's owner, Ms. Kawanami's son, would forgive her for playing it without permission. Hana had never met him, but she hoped he would have sweet dreams tonight too.

"Hana, would you come downstairs?"

It was Ms. Kawanami's voice, calling up from the shop.

"Yes, I'm coming."

Hana wiped away her tears and put the guitar back on the stand. She rushed down to the shop and saw Hikaru was there, holding a small cardboard box. She tried to make a cheerful face to cover up how she was feeling.

"Hi, Hikaru. How are you doing?"

"I brought some corn on the cob for you and Ms. Kawanami," he said, and opened the box. It was full of deep yellow, beautiful corn on the cob. "These are from the corn seeds that I brought from Kentucky, in America. My grandfather's old friend, Jack, gave me the best seeds from his farm. I didn't harvest many from the first planting, so I can't sell them yet, but please try them and let me know what you think. You can eat them raw or by steaming, boiling or grilling." Hikaru's eyes sparkled. Hana could see he was feeling proud.

Hana took the box with an apologetic expression. "Thank you, but I'm sorry that I'm always receiving presents from you. I haven't had a chance to offer anything back."

Hikaru waved his hands. "It's OK, no worries. Your sweet pumpkin chiffon cake was great, and my father loved it too. Oh, by the way, my father invited you to come visit the farm when you have a chance. He thought it would be good for you to know where the products you sell come from. Of course he wants to see you again too." Hikaru went a little red. "So, uh, would you like to come?"

"Of course she'll go," Ms. Kawanami answered for her. "She's always talking about your farm."

Hana's throat seized up.

"Is she?" Hikaru asked. "I mean, sorry, are you?"

"Well, I-"

"It's always Hikaru this, Hikaru that," Ms. Kawanami grumbled. "You'd think she wants to move in."

Now Hana's face was burning. "Yes," she said firmly, glaring now at Ms. Kawanami. "I would like to go. To see where the products come from."

"Yes, of course," said Hikaru. "The products. So, um, when would be the best time for you?" His face became very grave after asking this question, as if he was having deep thoughts.

Hana tried to calm her flushing cheeks. "Well, first I'd like to say thank you for the invite. Your father is very kind. And any time is good for me. What about next week, when the shop is closed?"

Hikaru nodded. "That sounds perfect. I'll come pick you up then."

"It's fine. I can go by myself if you give me your address."

Hikaru looked a little uneasy. "Well, it's pretty deep in the mountains, and you need to walk a long distance from the bus station. I'm happy to come pick you up, if that's OK with you." He smiled, then looked over at Ms. Kawanami. She was sitting in her chair now, behind the counter.

"Ms. Kawanami, my father said he'd like to invite you too, when you're feeling better."

"That's fine," she said quietly. "Hana can tell me about the farm."

Hikaru grinned. "Great. I'll head back then. See you soon." He hopped back in his truck and drove away down the market street. Hana watched his truck rumble along until he was out of sight.

After he was gone, Hana opened the box and touched the corn cobs. They were surprisingly tight and bouncy. She peeled the corn silk back from one cob, washed it and cut the corn kernels away with a sharp knife, then put the sliced fresh corn on a small plate.

"Ms. Kawanami," she said, "I'll watch the shop, so why don't you take a rest and have some corn upstairs."

"Oh, thank you," Ms. Kawanami said. She looked rather tired. Maybe the grumbling had taken the energy out of here.

Hana held her thin arm and helped her go up the stairs. Hana thought it must be difficult for her to walk up and down the steep steps every day. She poured some Hoji tea in a porcelain cup painted with blue flowers and set it in front of Ms. Kawanami, sitting on her chair in the kitchen. Warm steam rose off the cup as she held it in her wrinkled hands. Hana put the small plate with the sliced corn on the table between them with two forks, then took a bite.

It was like eating fresh fruit. The texture was crunchy outside and soft inside. The first bite tasted like popcorn and the second bite tasted like caramel. It was as sweet as a pineapple, and she didn't feel quite right to call it just ordinary corn. She could definitely feel it had been grown with care and love. She understood why Hikaru was proud of his grandfather's friend who'd provided the seeds.

Ms. Kawanami scooped up a couple of corn kernels using her fork, put them in her mouth and chewed. Her expression seemed somewhat uneasy. She had a hard time swallowing any food these days.

"Kato doesn't have to worry about his farm anymore," she said. Her voice was low and small but her eyes were sharp. Hana nodded at her and they both ate the corn silently.

It was the day before the start of a long national holiday weekend, so the market street was quieter than usual that afternoon. Hana closed the shop early, boxed up the leftover vegetables and fruits and swept the shop floor. The extra food would be picked up by a nearby charity center and delivered to an orphanage the next day.

Hana decided to make cornbread. She cooled down boiled corn cobs in ice water, then handpicked the kernels with great care, spread them on a tray, and put them in a pre-heated oven. While the kernels were baking nicely, she made buttermilk by adding lemon juice to warm milk and stirring it gently, curdling the milk quickly. She also prepared a mixture of self-rising flour, caster sugar, honey, eggs and butter. She took the baked corn kernels out of the oven and put them in the food processer with a pinch of salt. The blades whirled and the corn became a fine yellow flour, which she poured into a big bowl along with the other mixed ingredients. She stirred the wet dough well to remove all the air bubbles, then put it in the oven. Soon after, a sweet and savory smell floated in the air.

Hana turned the oven off and took the tray out. The cornbread was a deep yellow color, and well-risen. She poked the center with a chopstick, and no liquid ran out. She carried a thick slice and a glass of warm milk to Ms. Kawanami's room and slowly opened the door. Ms. Kawanami was sleeping on her side, half under the futon in her thick dressing gown. Age spots dotted her face like deep shadows.

Hana knelt by the bedside table and whispered by Ms. Kawanami's ear. "Ms. Kawanami, are you hungry? I made some cornbread from the Kato farm corn. It's soft, so it will be easy to chew and digest. Would you like to try some?"

Ms. Kawanami didn't reply, so Hana set the warm cornbread and milk on her bedside table and left the room. After cleaning the kitchen, Hana poked her face through the bedroom door to see how Ms. Kawanami was doing. The plate and the glass were both empty, which made Hana smile. Ms. Kawanami seemed to be having a good dream, as she was smiling.

Hana wrote out her recipe and edited her photos of the cornbread, then uploaded them to her blog. After that she sat at her desk and looked up at the red crescent moon through the open window.

On Monday morning, Hikaru came to pick up Hana in his truck. It was a day off for the vegetable shop, and Hana was worried about leaving Ms. Kawanami alone in the house.

"Are you all right to be alone?" she asked. "Shall I call Ms. Oyama?"

Ms. Kawanami frowned and waved her hands. "No, I'll be fine on my own. Don't worry about me. Kato will be waiting so get going."

"Are you sure?" Hana asked again. "Call me if anything happens, OK?"

"I told you I'm OK. Don't bother me. I've been managing this vegetable shop by myself for over thirty years. I know myself best." She turned around angrily, but her crooked back looked so small and thin to Hana.

"Ms. Kawanami, Hana will be back soon," Hikaru said, looking slightly concerned. "It won't take long."

"Who are these two to worry about me so excessively?" Ms. Kawanami muttered. "Do you think I'm a useless, feeble old woman?"

"No, not at all," Hana protested. "Then we'll leave now. I'll come back and clear up the shop later, so take a rest and see you then." Hana picked up her woven basket full of cornbread and closed the shop's glass door.

As soon as she opened the door to Hikaru's truck, Hana was hit by the smell of whiskey mixed with cinnamon. "Ah, it smells like Christmas!"

Hikaru grinned. "I made a reed diffusor from good handmade Kentucky bourbon; it was another present from my grandfather's friend, Jack. The fragrance was so beautiful, it seemed a shame to only drink it." Hikaru touched a thatch of reed sticks sticking out of a small brown bottle.

Hana looked at him with a new respect. "You've got so many talents, Hikaru. It's amazing. Do you think about what you're going to make every night before you go to bed?"

Hikaru closed the door and pulled on his seatbelt, smiling too. "I always liked to use my imagination. What are the other uses for this? What can I make using that? I used to ask my parents so many questions they got sick of it."

He started the truck and pulled away down the market street. He was focused on the road, so he didn't notice as Hana studied his face. He had good, sturdy cheekbones, a strong chin, and a light dusting of stubble on his cheeks.

"I'm sure they were glad about your inquisitive nature," Hana said with a smile, as he pulled off the market street and onto a bigger road.

"I don't know, really," Hikaru said, handling the wheel and changing lanes easily. "My mother died when I was young, so I don't have many memories of her, but my dad always encouraged me to do whatever I liked, as long as it wasn't illegal or a burden on other people." He fell silent for a moment and continued. "My father worried a lot when I first started farming, but it seems he trusts me more now. In fact, if I don't take the farm over now, there's no one else to do the work, and we'd have to sell."

Hikaru's hands tightened on the wheel, and green veins showed on his pale hands. Hana felt like she wanted to hold his hands and support him. Instead she put her hands in her pocket and looked out of the window, thinking about her mom's disappointed voice.

'What are you doing, Hana?' she might nag. 'The neighbor's daughter already graduated from university and got a good job. While other people are building their own careers, you're wasting time in Japan working at a useless photo studio. Is that really good enough?'

"Are you OK?" Hikaru asked. "You look pale. Should I open the window?"

Hana blinked and focused on him. "I'm OK, thanks. I feel slightly dizzy, probably because I haven't been in a car for a while." she touched the back of her hand to her forehead, and the skin felt hot.

"It's true that this truck bounces more than a regular car. I didn't think about it." Hikaru scratched his head.

"No worries. It's good to go out sometimes." Hana smiled.

"I'll open the window a bit. Let me know when you're cold." The window slid down and a cold breeze came in, touching her face and hair. "It's getting properly cold, isn't it? We may get a white Christmas this year." He paused. "How will you spend your Christmas, Hana?"

"I haven't thought about that yet," she answered calmly. "Ms. Kawanami is still not fully recovered, so I may just stay here and spend time with her. What about you?"

"I'll stay with my father and we'll talk a lot about managing the farm, probably. I don't have any special plans. He's still unwell, so I'll stay at home and look after him."

The truck passed Yotsuya crossing and headed toward the Imperial Palace. Lots of people were jogging in a big circle around the Palace. Some of them were in shorts and thin gloves. Hana inhaled and exhaled deeply. Her breath made a white fog.

Hikaru turned to her. "What's your hometown like, Hana?"

She smiled. "My hometown's near the sea, in the southern area of Korea, with a big mountain nearby" she thought for a moment, and couldn't help imagining the nights spent walking with Jin, beside the black winter sea. She pushed the memory away and kept talking. "There're not so many people there, like Tokyo, so it's quiet. People are friendly, and there's lots of fresh seafood."

"It sounds lovely," said Hikaru. "I'd love to visit sometime." He thought for a moment. "Chiba has mountains and the sea, but my place is out in the total countryside, so it must be pretty different from your hometown."

"I've never been to Chiba, or really into the Japanese countryside, so I'm excited to visit your farm."

This seemed to cheer Hikaru up a little. "It's the season of Chinese cabbage and long white radish, so we're growing lots of them on the farm now. The cabbages are good for nabe hot pot or shabu shabu stew. It's good to steam and garnish them with fish dishes too."

The truck passed Kasai Rinkai park while Hikaru was talking. People were watching birds on the sea or walking their dogs, and some kids were flying big kites on the grass. Hana thought Miyo would be having an afternoon nap in his cat house around this time. She felt cozy and it made her yawn.

"It's tiring to just sit there, isn't it?" Hikaru said. "We'll get onto the highway soon and it won't be long after that. My farm is in the suburbs of Tateyama, in Chiba. It's a peaceful place, really. We may be able to see the sea today, since the weather is nice and clear."

Hana yawned, then quickly covered her mouth, cheeks flushing with embarrassment. "Sorry, I am getting a bit sleepy, but I'm not bored, I promise." She tried to think of another topic. "How's Mr. Kato doing these days?"

Hikaru took a little breath and glanced at Hana. "I think you probably know my father's been sick. Did you know he had surgery for thyroid cancer last year?" Hana nodded. Ms. Kawanami had told her the details. "Well, I think the farm caused it. We were both born and raised there, since my great-grandfather started it. We've always tried to grow crops as naturally as possible, but some crops need pesticides. I think chemicals from those pesticides got into my father's body and caused the cancer." He paused for a moment. "These days I feel like my mom died early because of that too." He gave himself a little shake and brightened. "Anyway, my dad got better after the last surgery. He lost a lot of weight though, and he doesn't have much energy."

Hana thought about that for a moment. "Ms. Kawanami said Mr. Kato must have no worries now, because you're doing a great job. I'm sure the cold weather isn't helping. He'll get better soon, once it's warmer."

"I hope so too. Since his surgery, I've been using only organic methods." There was another thoughtful pause. "My father supports me, but I know he still worries about things. Organic farming requires a lot of extra work, and we can't produce as many crops as with ordinary farming. I need to learn more and find efficient ways of running the farm."

They both sat in silence for some time. The truck passed Tateyama Castle, which looked like a big fort made of snow. It was as beautiful as a Disney princess' castle, and Hana was impressed. The truck soon passed a big sports center with empty outdoor tennis courts, then finally rolled onto unpaved roads in the mountains.

"Let's go up to Tateyama Castle next time," Hikaru said. "The view is nice up there. The roads here are quite bumpy so fasten your seatbelt." He changed to first gear, and the truck made a loud noise as it drove up the sloping road. They made some turns, and after a while

Hana saw a sign for 'Kato Farm' handwritten on a big piece of old wood.

"Here we are. It was quite a journey, wasn't it?" Hikaru stopped the truck and opened the door. Mr. Kato was standing in the fields, waving at them over the wooden fence. Long rows of crops stretched away beyond him. Bright green radish leaves shone in the afternoon light, dancing backwards and forwards in the wind. Chinese cabbages were opening their big green leaves and showing off their pure white hearts, like blooming flowers. Hana was fascinated by it all.

Mr. Kato came around the fence and walked over to them, wearing a thick chestnut brown wool jumper, black waterproof pants and black wellington boots.

"Thank you for coming to this faraway place," he said, wrinkling his eyes in a smile. "It's good to see you, Hana."

"Mr. Kato, it's lovely to see you again, thank you for inviting me." She held out the bread basket. "I've made some cornbread from the corn that Hikaru planted."

Mr. Kato took it and shook her hand with a smile. His hand was so cold and thin. Hana felt that if she held his hand too firmly, it would crush like ash. She wished she could share some of her warmth with him.

"Please come on in. It's cold outside."

Mr. Kato guided Hana to their traditional Japanese house, built out of wood with a high triangular roof. The wood looked well-maintained, with a lovely sheen. The tall wooden deck around the edge of the house looked like perfectly tempered dark chocolate. Hana imagined sitting there with a piece of cold watermelon, listening to cicadas sing on a sunny summer day. She touched the deck gently, feeling a warm, strange kind of nostalgia.

"My mother and I used to sit here and watch flowers and birds while drinking cold plum tea," Hikaru said. He had a sad expression, as if he'd read Hana's mind.

"It must have been lovely," she said. "I can picture it in my head like a scene from a movie." She put her hands out to catch cold white petals falling from the sky.

"It's snowing," Mr. Kato said. "You'll get wet. Take your shoes off and let's get in."

"Thank you." She took her boots off and stepped onto the deck. The cold wooden floor made her brain freeze and her shoulders tremble. Hikaru turned her boots around and put them underneath the deck to keep them dry, while Mr. Kato opened the paper sliding door.

Inside, a warm orange fire in a square, open Irori fire pit made the traditional tatami-mat room feel lovely and cozy. A long iron pole hung down from the ceiling, with an iron pot hooked on the bottom just above the licking flames, gushing steam. In the center of the Irori, reddish-gray ash and dry chunks of wood were slowly burning, warming up the whole house. Past the fire, long tube-shaped paper lamps sat either side of a set of paper sliding doors, decorated with paintings of flowers and leaves in black ink. A big paper kite hung down from the ceiling.

Hana immediately fell in love with the room. "I've never seen a house with so much character and personal touch!" she said. "All the furniture and belongings seem to be alive."

Mr. Kato smiled. "This house is over a hundred years old. It's old and requires a lot of maintenance. Young people don't want to live in these houses anymore." He pointed at a thick cushion on the floor. "Please, have a seat. What would you like to drink?"

Hana sat on the cushion slowly, still looking around the room. "I'm envious Hikaru gets to live in this beautiful house. Mr. Kato, what are you going to drink?"

"I'll have Rooibos tea," he replied.

"Then so will I."

"Sure, I'll bring the tea," said Hikaru, passing a wool vest to his father and heading through into the kitchen.

Hana looked at Mr. Kato's thin and tired-looking face as he took off his jacket and put on the wool vest. "You must be very proud of Hikaru," she said. "He's such a hard worker."

Kato sat down opposite Hana. "Ah, how time flies. I feel like it was just yesterday that Hikaru was learning how to walk. He was such a tiny, sweet, loving boy." A shadow seemed to pass over his face briefly. "Maybe he mentioned, I lost my wife when he was still young. I was busy with the farm, so I couldn't spend much time with him, but he's grown up now and taken over, so yes. I'm proud and happy." His eyes wrinkled again in a smile.

Hana smiled back. "I know Hikaru's also proud of you." She paused then went on. "He told me he started organic farming for your health. I'm sure you'll get better and the farm will be thriving again soon. Plant new seeds in spring, enjoy flowers in summer and harvest in fall. Only good things will come."

The crow's feet at the corners of his eyes wrinkled up more. "I know he will." He picked up an iron poker and dug into the Irori for a moment. The embers rustled and glowed orange. When he spoke again, it was with his eyes focused on the fire. "Hana, this may sound strange, and I don't want to frighten you, but I feel I don't have much time left." He put the poker down and took a slow breath. "I see my wife in my dreams every night. She's standing under a big apple tree, waving at me. The apple flowers are in full bloom and she's smiling." He paused for a moment and looked up at her, as if willing her to understand something. "I think it's not bad to say goodbye like this; not giving everyone too much of a burden. I haven't said this to Hikaru, since I know he'd just worry, though he may have noticed it already." He stopped talking and seemed to be lost in thought. "I'm not saying this just because he's my son, but Hikaru is a good man. He's rather sensitive, but he has a warm heart. Please support him if I'm not here anymore." Kato's voice cracked at the end.

Hana didn't know what to say. She felt her cheeks flush and bowed low over the cushion, though she didn't know why. "No, please don't say that. You'll get better soon. You should." She tried to think of something more to say, because Mr. Kato was looking at her so honestly. She reached out and took his cold, thin hand. "I don't know what I can do, but I promise I'll do my best to support him. I'll also help at the vegetable shop more, so Ms. Kawanami can recover faster. The Kato farm fruits and vegetables are always popular, so I'm sure the new organic products will definitely do well too."

Mr. Kato smiled, but his eyes looked rather sad. "Thank you for saying that."

The orange fire made a crackling sound in the Irori fire pit, and Hana gazed into the flames.

A few moments later, Hikaru came into the room holding a big wooden basket.

"Thank you for waiting so long," he said, then looked at them both sitting silence. "What have you been talking about so seriously?"

"We were talking about new apple trees," Hana said quickly, in a high voice.

"Yes," Mr. Kato went on, "I've been thinking about what types of trees will be good for the Japanese climate and soil."

"You've got plenty of time so there is no rush," Hana continued, but Mr. Kato said nothing more. Hikaru looked between them with a slightly suspicious expression, but didn't say anything as he put the teapot and teacups on a long square table at the edge of the Irori. He put on a heatproof glove and unhooked the hanging pot to pour hot water into the teapot. A subtle savory fragrance steamed out.

"I mixed Rooibos and Earl Gray together. I hope you like it." Hikaru poured the tea into the white glazed teacups, then laid out two big wooden plates; one stacked with Hana's sliced cornbread, the other with six big oranges, half of them fresh and half of them a crinkled brown, as if they'd been baked.

"This bread looks tasty," Mr. Kato said, studying the yellow cornbread.

"I hope it tastes OK," Hana said. "The tea smells lovely." They all tucked in.

"This is so moist and soft," Mr. Kato said, while chewing a big bite of cornbread.

"Yes, it is," Hikaru agreed.

"You have a great talent for baking." Mr. Kato seemed to really be enjoying the cornbread.

"It's because the corn tastes great, so really Hikaru did a good job." Hana glanced at Hikaru.

"Ah, Jack's special seeds." Mr. Kato nodded. "He was a great friend of my father, and a great farmer too."

"Jack gave me some handmade bourbon as well, but I'm saving that for Christmas." Hikaru lifted one of the oranges. "Now, this is a local Japanese orange called Iyokan. It's somewhere between a citron and a mandarin. It's good to eat on its own but we make it into a jam or chutney too. We also like grilled Iyokan. Do you want to try one?" Hikaru held the bright orange out.

"Sure." Hana took the big Iyokan. It looked freshly cut, with sappy green leaves on top. She peeled its thick and shiny orange skin, releasing a wonderful citrus smell. She tore the Iyokan into slices and had one bite. The taste popped in her mouth immediately.

"It's so unique," she said. "It's a bit like an orange, mandarin or citrus but it still tastes different. It's sweet, sour and slightly bitter." She popped another slice in her mouth. "I can eat this all day."

"Try it grilled. It tastes quite different." Hikaru handed her one of the crinkled, baked Iyokans. The skin was warm, slightly crunchy and dark brown. Hana peeled the skin and tasted a slice slowly.

Her eyes flared wide. The taste was stunning. She chewed and swallowed quickly. "It's amazing that food can taste completely different, just by being cooked! It got a lot sweeter, juicier and less sour. The texture is also a lot softer than the raw Iyokan. It's my first time trying grilled fruit, but it's a delicacy indeed."

Hikaru grinned widely. "I'm glad you like it. Dinner will be ready soon."

While Hana finished the whole Iyokan by herself, and Mr. Kato drank his tea slowly, Hikaru prepared the ingredients for a nabe hot pot. Soon he had a large cast iron pot boiling and bubbling on the Irori fire, filled with creamy chicken stock, tofu, Chinese cabbage, leeks, chicken meat balls, thinly sliced beef, carrots and Shiitake mushrooms. The food looked like a work of art, and only took a few moments.

"They're all mostly cooked now, so you can try the vegetables first," Hikaru said. "The rest will stay warm while we eat." He scooped generous portions of Chinese cabbage, leeks and tofu into small bowls and sprinkled thinly chopped spring onions on top. He also poured citrus soy sauce into small sauce bowls, then presented the feast on the Irori side-table.

Hana couldn't help but admire his skills. "Hikaru, you're like a professional chef. Everything looks amazing and smells so good."

"Thank you. I hope it tastes good."

Mr. Kato, Hikaru and Hana each dipped a stalk of hot Chinese cabbage in the citrus soy sauce and chewed slowly. The cabbage melted in Hana's mouth. She drank the soup and ate the soft tofu, feeling her body getting warmer and healthier from the inside. The chicken meatballs disappeared without needing to be chewed, and the thinly sliced meat was so tender. The room was still but for the sound of the fire spitting, the nabe hot pot bubbling and their chopsticks clacking. Outside, thick fluffy white snow fell silently past the windows.

13. Toshikoshi soba on New Year's Day and carrot cake

The New Year countdown began. Hana sat at the desk in her room and lifted her New Year's resolution paper. "Ten, nine, eight, seven," said the radio presenter, counting the numbers down in an excited voice. Hana opened the window by her desk and used a cigarette lighter to set her resolutions on fire. The paper burned with a slow, red flame. Hana made her wish while the paper was burning down.

"Three, two, one!" Fireworks popped in the dark sky over the market street. It was her first New Year's in Japan.

Hana posted New Year cards to the Kimura photo studio, the Sakura Japanese school, Mr. Abe, Nok, Ms. Oyama, and the Kato farm. All that was left was to call her mom.

"Mom, Dad, Happy New Year!" she said cheerfully. "Are you still awake?"

Her mother didn't even say hello. "Stop your nonsense trip right now, Hana! Come back home and get a job."

The sudden harshness made Hana instantly depressed. She managed a quick conversation then hung up the phone, closed the window and went out to the kitchen. Ms. Kawanami was watching TV in her bedroom, wearing a thick cotton dressing gown. Her face looked tired and pale.

"Ms. Kawanami, I thought you were sleeping. Happy New Year! I hope you'll recover fully and be healthy again in the new year."

"You too have a good new year," Ms. Kawanami said in her croaky old voice. "I ordered Toshikoshi soba from the soba noodle shop nearby, but I forgot to tell you. It's in the fridge."

Hana smiled. "Sure, I'll bring it."

She took the soba noodles and the broth pot out of the fridge, simmered the broth with a spoonful of soy sauce, added the noodles sliced root vegetables and shrimp tempura, then poured the hot broth into two bowls and garnished them with thinly sliced spring onions.

"Toshikoshi soba is ready!" she called, laying the bowls out on the kitchen table. Ms. Kawanami and Hana sat opposite each other and ate the noodles and drank the broth. The hot liquid warmed up Hana's cold body.

"All our bad luck will be chewed up with these noodles, and only good things will come in the new year," Ms. Kawanami said, though her thin and wrinkled hands seemed to be having a hard time holding the soba noodles with her chopsticks.

"It's slippery, isn't it?" Hana handed a spoon and a fork to Ms. Kawanami.

Ms. Kawanami frowned. "Are you treating me like a child? I'm old but I'm not so feeble that I can't eat with chopsticks anymore."

"Not at all," Hana explained smoothly. "But it's not easy to hold the noodles, so I'm going to use a spoon too." Hana cut the noodles with a spoon against the ceramic bowl, then scooped them up. Ms. Kawanami watched grumpily for a moment, but soon copied Hana and started eating slowly. Hana soon finished her noodles and broth but Ms. Kawanami hadn't finished even half of the small bowl.

"You hardly touched your food. Why don't you have some more?"

"I'm full now," she said primly. "Thank you."

Hana watched her go back to her room. Her small back was more crooked than ever.

The market street was empty the next day. A lot of shops were closed for the New Year holiday.

"There are no customers these days," Hana said to Ms. Kawanami in the morning. "Why don't we close the shop so you can take a rest? You're not well these days."

"Feeling unwell, the weather's not good, there are no customers," Ms. Kawanami muttered. "Making excuses and taking time off are bad habits in business. It's difficult and it takes time to earn trust, but it's easy to lose it all."

Ms. Kawanami was as stubborn as a rock. Hana gave up on trying to persuade her, and decided to sit with her in the shop for company, sipping hot tea together. When Hana was away doing chores, she usually put the radio on so Ms. Kawanami didn't feel lonely or bored.

"Stay warm and don't catch a cold," Hana said, putting a tartan wool knee blanket on Ms. Kawanami thin legs.

When she had some free time after the shop closed, she went through the photos and recipes of her recent bakes and posted them to her blog. To her surprise, she found she had another comment.

'Hello, I've never left any comments before but I've been enjoying your blog. My boyfriend's 15th birthday is next week, so I'd like to give him a present, but I don't have much pocket money. Is there any cake that I can make easily? I don't have an oven at home either and I've never baked before. Sorry to bother you, but it would be great if you could give me some advice. Thanks, Amy.'

Hana started thinking right away. An easy and inexpensive cake. She checked her recipe book and found a Castella sponge cake that she'd made for Jin at university. The recipe was simple and easy to follow for a high school girl. Hana wrote her back.

'Hi Amy, thanks for your message. I recommend Castella, it's a Portuguese sponge cake which can be made easily in an instant cooker or a slow cooker. I used to make it for my boyfriend at university. The ingredients are eggs, flour, sugar, vegetable oil, honey and milk. That's all.' She added precise quantities of the ingredients first then started explaining the baking steps. 'Separate the egg whites from the yolks, beat them until they are stiff, add sugar, flour, honey, milk and vegetable oil and mix them carefully so as not to lose the stiffness from the eggs. Put the mix in the oiled pan of the instant cooker and push the start button. Honey helps the texture become moist and slightly fluffy. Take the cake out of the pot once it's cooked, and when it's cooled down put it in an airtight plastic tub. It gets softer and tastier the next day. Good luck! Hana.'

After Hana sent the message to Amy, she wrote an email to Jin. It was a long time since she'd sent him an email.

'Hi, Jin. Happy New Year. How are you doing? I received your postcard and the dreamcatcher. I thought I would send you an email straightaway, but I needed some time to think first. There are lots of questions I want to ask, but I know you probably won't reply. I'm doing all right. It was tough in the beginning and I missed you so much, but I'm getting used to it slowly. I'm trying to understand why you left me without telling me anything. I don't know what the reason was, but it must have been something difficult to explain. I sometimes get upset or confused still about the whole thing, but I believe we'll be able to see each other at some point again.

'Tonight I burned my New Year's resolution paper. You remember? We stayed together on the Beauty Bench on the night of 31st December last year. We hid our New Year's resolutions from each other and listened to the countdown together. Now I wonder what you wrote on your paper. I wished for us to live happily together. It feels like that was a long time ago though. I wish I knew where you are and what you're doing right now.

'By the way, how did you know my address? I don't think I ever told anyone that I'm staying here. Perhaps it's not important. Anyway I'm not sure if you'll read this email, but Happy New Year. Hana.'

Su Young Lee

14. New Year's morning, in Tokyo

Hana turned the laptop off and turned the TV on. On the news, the weatherman said it was the coldest and wettest winter for the last ten years. Lots of places were flooded by heavy snow and rain. Hana was reminded of the winding hilly roads on the way to the Kato farm. As soon as Hana thought of Hikaru, the phone rang. Ms. Kawanami answered it, then called across the hall.

"Hana, come over here."

"Sure." Hana hurried to Ms. Kawanami's room.

"Kato just called me," Ms. Kawanami said. "It seems Hikaru slipped on the wet road and sprained his ankle. I'm worried, as Kato is still not in good shape yet."

Hana's mouth went completely dry. "How badly is he hurt?"

"He went to the hospital this morning and has a cast. Kato says it's not a fracture, fortunately, but he won't be able to walk properly for a while."

Hana's mind raced. She started thinking about the things they could take to the hospital. Some flowers, maybe, but would Hikaru like that? Maybe not. Some cakes, then! She'd have to bake some, but was there time? "We have to go see him."

"I said that," Ms. Kawanami said calmly. "But Mr. Kato was very firm. He wants us to enjoy our New Year rest. You in particular. Hikaru said that."

Hana blinked. "What? He doesn't want us to come?"

"It's not like that," Ms. Kawanami chided. "I think he's proud. Probably he's embarrassed he slipped. Mr. Kato said Hikaru didn't even want to tell anyone."

Hana considered that. "He's too proud to tell me." She wasn't really sure what it meant.

"That's it. Anyway. He's not so hurt, and Mr. Kato said he's home already. You can see him soon."

Hana nodded seriously. That was annoying, but she knew men were sometimes too proud. Well, visiting him wasn't the only issue. If Hikaru couldn't work, and Mr. Kato was still sick, who would harvest the fruits and vegetables from the farm?

"What about pausing our orders from them for a while," she suggested, "so Hikaru doesn't have to worry about us at all, until he gets better?"

Ms. Kawanami nodded. "Yes, that's a good idea. He must have lots to do at home, so we shouldn't give him any extra burden."

"Why don't we close the shop until then?"

Ms. Kawanami made her usual stubborn face. "No, I need to open the shop no matter what happens."

"OK, fine." Hana gave up easily, as she knew Ms. Kawanami was more stubborn than a rock, and it was impossible to change her mind.

During New Year's week there were almost no customers at all. The market street was totally empty.

Even the cats didn't show up. They must have gone for their own family gatherings and house parties.

Hana organized the vegetable boxes in the back of the shop, trying not to think about proud Hikaru and his sprained ankle. They were running out of fresh fruit but there were still plenty of onions, carrots, potatoes, sweet potatoes and radishes left. Luckily, they were all healthy looking. Hana took some small sweet potatoes from a box and put them in a basket. Upstairs she washed them, cut them in half and steamed them in the bamboo steamer until they made a lovely sweet smell. She peeled their bright yellow skins off and mashed them with milk and honey in the blender. She poured this sweet, warm potato latte into a big mug and sprinkled it with tiny bits of cinnamon powder. It would be a good healthy meal for Ms. Kawanami.

Hana opened Ms. Kawanami's door, and found her looking out of the dark window from her bed. "You haven't had anything today, have you?"

Ms. Kawanami shook her head. "I don't have any appetite. You go ahead and have dinner."

"I made a sweet potato latte for you. It should be easy to digest and kind on your belly." Hana put the mug down on her bedside table.

Ms. Kawanami's age spots seemed to be darker under the dim light. She looked dully at the latte. "When did you make this?"

"Just now. Drink it, it's good for you. You have no energy these days, so you should eat well to get your strength back."

"Thank you." Ms. Kawanami picked up the mug. It seemed huge in her thin, shivering hands. She looked at the mug, then looked up at Hana suddenly, as if the latte had made her think of something. "Is it all right for you to stay here over New Year? You don't have to go home?"

Hana thought about telling Ms. Kawanami that she was unwelcome at home, just a burden to her parents, but she felt bad to badmouth her parents.

"My parents are busy working, so they're hardly at home," she mumbled instead, then looked for a way to change the subject. "What about your son in Hokkaido? Is he doing all right?"

Ms. Kawanami drank the sweet potato latte slowly instead of answering the question.

"Thank you for the drink. I feel much better now." Ms. Kawanami laid down on the bed and turned over. It felt sad and lonely to see her crooked back.

After the New Year's celebrations, the market street became lively again as people came back from their family gatherings. A chubby middle-aged lady holding a big basket slid the vegetable shop door open, and Ms. Kawanami greeted her.

"It's good to see you again. Did you have a good holiday?"

"Yes, I did," the woman said. "My son and his family came back to Japan from Singapore for Christmas. He got an expat deal in Singapore two years ago. It's a good place to raise children. There are many international schools to choose from. It was nice to see our grandchildren and the house was cozy, filled with people again. They've gone back now, and the house is empty again." The woman seemed both sad and relieved. "How have you been?"

"It was a calm and relaxing holiday," Ms. Kawanami said.

"I hope you get better soon." The lady held Ms. Kawanami's hands. "You're even thinner than a few weeks ago."

"Thank you," Ms. Kawanami said primly, pulling her hands back. "I'm afraid we don't have many items this week, as the Kato farm is on holiday now. Also, every item is fifty percent off since they are not freshly picked today."

"Oh, I see. No problem." The woman started looking at the vegetables in the shop. "How's Mr. Kato doing these days?"

"He's still recovering. His son Hikaru sprained his ankle, so they're having some time off. When he comes back, I will check how things are going."

"Ah, that's bad luck. Please say hi to him when you have a chance."

Hana listened to them talk from the upstairs kitchen while she was cooking. She knocked the soil off some carrots and washed them, then shredded them in the food processor, releasing a fresh earthy smell with a hint of good soil. She poured self-rising flour, a pinch of salt, cinnamon powder and brown organic sugar in one bowl, then poured grapeseed oil, vanilla extract and large free range eggs in another, whisked them then combined the two mixtures carefully. To this soft batter she added the shredded carrots plus some pecans, pineapple pieces and raisins, then poured the mix in an oiled tray and put it in the pre-heated oven.

While the cake was baking, Hana made cream cheese icing with icing sugar and lemon juice. Her movements around the kitchen felt as smooth and sleek as the surface of the icing.

"Hana, could you come downstairs?"

It was Ms. Kawanami.

"Sure." Hana washed her hands and went downstairs. The Kato farm's white truck was outside the vegetable shop. Hikaru stepped out of the truck with his leg in a cast.

Hana ran over to support him. "Are you all right?"

Hikaru managed to blush, grin and look surprised all at the same time. "Thank you. Yes. I sprained my ankle a few days ago. My leg is mostly better now and the doctor will remove my cast next week."

"Oh," Hana said, then remembered to be surprised. "That's terrible you hurt your leg! Oh, poor Hikaru." His face reddened further. She didn't want to embarrass him though. "But what a relief that the doctor says you'll be all right! Why didn't you tell us?"

His cheeks went redder. "It was nothing, really. Just a small thing. I didn't want to worry you."

"Well, I'm glad you're all right! Here." Hana pressed close to try and support him as they walked to the shop.

"Hikaru," Ms. Kawanami said, smiling. Was that a wink, just for Hana? "It's good to see you; I was about to call. How's your father doing?"

Hikaru nodded seriously. "He's doing well, thank you. He said hi to you and Happy New Year."

"Sure, Happy New Year to you too." Ms. Kawanami nodded.

Hikaru opened the truck and moved some vegetable and fruit boxes around. Hana had to help him carry the boxes into the shop.

"Wait a minute, Hikaru," Hana said, as she carried the last box into the shop. She ran upstairs, took the carrot cake out of the oven and cut it in half. The delicious sweet smells of cinnamon and carrots filled the kitchen. She put half the cream cheese icing in a small tub and the hot carrot cake in a bigger tub, then put both tubs in a paper bag and hurried downstairs.

"Hikaru, have this with your father later." She handed the paper bag to Hikaru, standing outside the shop by his truck. "The cake is still hot so I couldn't put the icing on, but spread it on the cake when you eat it."

Hikaru nodded quickly. "Thank you. It smells great. Ah, also thank you for sending the New Year's card. My father was pleased. Oh, and also." Hikaru opened his truck and took out a small wrapped box. His cheeks looked so red they had to hurt, like a Snow White apple. "I know it's a bit late, but I brought a small Christmas present for you." He handed the box to Hana.

"Ah, I'm sorry." Hana felt her own cheeks redden. "I haven't got anything for you."

"No, no need to apologize. This cake can be my present from you. And thank you for coming to our house before. I know my father appreciated it too."

Hana gave a little bow. "It's so sweet of you to say so. Please say hi to Mr. Kato."

"No worries." He gave a little bow too. "Well, I'd better get going."

"Sure, drive safely." Hana waved at Hikaru until his truck was out of sight.

Afterward she went up to her room and carefully opened the wrapping paper on her present. Inside was a bright yellow woolen scarf with two red cherry stitches at the edge. It was warm, soft and made her smile to touch it. She put it on and looked at herself in the mirror. It had been a long time since she'd looked at herself in the mirror. Somehow she looked like a whole different person. She fixed her hair and touched her still-pink cheeks. The yellow wool scarf looked good on her.

She went to the kitchen wearing the scarf. She cut a big piece of carrot cake and spread icing on top, then took a photo of the cake, wrote the recipe down in her book and opened her laptop. There was another comment on her blog.

'The slow cooker Castella was a big success! My boyfriend loved it. Thanks a lot. Amy.'

Underneath the comment there was a photo of a light yellow cake with fifteen colorful candles. Hana laughed out loud.

"What's so funny?" Ms. Kawanami called, walking slowly up the staircase.

Hana popped her head happily out of the bedroom. "I just got a great message from a friend. Oh, I made a carrot cake! Please have a seat, I'll serve it with hot tea."

"You look good in the scarf," Ms. Kawanami said calmly. "He's a real gem."

"Yes, he is." Hana touched the soft scarf gently.

15. Cranberry scones and the dreamcatcher

The cold and gray weather continued, and Ms. Kawanami kept getting weaker and weaker. She often stayed in bed and didn't have enough energy even to go down to the shop. The shop had fewer customers than usual, but Hana grew twice as busy trying to fill up Ms. Kawanami's absence.

At the photo studio Hana explained the situation to Yoko. "I have some extra work to do, so it would be helpful if I could reduce my hours a little. Would that be OK?"

Yoko looked up at Hana. "Is anything wrong?"

Hana shook her head. "No, nothing really."

Yoko gave a mischievous smile. "Oh, perhaps you're busy going on dates? That wool scarf looks like it was hand-knitted. Is it a present from your boyfriend?"

Hana smiled shyly. "No, it's not."

Yoko turned the page of a new photo book while having a sip of hot black coffee. "It's fine to take some time off during winter. We don't have many customers right now. But let me know if you need any help though."

Hana nodded. "Sure, thank you."

Now Hana's daily routine involved waking up early, organizing the fruits and vegetables in the shop, working in the photo shop, coming back to the vegetable shop, closing the shop, then preparing Ms. Kawanami's meals as well as food and water for her stray cats. She was exhausted most nights, and fell asleep immediately as soon as her head hit the pillow. She was too tired even for dreams.

The phone was ringing. Hana opened her eyes and realized she must have fallen asleep without even taking her jacket off. Her phone screen said it was barely 10 pm. She answered with half-open eyes.

"Hello?"

"Hi Hana, it's Abe from the Sakura Japanese school. I'm just checking in, are you all right?"

"Uh, sure?" Hana said.

"That's good." Mr. Abe paused a moment. "We were wondering why you're not coming to the Japanese school these days. Is everything OK?"

"Ah, sorry," Hana said, rubbing her eyes. "I haven't had a chance as I'm so busy these days."

"Ah well." Mr. Abe sounded disappointed. "Are you at least in training? The Tokyo Marathon is only a month away."

The words 'Tokyo Marathon' hit Hana like a bucket of cold water, waking her right up. What with Ms. Kawanami getting sick, Jin's letter then Hikaru's injury, she'd completely forgotten about the marathon. "Uh, no..." she murmured, feeling embarrassed.

"Not training!" Mr. Abe exclaimed. "Whatever's going on, it must be pretty big to distract you from the marathon. You were so keen before! Well, just listen to me, Hana." His voice took on a lecturing tone. "No matter how busy you are, you should start training for at least five miles a day or you'll never be able to complete it. You know that, right?"

Hana sighed. "Yes, I know."

"And let's have a meet up for a strategy session soon."

"Ah, OK?"

After hanging up, Hana lay perfectly straight on the bed and looked up at the ceiling for a while, wondering what a strategy session for a marathon was. She didn't know how she'd forgotten about the marathon so completely.

The wooden dream catcher that Jin had sent from America was hanging on the wall still. Last summer, she'd applied for the marathon hoping to run it with Jin together. Now it was just a month away. She took her almost-brand-new running shoes out of the cupboard. The marathon was just one more task on top of her huge to-do list. She closed her eyes and invited sweet dreams to come.

The next morning she woke up early in the morning and opened her laptop. There was an email from her other Sakura school friend, Nok.

'Hana, how are you doing? It's been a while. I haven't been to the Japanese school for quite some time, but I heard everyone is doing well.

'I have some sad news – I had a miscarriage three months ago. I didn't tell anyone, I just went to be with my husband and family in Thailand for several months. It was heartbreaking, but we're back in Japan now, and we have a son! We adopted him from an orphanage near my hometown. He's a sweet boy, only four years old, but he's shy and traumatized after being abandoned by his family. He wets the bed and cries in the middle of night.

'It must be hard to get used to this new environment. It will take time for him to make friends and be comfortable here. I'd like to take him to Sakura Japanese school too, but I think he'll be scared. It would be so great if you could come visit us sometime, and give him some advice about living in a foreign country. Let me know if you're available. Of course it's OK if you're busy. I hope all's going well with you, and let's keep in touch.

'Nok.'

Hana was reminded of Nok's calm and soothing voice, and all the ways she'd supported her, and replied immediately.

'Thank you for your email, Nok. I'm so sorry to hear your sad news, but I'm also glad to see you and meet your son soon! Congratulations on adopting him! Let me know when you're available for a visit, and I will be there. Hana.'

Straight after that, Hana threw herself into her chores. There was so much to do, but she got most of it done by mid-morning, then strapped on her running shoes and set out for her first training run in weeks.

It was cold out, and the air was sharp in her chest. She ran at a gentle pace to the frog pond park, around some sports fields and back around the hill where Jin's old apartment was. After three miles she was panting hard and had a sharp pain in her side. After four miles she had to stop and walk back to the vegetable shop.

She'd lost all her progress. It was disheartening, but when she got back there was a reply from Nok, and that cheered her up. She vowed to herself to run for at least five miles every day until the weekend, when she'd visit Nok for lunch. It would be her reward for working so hard.

Each day she did her chores, ran, and thought about Mr. Abe too. She didn't want to let him down. She managed to hit five miles on the Friday, then it was the weekend and Hana was definitely ready to celebrate.

Hana cycled the long journey to Nok's house, enjoying the pumping feel of her tired leg muscles. In her basket she'd packed a bag of cranberry scones with Tiptree raspberry jam and clotted cream from Cornwall, England. She bought a bunch of white tulips in a flower shop on the way, then enjoyed the changing views of the cityscape as she cycled along, past thin wooden houses, trees, electric poles with multiple layer of electric wires and gray concrete apartment buildings.

In Tama Center at the very edge of Tokyo Prefecture, the cold wind was fresh and crisp. She parked her bicycle, then rang the doorbell of Nok's familiar two-floor wooden house.

Nok smiled brightly when she opened the door. "Hana, thank you for coming all the way here!" Behind her stood a small, thin boy with Bambi eyes. "Say hello," Nok said, gently stroking his shiny black hair. "This is Hana, a good friend of mine."

"Hello, young man. What's your name?" Hana waved at him but he didn't wave back.

"I brought you some sweets. Would you like them?" Hana handed him the bag of scones and jams. The boy hesitated but took the bag, which covered up his whole face and shoulders.

"Bicycle bakery lady!" Nok cheered, smiling widely.

Hana smiled back, and handed over the white tulips. "These are for you."

"Oh, thank you!" Nok said brightly, holding them in front of the little boy. "These are such beautiful flowers, aren't they?" She looked back up at Hana. "Please come in. My husband wanted to be here and meet you, but he had to work."

Hana nodded and followed Nok and her new son inside the house. A clutch of yellow daffodils sprayed up from a big blue and white Arita vase in the living room.

"Would you like to sit on the sofa? I'll bring some tea." Nok disappeared to the kitchen. The boy was standing awkwardly by the corner of the sofa, still holding the sweets bag.

"Shall we sit down together?" Hana asked, pointing at the sofa. The boy slowly came to Hana and touched her yellow scarf. "Do you like it?"

The boy nodded instead of answering.

"Thank you. My friend made it for me. It's a Christmas present." The boy put the bag of scones down and sat next to Hana.

"My name is Leo," he said. He had a tiny but cute voice.

"Oh, that's a great name. My name is Hana. It means the first in Korean and flower in Japanese. I'm from South Korea and I've been living in Japan for over six months now." Leo gave a tiny nod. "Does that sound like a good name?"

"Yes," Leo replied in a slightly bigger voice.

"I think Leo's a wonderful name, too. It means lion, doesn't?"

The little boy nodded.

"So you must be brave and strong, like a lion. When I look at you, that's definitely what I see."

Leo smiled, showing his missing teeth.

Hana mimed being afraid. "Oh, be careful, you'll scare me, showing your fierce teeth like that!"

Leo laughed.

Just then Nok came bustling back in with a tray carrying a glass pot of lemon grass tea. "What have you two been talking about?" she asked brightly, setting the tray down. "He never talks to anyone he meets for the first time. It's amazing Hana."

"We just introduced each other. Leo said my name was pretty. Right?" Hana smiled at Leo. He ignored Hana and looked down at his small feet. "The tea smells lovely," she went on. "I've baked some cranberry scones too. Shall we have these with the tea?"

Nok smiled widely. "That sounds lovely. Leo is a lucky boy." She got up to fetch plates and cutlery from the kitchen.

Hana looked at the shy little boy. "Leo, have you had a scone before?" Leo just shook his head. Hana plucked one of the scones from the bag and held it up. "A scone is a kind of bread, made in the eleventh century in the southern part of England." She turned the scone before him, letting him get a good look at it. "People in England have enjoyed tea, scones, cream and jam as an afternoon snack for many, many centuries. It's called cream tea. Now, there are two ways of eating scones."

Nok popped back in, and Hana took a knife from her tray and cut the scone neatly in half. Leo studied what Hana was doing carefully.

"In the area of Devon, people put the cream on their scone first, then the jam. In the area of Cornwall, people add their jam first then put on the cream. Which way do you like?"

"Devon," Leo said quickly, his eyes shining like stars.

"That's a very good choice," Hana said thoughtfully. "I'll try Devon style like Leo today. What about you Nok?"

Nok smiled. "Shall I try Cornwall then?"

"That's also a good choice." Hana smiled at Nok.

Everyone cut and loaded their own scone in their own way, then tasted it while drinking tea. Leo enjoyed the scone so much he got cream on his nose.

"How is the taste?" Hana asked. "Is it good?"

Leo nodded enthusiastically. Nok looked happy. Leo had another big scone with cream and jam then wiped his nose and hands with a tissue. His face looked much more relaxed and happier than when Hana had first met him half an hour ago. Hana looked at Leo's small face and started talking.

"Your mom says you're having a tough time settling in here, is that right?"

Leo instantly looked at the ground.

"It's all right," Hana said. "I had a tough time too. I came to Japan because I was following my best friend. By the time I got here, he'd already left. Nobody knew where he was exactly. I was thinking to go back, but I realized there was no one who would welcome me at home. My parents didn't like me really. I had nothing to do and nobody to see. Still, I didn't want to give up, so I thought I'd start a new life here by myself." Hana stopped talking and thought deeply for a moment. Leo was leaning in now, listening sincerely.

"Soon after that, I met your mom. I met other friends too. I found a place to stay and a part-time job. I was lonely from time to time but I was cheered up by the good people surrounding me. Don't be afraid, Leo. You're a lion, remember? If you open your heart, you'll make lots of friends and a lot of good things will come to you. You're not alone." Hana held Leo's small hands softly. His big shiny black eyes were like fresh flowers with a few drops of morning dew. Hana opened her bag and took something out.

"This is called a dream catcher. If you hang it over your bed, these spiderweb-looking strings will catch your bad dreams and carry them away. I don't have any bad dreams now, so I'll give you this one. If you don't need it anymore, you can give it to someone who needs it." Hana solemnly put the dream catcher on Leo's small palm. He touched the surface of the dream catcher with his tiny fingers.

Nok put a hand on Hana's arm, her eyes shining brightly, and mouthed, "Thank you."

After that, Hana and Nok caught up on some gossip; the school, the vegetable shop, even a little about Hikaru, but not too much. Throughout, Leo didn't put the dreamcatcher down once.

"When are you coming back?" he asked, looking up at Hana when she was about to leave.

"Whenever you want me to come back" she said. "Like your mom and I became friends on the first day we met, you and I just became friends now. Isn't that right? I'd like to be good friends with you. If you make new friends, would you introduce them to me next time?"

"Yes, I will," Leo replied and blinked his big Bambi eyes. They were spotless, deep and transparent. The two of them shook hands and made a promise to each other. On the cycle ride home, Hana wished for Nok and Leo's happiness. She saw a Tokyo Marathon advertisement on the train and redoubled her commitment to run the whole thing without fail. Jin could watch her run from somewhere far away or not at all, it didn't matter. She wanted to run it for herself.

She continued her training hard the very next day.

"Don't catch a cold," Ms. Kawanami said with a worried face, looking at Hana as she came in after finishing another five-mile run. "Wear more clothes while running and be careful of cars passing by."

"Sure, I'll be careful."

Hana took her gloves off and wiped away the sweat on her forehead, then went upstairs and recorded her time and distance in her diary. Just as she finished, her phone rang. She looked at the screen; it was Mr. Abe.

"How was your training today?" Mr. Abe asked. "How do you feel?"

"It's not bad," Hana said, wary of sounding too confident. "I'm feeling OK, really. I'm doing five miles a day now."

"That's great! So do you think you can complete the whole marathon?"

"I think so."

"That's excellent. Good luck." Mr. Abe's voice became serious. "Let's have lunch before the marathon. We can talk about your marathon strategy."

Hana didn't know what to expect from that. "Marathon strategy?"

"Sure! You have to have a plan, like a military campaign."

Hana smiled. "OK. I'll see you soon, then."

After the call she had a shower and opened her laptop. She uploaded the scone recipe to her blog, along with photos and a comment.

'I'm going to run the Tokyo marathon. Wish me luck to complete it.'

To her surprise, a reply came in immediately.

'Good luck! You can do it. Amy.'

Hana smiled. Amy, her first fan.

The temperature dropped dramatically the next morning. It had snowed in the night, and it was below zero degrees outside. Hana felt like a rusted robot. It was hard to wake up and her joints made creaking sounds, and there was a pain in every muscle whenever she moved.

Still, she got up and put on a thick jumper, padded trousers and wool socks. It was still before dawn but she had a lot to do: chores in the shop, work in the photo studio, warm-up exercises and her training run. Ms. Kawanami was up and making tea in the kitchen.

"It's really cold this morning," Hana said, blowing warm air on her fingers. "Did you have a good sleep?"

"The boiler doesn't work so I should take a look."

"I can do it," Hana said, trying to stop Ms. Kawanami. "You don't need to go down just yet."

"I'm fine," said Ms. Kawanami, pulling her arms sharply away. "I can check it by myself." She bustled over to the steps. A few seconds later Hana heard a heart-stopping series of thuds. She rushed down the stairs to the shop, where she found Ms. Kawanami lying on the concrete floor at the bottom, making a low painful noise. Her forehead was bleeding.

Hana dropped to her knees by her side. "Ms. Kawanami, Are you OK?" Hana tried to help her up but Ms. Kawanami couldn't move an inch, so she called emergency services immediately.

"Please send an ambulance right now. An elderly lady fell down some steep steps and now she's bleeding." Hana's voice was trembling.

The emergency operator asked some questions, but they were hard for Hana to hear over the rushing of blood in her head. All she could make out was the word 'ambulance'. She put the phone to one side and leaned over Ms. Kawanami.

"Ms. Kawanami, can you hear me? Can you see me?" Hana raised her voice but the old lady seemed to be losing consciousness. Hana's tears dropped on the floor.

The ambulance arrived and two crews lifted Ms. Kawanami and put her on a stretcher. Hana got on the ambulance with the crew. They dressed her bleeding forehead and put an oxygen mask on her face. The ambulance drove swiftly and arrived at the hospital, where they moved her on a gurney direct to the X-ray room in the emergency center. Hana waited anxiously outside.

After a while, Ms. Kawanami was moved to a patient's room.

"How is she?" Hana asked the doctor, feeling sick with worry.

The doctor spoke slow and carefully, holding up an X-ray chart. "She got a shock from the fall and passed out, but she'll soon be conscious again. Her forehead is bruised but it will heal soon. However, her hip was cracked in the fall, and it will take some time to heal." He pointed on the X-ray chart. "Here, can you see the line?"

Hana couldn't see it. It was hard to even focus on the chart.

"She needs to stay in the hospital for a few weeks at least," the doctor went on. "It's crucial that she not move and rest well at this stage. We'll check her condition on a daily basis."

Hana cried some more, even though it seemed to be good news. "Oh, thank you. I was so worried about her."

The doctor gave a sympathetic smile. "Elderly people have very low bone density, so their bones can easily crack or fracture. She was lucky her bones were not completely broken. But if she doesn't keep moving her body, she'll lose more muscles. Once the muscles are lost at her age, they don't come back, so please take good care of her and help her move around."

"Yes, I'll do that." Hana nodded. The doctor left and Hana was left in the empty patient's room with the sleeping Ms. Kawanami. Hana just watched her silently, hardly even thinking. At some point, as Hana began to doze off, Ms. Kawanami opened her eyes.

"Where am I?" she asked, her voice dry and cracked.

Hana leaned in and held her cold hands. "You fell down the steps. Do you remember?"

Ms. Kawanami frowned. "I can't move my body."

"Your hip bone got cracked so you need to stay in the hospital and be treated well," Hana explained in a soft voice. "The doctor said you shouldn't move for a while."

Ms. Kawanami shook her head slowly. "I've lived too long."

"Don't say that. The doctor said you'll be better soon. Then you can go home. I'll look after you. Don't worry."

"Thank you," Ms. Kawanami said, with a blank facial expression. Her voice sounded like it was full of air.

16. Tokyo marathon, Tokyo banana and Ms. Kawanami

The day before the Tokyo marathon, Mr. Abe and Hana met in the restaurant near Sakura Japanese school. Hana ordered tofu salad and an eggplant tomato pasta, thinking about a newspaper article that said soft and plain foods were the best to have before a marathon. Mr. Abe ordered a tempura dinner set with miso soup.

As they ate, they studied the map of the marathon on the table before them. Mr. Abe and Hana looked at each destination seriously: Tokyo ward office, Iidabashi, the Imperial Palace, Tokyo Station, Ginza, Asakusa and Odaiba. Mr. Abe pointed at Tokyo Tower and Kaminarimon gate in Asakusa with his index finger.

"Try to take a break in these spots, Hana. There are plenty of toilets during the course, so that shouldn't be a problem. And look, they give out bananas at the ten-mile points! If you get tired, think of bananas and run." He smiled. "Did you hear they've arranged for special bananas for the Tokyo marathon? I heard they're especially sweet and tasty. Let me know how they taste."

Hana thought about monkeys eating bananas in the jungle, and wondered if they would like to try the special, sweet Tokyo bananas too. Mr. Abe was too focused on the map to notice Hana spacing out.

"Ah, there are some quite high hills around the twenty-mile point. This one looks especially high. Save your energy and run slowly here. What's your average pace so far?"

Hana pulled herself out of thoughts of monkeys running up hills. "Eight to-ten minutes per mile."

"Hmm, then keep that average until ten miles," Mr. Abe said thoughtfully, "then speed up a bit after the halfway point, if you have the energy. Does that sound good?"

"Yes, sure." Hana nodded, but now she was thinking about Ms. Kawanami in hospital. She spent most of each day sleeping as she recovered.

It was dark outside when they left the restaurant. The wind was cold and sharp. Mr. Abe tightened his black and green cashmere tartan scarf.

"I'll wait for you at the Iidabashi crossing and at the finish line in Odaiba. I have some other students to support too, so I may not be able to see you but if you spot me, shout."

"Sure, I will."

"Rest well and see you tomorrow." Mr. Abe held his hand out and Hana shook it like a good little soldier.

Hana walked over the empty crossing, bought a can of hot oolong tea and a carton of orange juice from a convenience store and went back to the hospital. Ms. Kawanami lay in bed watching the dark window with her eyes half-closed.

"How do you feel today?" Hana asked, sitting on a stool next to the bed.

Ms. Kawanami turned her face slowly to look at Hana. It seemed like it was a big effort. "My head is full of fog and I feel dizzy," she said slowly. "I feel like millions of ants are running around in my brain. I want to go home now."

Hana leaned in. "The doctor says you need to stay in the hospital so they can check your hip. But it won't take long. Please be patient."

"I don't know how long I need to stay in this stuffy hospital," Ms. Kawanami complained. "I want be in the shop and die in my own house quietly. I don't want to be a burden to anyone." Her tired face was filled up with dark age spots.

Hana poured the hot oolong tea in a brown porcelain cup and handed it to her. "Sure, you'll walk home healthily and work in the shop again soon, so don't worry. But you need to do your rehab, eat well and take your pills without skipping."

Ms. Kawanami made a face, but drank her tea and laid back on the bed. Hana pulled the thin blanket up over her; it looked almost heavy on her bird-like, bony shoulders.

"How's your marathon practice?" Ms. Kawanami whispered.

"Oh, it's going well," Hana said. "Tomorrow is the marathon day. I'll take lots of photos and show you later."

"Don't run too fast," Ms. Kawanami cautioned. "Run slowly and be careful not to get hit by other people and fall." Her voice had no strength in it.

"Yes, I'll be careful about that, thank you. I hope you can sleep with no headaches or pain tonight." Hana watched Ms. Kawanami fall asleep then left the room quietly.

Hana walked out of the hospital, past the park and the empty market street. Her footsteps made loud echoes in the darkness. She blew hot breath on her freezing hands; it came out white like cigarette smoke. She opened the glass door of the vegetable shop and walked upstairs slowly.

Her cold room had the smell of Ms. Kawanami. She opened the window and a chilly wind hurried in, as if it had been waiting outside for a long time. A full moon shone in the dark sky, partly covered by cloud. Someone was grilling mackerel in a house nearby. Someone was watching a TV show by Sanma Akashiya in the opposite building across the road. There was a light coming out of the screen as big as a square of tofu. Someone's voice, someone's laughter, someone's grilled mackerel smell were all floating around the empty streets.

Hana closed the window and watered her peppermint plant pot. It reminded her of the early days in the guest house. Over six months had passed. Time flies, she thought.

She turned the radio on. The Last Waltz violin duet was playing on the classical channel. She took her running shoes out of her shoe rack and fastened a thin GPS chip onto her shoelaces while listening. She could hear her heart beating loudly. She touched her soft pajama sleeve and looked at her toenails. The nail varnish was coming off. She felt more relaxed after preparing her clothes and shoes in a neat pile underneath her bed, like she was well-prepared for a big earthquake.

That night she dreamed she was dancing a waltz in a long red flared skirt and a long black shirt on a bright stage. Ms. Kawanami was sitting on a chair nearby, drinking hot tea and looking at her with a satisfied face.

The alarm went off right at the moment Hana opened her eyes. She pulled the curtains open and was happy to see a bright and blue sky through the window. She could still feel the movement of her feet and the texture of the skirt when she danced.

She had a long bath to relax her muscles, then had a breakfast of protein water, a banana and some plain bread. She put on her thin windbreaker, fastened the number tags to both the front and back of her jacket, and laced up her running shoes.

When she arrived at Tokyo city hall, the streets were crammed with people, runners, volunteers, families and friends. She gave her bag to one of the volunteers on a big transport bus, so she could pick it up at the finish line. She slowly walked over to group J, at the back of a huge mass of people. Hana felt both excited and nervous that she would soon be running the marathon with thirty thousand other runners. A volunteer in a red hat came over to group J, holding up a sign.

"Ladies and gentlemen," he announced, "this group will run last, so you don't have to feel any pressure to win the marathon." He smiled. "Please relax and enjoy running. Also, if you want to use a bathroom, please use it before the marathon starts."

Hana took a deep breath and stretched her muscles. Her whole body felt stiff in the cold weather. There was a countdown to the starting pistol, and the whole crowd grew silent as the numbers approached zero. Hana counted down along with it, slowly and thoughtfully in her head.

5, 4, 3, 2, 1.

When the starter's pistol fired, a movement like a rippling tide passed through the crowd. The sounds of cheerful orchestral music, people cheering and fireworks bursting got mixed up all at once. Thin white confetti fell down from the sky, the tiny papers just like cherry blossom flowers. Hana watched them fall and picked up one which landed on her shoulder. It was fragile and half transparent, so she could see through it to her fingers. She carefully put it in her pocket and started running along with the other runners, as the mass of people began to move gradually forward.

Together they entered the big straight road which led through Ichigaya and Iidabashi. For the first thirty minutes she could hardly see anything but other peoples' backs, they were so tightly packed in, but soon the group spaced out a little, and she saw cherry blossom trees on the side of the Kanda River. The pavements either side were just as crammed as the road, full of people watching and supporting the runners. She remembered that Mr. Abe said he would wait around here, so she moved to the edge where she quickly found Mr. Abe doing high fives and offering salt candies to runners with great enthusiasm.

"Mr. Abe!" Hana shouted and ran over.

"Hana!" He called back and checked his wristwatch like a coach. "Well done, your time is very good so far. How's your condition?" He studied Hana's face closely.

"Yes, I'm good," Hana said, nodding fast with the excitement.

"Wonderful. Don't speed up yet and enjoy every moment!" Mr. Abe handed her some salt candies and mini chocolate bars. "I'll stay here for a while waiting for other students and move on later. I'll see you at the finish line. Good luck!" Mr. Abe flashed a big smile and gave Hana a high five, then Hana was away again.

She felt good. She ran past the Imperial Palace and hit the first roundabout. A man in a Super Mario costume was running fast among the front runners.

"Mario, good luck!" People cheered him along and he waved back at them. Before Hana could take out her phone and snap a photo of him, he disappeared into the crowd like magic.

She sped up and entered Ginza crossing. Two guys in highball and pork cutlet costumes were running in front of her. The highball had long thin legs like sausages and the pork cutlet had a round chubby belly like a potato. They were singing a song with strange lyrics: 'Highball and pork cutlet are a good pair. How can you live without highball and pork cutlet?'

People cheered, applauded and gave them high fives.

"Highball, pork cutlet, you look cool!"

"Good luck!"

Hana ran another five miles then saw volunteers handing out bananas to runners.

"Tokyo bananas. Have a banana. Boost your energy!" they called. Hana stopped and took a banana from the stand. She was thirsty and felt slightly hungry. She peeled the perfectly yellow banana skin and took a bite. It felt like swimming in a river after walking in a desert for hours. It was sweet, juicy, soft and gave her a burst of instant energy. She finished the whole banana in seconds and started running again.

The next ten miles were a slog. She barely thought about anything, just putting one foot in front of the other. At the twenty-mile mark she was slowly running out of energy. Her head felt empty. Around the time she was losing any feeling in her legs, she saw a big flag stating '5 miles left' at the top of a high hill. Halfway up the hill, she saw a tall and thin guy carrying a big cross on his shoulder. He wore thin white clothes and leather sandals with no socks. His beard and long hair covered most of his face so she couldn't see his expression clearly but his eyes were sparkling. He seemed rather tired but he kept pushing his legs forward like every step was part of a prayer.

Hana started running out of breath, so she slowed down and tried to take a break by just walking. Music rang through the blue sky at the midpoint of the hill. It was from Rocky, 'Going the Distance'.

"Runners, just five miles to go," volunteers encouraged at the sides. "Almost there. You're doing a great job!" Hana's head was like a blank canvas. Her legs felt like they were floating above the ground, stepping on marshmallows. The sounds of clapping and cheering overlapped and became like a big lump of cloud. Hana heard a voice singing with a guitar accompaniment in the distance. She sped up; the closer she got to the guitar sound, the more the cloud in her head cleared. A young man with a guitar slung over his shoulder was singing a song. It was more like rough breathing rather than singing, but he was still moving forward step by step.

'What if Jin's running next to me right now?' she wondered. 'What if I'm actually running with Sok and my university friends? What are they doing? What am I doing? Where am I going?' Her throat got hot like she'd drunk a straight shot of bourbon in one go.

When she finally reached the end of the marathon, the clock in Odaiba square pointed at five hours and thirty-two minutes. Hana passed the finish line and laid down on the floor in an empty playground. Her feet and mouth were burning hot but her soul felt full and sweet. She got control of her breathing, drank a whole bottle of water then sat up and watched runners crossing the finish line. Each one looked like they were having a big bite of soy sauce rice cake. Soft, fluffy, sweet, salty, sticky. Mixed-up feelings and dull pain from their tired legs and back. She could feel lots of emotions from the runners' faces.

The cool breeze off the river had a fresh grass smell. Hana stood up slowly and walked over to a container truck surrounded by volunteers.

"Congratulations!" A volunteer handed her a medal with a big smile, along with a goody bag. "Here are some items for you."

There was a pain-killing spray for her legs, a bottle of water and an energy bar in the bag. Hana sprayed her tired legs and drank the water while checking her phone. There was a message from Mr. Abe.

'Hi Hana, have you enjoyed your big run? I'm very proud of you. My knees are aching now, so I'll head back, but I'll see you at the school sometime soon.'

Hana smiled and sent a text to Mr. Abe saying that she'd finished the marathon successfully, then sent another to Nok as well. She was thinking to call Ms. Kawanami but she wanted to tell her face-to-face. She would definitely be pleased. Hana felt a flush of excitement and tried to hurry back to the hospital. The buses near the finish line were all full of runners though, so she had to wait a long time to get on. She fell asleep as soon as she got a seat.

She woke up to the announcement of the bus's final destination. She wasn't sure where she was, and her body felt like warm melted chocolate on the seat. She stood up slowly, lifting her heavy legs step-by-step, and got off the bus. Her head was foggy and her mouth felt like she'd taken a big gulp of sand. The wind was cold and it was almost dark. She got on a train and changed to another line in Shinjuku station. When she finally reached the hospital, it was completely dark out. There were not even any stars in the sky.

In the hospital she took an elevator then opened the door to Ms. Kawanami's room, but the bed was empty and the room was completely clean. A nurse came in a moment later.

"Could you please come in the other room?" she said. "I'll call the doctor."

In the next room over, Ms. Kawanami was lying on a bed. Her face was calm and her body was extremely thin. Her face was covered by a translucent mask that pumped air in and out of her lungs.

Hana stared. The doctor entered and looked into Hana's eyes with sympathy.

"Would you have a sit down? We have some difficult news to tell you." He pointed at a chair in the middle of the room.

"What is it?" Hana asked quickly. "What happened to Ms. Kawanami?"

"I'm afraid Ms. Kawanami's brain stopped working this afternoon," he said softly. "If the respirator is removed, she will stop breathing and her life will come to an end. We checked her admittance paper, but it seems she has no next of kin. You brought her into the hospital, so I'm afraid it's your decision if she should continue on the respirator or not." He paused for a moment, letting the news sink in. "Please, take your time and think about it."

Hana's bag slipped from her shoulder. It fell on the floor with a big clattering noise. The nurse standing nearby held Hana's shoulders gently.

"This is the letter Ms. Kawanami gave us a while ago," she said, handing over an envelope. "She asked us to hand it to you if something happened to her."

Hana opened the letter with trembling hands. There was a pink hydrangea painted on the thick white paper. The handwriting was small, thin and almost transparent, lacking any energy. It looked like Ms. Kawanami had spent a long time on it, as the Japanese characters looked like paintings rather than text. But it was definitely Ms. Kawanami's handwriting. Hana began to read.

'Hana. I'm sorry to ask you for a favor in this letter. When you read it, I probably won't be alive anymore. Every day, small worms are eating up my brain slowly. I feel foggier and dreamier each day, every day. It is not bad, but I notice death is coming step-by-step towards me. I wish I could disappear like a bubble or a breath of wind, but human beings need to be responsible for themselves until they die, and even when death comes. Once my brain stops working, don't hesitate. Let me go in peace, and donate my organs and body to people who need them.'

Hana closed her eyes and opened them again full of tears.

'I prepared a simple funeral, so call this number and they will take care of everything. It is better not to tell anyone about my death until the funeral is completed. Instead, please post the letters that I saved in the wardrobe in my room after everything is done. That will be good enough.'

Her handwriting got smaller and thinner. The characters were losing their shapes and becoming more like abstract watercolor drawings.

'I remember the day I saw you crying like a kitten in the rain. Even then I saw the hope in your eyes. It felt like a wind blowing across an ocean which was still for decades. I don't believe in God, but I believe someone sent you to me with a reason. I hope you weren't hurt by my harsh words. I wanted you to be stronger and to be able to take care of yourself. You're kind and gentle, but you're also as resilient and strong as a bamboo shoot. You still haven't found your own path yet, but I know that you will. Be confident, be yourself. You can do anything and everything you want. You were my only family and a little light to shine on the last chapter of my life. Thank you.'

Hana put the letter to her face and burst into tears. The letter had a grass tatami smell. Ms. Kawanami's handwriting got smudged by Hana's tears. She read the letter again and again while stroking the watercolor writing.

Once Hana signed the paper that the hospital provided, everything moved on quickly. They removed the respirator, and Ms. Kawanami just lay still, like nothing had happened at all. Her chest didn't rise or fall. She didn't make a sound.

The hospital staff took her body to an operating room. Afterward, they said her cartilage and the valves of her heart would save three young patients. The parents of the patients might want to meet Hana to show their appreciation, but she politely declined through the hospital staff, saying she had simply followed Ms. Kawanami's will.

A funeral director came to the hospital the next day. He wore a well-ironed black suit and dressed Ms. Kawanami in a clean white gown. He brushed her hair neatly and put gentle makeup on her face, all the while displaying a professional and polite manner. When he put subtle pink pearled lipstick on her lips and light blusher on her cheeks, Hana almost thought she would open her eyes again. She looked peaceful and happy.

"Thank you for looking after her so nicely. I feel she may come back to life again."

The gray-haired funeral director nodded solemnly. "Thank you for your appreciation. It's my job to respect people in eternal peace, just the same as people who are alive." He was silent for a moment, carefully and methodically putting away his make-up and tools. "She'll be cremated after this. We'll put her ashes in a small box which will be sent to the shrine she arranged in advance. They will contact you once you can visit her." It seemed there was a warm light shining on his face.

Three days later Ms. Kawanami's ash box was sent to her family shrine in the suburbs of Tokyo. Her full name, Chieko Kawanami, was inscribed alongside her family members' names on a long thin piece of wood, which was placed in a family tomb. A monk sang sutras in an enchanting voice, hitting two wooden blocks together. The sounds spread a beautiful calm harmony throughout the shrine. Hana watched as the incense burned slowly and the smoke disappeared up into the air. The sky was crisp and spotless blue. The incense smoke looked smudged through her teary eyes.

The vegetable shop was full of a dry onion smell when she got back. As she walked up the lonely stairs from the shop, she thought it was time to say goodbye to this loving, sad place.

She opened the door to the second floor and walked along the dark wooden boards to Ms. Kawanami's room. The grass smell from the tatami mats made her feel like

Ms. Kawanami was still alive. In the doorway she took a deep breath and closed her eyes, trying to memorize the smell so she would never forget it. Then she went back to her room.

The whole thing was like a dream. She would miss Ms. Kawanami and everything she'd experienced here. She had a long, warm shower, changed to clean pajamas and fell onto her tiny single bed. The mattress made a squeaky noise. She felt like she was floating on the sky. It all felt surreal. She hadn't slept properly since Ms. Kawanami died. Now she fell asleep swiftly and felt into a long and endless dream.

17. Fruitcake with dried figs in sherry

Hana had endless monotonous dreams. She woke up several times with a dire thirst, but each time she had a sip of water and went straight back into the endless tunnel of dreams. She heard the faint sound of birds chirping, the loudspeaker announcements from a truck buying and selling second-hand TVs and refrigerators, the hubbub of drunken young people singing and shouting. She felt sunshine, darkness, moonlight and clouds pass across her closed eyes. Apart from those, she had no sense of time or space.

The phone was ringing with a sharp electronic blare. It broke through the silence of the house, but Hana thought she was still dreaming. The phone kept ringing until Hana finally opened her dry eyes. She blinked and slowly climbed up from her tedious long well of dreams. At first, she didn't remember where she was, then she saw the Martin vintage guitar and realized she was still in Ms. Kawanami's house.

Her throat was like a desert, hot and dry. She felt dizzy when she got up from the bed, and had to hold the headboard so she wouldn't fall over on the tatami floor. She could feel her blood pumping and her nerves jangling with every step she took. There was a sharp feeling in her swollen muscles, still weary from the marathon, and a fever in her head. She switched on the light and picked up the phone with half-closed dreamy eyes.

"Hello, who's calling?" Her voice sounded like it was split in half, croaky and raw.

"Good morning, this is Kazuhiko Sato from Matsui law firm. Is that Hana Lee?"

It was a calm middle aged man's voice, and it took Hana a moment to process what he'd said. A law firm. Her mind worked slowly. Had she made some kind of mistake? She took a breath and answered.

"Yes, this is Hana Lee."

"I would like to have a meeting with you regarding Ms. Kawanami," the man said, then went on. By the time Hana felt fully awake, she was holding a piece of paper in one hand and the phone in the other hand. There was the law firm's address and a meeting time written in a hurried way on the piece of paper. The wall clock's hands pointed at 8:30, but she wasn't sure if it was morning or night. She opened the curtain. Someone was cycling on the dark market street. The light from their bicycle headlight looked like a firefly glowing in a black sky.

She looked down at her feet. Her toenails were swollen with purple-black bruises. She moved her toes but couldn't feel anything. She looked at herself in the mirror. Her hair was tangled and had no shine. Dark circles hung like dirty lace curtains under her eyes. The black dress she'd worn to the funeral the day before was wrinkled.

She looked at the white ceiling then at her bruised black toenails then at herself in the mirror. The person there didn't look like her. It didn't look like anyone she knew.

She brushed her tangled hair with her fingers, then went to the kitchen and opened the fridge, wincing at the sharp blue-white fluorescent light. She screwed up her eyes and took out the carton of soymilk. She took a glass off the shelf and poured the soymilk in it, then drank it slowly. The cold liquid spread through her like a strong mint candy.

She turned the bathtub shower on and put the plug in the drain, so hot water gathered in the tub. Once she put her cold feet in the warm water, she felt a strange sparkle in her swollen feet. She sat down and let hot water spray on her head and down her face. She lathered with shampoo, and bubbles ran down her hair, face and shoulders.

The same old questions came back to her, circling her head like the endless dreams. What should she do now? Where should she go? Should she go back home or stay there longer? She couldn't see any clear way forward. She thought about how she'd barely spoken to her parents since she'd come to Japan. Her friends had all finished university and were now getting good jobs. Some of them were already thinking of marriage and building their careers.

She knew her mom was disappointed in her, and that made her sad. What was Jin doing now? She felt like she was all alone again, just like when she was crying outside the vegetable shop on that rainy day. The more she tried to find an answer, the more it was getting away from her like dry sand slipping on her open palm.

She finished her shower, put the black funeral dress in the washing machine and changed into a white wool jumper and jeans. She went to Ms. Kawanami's room and opened the dresser. As she'd mentioned in the letter, there were postcards in one of the drawers. Each one had a thank you and goodbye message. They were simple and concise, just the same as Ms. Kawanami's character. Hana thought that these postcards had been written quite a while ago, because her handwriting was clear and strong compared to the letter she'd left for Hana in the hospital.

There were twelve postcards in total. Hana checked the names and addresses looking for the family name 'Kawanami', in case one of them was for her son, but it wasn't there. She sat down and wrote out twelve more letters to go with the postcards.

'Hello, my name is Hana, and I've been working with Ms. Kawanami in her vegetable shop for the last several months. I'm sorry to inform you that Ms. Kawanami passed away three days ago. I'm enclosing the postcard that Ms. Kawanami prepared in advance. Her ashes were interred in a shrine in the suburbs of Tokyo after the funeral. It was a simple one according to her will. I'd like to say thank you for your support on behalf of her. I will leave the vegetable shop next week, and I'm planning to organize a small wake before that. Please come to the second floor of the vegetable shop this Saturday at noon if you're available. Ms. Kawanami's family members will be especially welcomed.

Warm regards, Hana Lee.'

She put on a thick wool poncho with a hat and opened the shutters of the vegetable shop. A cold breeze came through the small holes of the poncho and set her shivering. She walked along the dark and empty market street and stood in front of the postbox at the end of the road. She opened her canvas bag and put the letters in the postbox one by one. She heard exactly twelve envelopes drop in the postbox, then sighed with a feeling of relief.

She went to a supermarket and bought bread, milk and flour then came back to the house. She found a small round glass jar of Hoji tea on the kitchen table. She'd left it there and forgotten to bring it to the hospital. She opened the lid and the subtle earthy smell rose up, reminding her of the times she'd drunk tea with Ms. Kawanami over the kitchen table, talking about their days. She missed that routine.

She boiled the kettle and poured hot water over Hoji tea in a porcelain cup that Ms. Kawanami used to use. She diligently watched the tea leaves as they sat down at the bottom of the cup, turning the water a light brown color. She took a sip but the taste was different from how Ms. Kawanami made it. She wished she could taste her Hoji tea. She held the hot teacup, sat down by the window in her bedroom and stared at people walking by in the dark. A breeze blew in and made the bottom of the curtain dance.

When the tea was finished, she went back into kitchen, opened the paper bag from the supermarket and took the flour out. She'd stopped baking since Ms. Kawanami first went into hospital, and this might be her last chance to do it again here. That thought made Hana sad. She opened the cupboard and took out the big glass jar of dried figs from the Kato farm. When she opened the lid the strong sweet fragrance of figs fumed up. She took the best-looking ones out and poured sherry over them to soak in a small bowl. Soon they softened up and became a rich golden brown color, as beautiful as the wheat fields from The Little Prince. She closed her eyes and inhaled the rich fragrance.

She mixed butter, eggs, milk, sugar, cinnamon, nutmeg and flour in a bowl, then cut the sherry-soaked figs into pieces and folded them in. She placed parchment paper on the bottom of a pound cake mold and poured the batter over it carefully, got rid of the air bubbles with a few firm taps then put the mold into the pre-heated oven. Soon the whole house smelled like sweet and elegant fruit liquor.

She planned to pour the leftover fig-infused sherry on top of the baked cake each day, then put marzipan on the top and serve it to the guests for Ms. Kawanami's wake on Saturday afternoon. Other than that, she felt mostly ready to leave the vegetable shop behind. She started packing her clothes and belongings, throwing away unnecessary items at the same time. One final important thing to do before her departure was to go meet the lawyer.

The next morning Hana woke up early as usual, had a quick shower and drank a Hoji tea with toast while reading the newspaper. She put on a peach-pink long padded coat over a black and green tartan wool dress with a white fur hat, then she left the house and headed to the lawyer's office in Ichigaya. It had been a while since she'd taken a train or met someone new, so she felt nervous.

The lawyer's office was on the banks of the Kanda River near Ichigaya station, an old building with no elevator. The paint was peeling off here and there on both the outside and the inside of the building. Hana walked up the steep staircase to the fifth floor, took a deep breath and knocked on the black metal door of the lawyer's office. A balding middle-aged man in a dark blue suit opened the door.

"Hello, I'm Hana Lee," Hana said in a quiet voice. "I have an appointment with Mr. Sato."

"Yes, I'm Kazuhiko Sato. I've been waiting for you. Come on in." He opened the door wide and guided her in. Through the window of the office, there was a clear view of the Kanda River and the Sobu line rail tracks. A dark wooden coffee table stood in the middle of the room, clearly treated well with a nice shine.

"Please have a seat." Mr. Sato pointed at a dark brown leather sofa with some scratches on the corner.

Hana perched on the edge of the sofa. "Thank you."

"How was the journey?" Mr. Sato asked, smiling. "Was it easy to find the office? What would you like to drink?"

"Yes, it was easy to find, and I don't need anything to drink, thank you." Hana said it all quickly, then coughed. Her throat was completely dried out and she was almost shaking with worry about what the lawyer might say. She cast her mind back over everything, trying to guess where she'd made a mistake.

She'd held the funeral according to Ms. Kawanami's instructions. Ms. Kawanami's bills were automatically paid through her bank account, so she wouldn't have any problems with that. Hana was going to leave the house by the end of next week, once she'd had a meeting with Ms. Kawanami's close friends or family members, thanks to the twelve letters she sent. The lawyer would surely take care of any other matters. Hana thought it all over and tried to reassure herself that she'd caused no problems while living with Ms. Kawanami.

"Mr. Sato," she said, trying to sound confident with her hands folded neatly on her lap, but her voice still trembled slightly. "I understand you want to discuss about Ms. Kawanami. I wonder if I've done something wrong."

"No, not at all," Mr. Sato said, and took a leather briefcase from his big black metal cabinet. "In fact, Ms. Kawanami left the building to you." He put the briefcase in the middle of the coffee table.

Hana's mind went as blank as a piece of white paper. "I beg your pardon?"

"Yes, let me see," said Mr. Sato, leafing through the papers in the case. "Ms. Kawanami's building still has a five million yen mortgage outstanding, and the payments get deducted with interest on a monthly basis, but she already paid her inheritance tax, paperwork and stamp duty costs separately in cash. Of course, the building needs to be maintained and assessed against government regulations on a yearly basis, at least, if you intend to keep it as a shop that sells fruits and vegetables." He looked up briefly at Hana, then back to his papers.

"Additionally, insurance is required to cover the building, the road in front of the building and the customers who use the road and the building respectively. Plus property tax and other bills need to be paid. The building is over fifty years old and proper checks should be done soon, with some repairs likely to be required before the title can be transferred. But all the paperwork will be done through us, so there's no need to worry. It is a small two-floor building, so it's not a large inheritance, after deducting the mortgage and the repair costs. But I believe it meant a lot to Ms. Kawanami, and that she wanted to pass it along to someone." Sato paused and took a breath, looking up again.

"Of course it is entirely up to you to make any decision about this matter. If you renounce your inheritance, the building will go to the bank which holds the current mortgage." He held out a thatch of complex-looking papers; some of them tatty and worn, some fresh and new in neat yellow wallets. "Here are the relevant papers; registered copy of the building, water supply, boiler maintenance, gas certificate, mortgage deed and all other bills and papers regarding the building. These are copies of the papers for you, so please take them with you, have a look at them and let me know if you have any questions." Mr. Sato went through them all, explaining it all to her like a school teacher, putting sticky notes on important papers as they went through them.

Hana felt her brain melting like a broken cotton candy machine. It reminded her of the wind and the sun on the uphill in Odaiba, with her legs heavy and tired in the last stretch of the marathon. She closed her eyes and took a deep breath.

"Are you alright?" Mr. Sato was looking at Hana with a worried face.

"Yes... I... I heard Ms. Kawanami had a son in Hokkaido." She mumbled.

"Hokkaido?" Mr. Sato adjusted the arm of his black glasses and opened his mouth slowly. "In fact, Ms. Kawanami's son died ten years ago, from injuries sustained in a car accident. A hit and run. I believe he was a famous chef." He paused, studying Hana's eyes. "He studied in Italy and had a restaurant in Hokkaido for a time. Ms. Kawanami remortgaged her shop to cover the cost of his brain surgery. Tragically, he did not recover; the damage was too great." He paused a moment longer, as if reflecting on how much more he should say. Maybe he saw the tears welling in Hana's eyes. "I believe she tried her best to save her son's life, but it was outside her power. I think it was not easy for her to let him go. I saw her many times throughout this process. Fighting the hospital. Fighting the government, who wanted to shut down his care." He let his hands drop to the table. "She held on to him for many years, Ms. Lee, until his brain finally stopped working altogether. She never gave up hope."

Hana didn't know what to think. She took the big envelope of copied papers and left the lawyer's office. She sat on a bench on the Sobu line platform and watched light and fluffy cherry blossom petals fluttering out over the river, blowing pink and transparent on the wind. One landed in her lap. It reminded her of the colorful toppings on vinegared rice she'd made several times with Ms. Kawanami. Ground boiled shrimp, diced marinated raw red tuna with soy sauce and rice wine, pan-fried egg omelets cut into long strips, boiled lotus root slices with soy sauce and dark brown sugar, all made by Ms. Kawanami's wrinkled thin hands. Hana had laid out a thin layer of vinegared rice in the big bamboo basket then placed the various toppings on top; a duet ensemble between Ms. Kawanami and Hana, performing in perfect harmony.

Hana carefully picked up the cherry blossom petal and put it in her pocket.

A purple-orange sunset was slowly coming down over the train lines. Hana got up off the bench and took a train. She watched the sunset on the river through the window. Back in the vegetable shop she walked up the dark steps to the second floor. She breathed in the tatami smell, and the smell of Ms. Kawanami's handmade pickled vegetables and plums. It felt like Ms. Kawanami would open her bedroom door and greet her any second.

She sat down at the little desk in her bedroom and opened the window. A high school girl in a school uniform was ringing her bicycle bell as she cycled along the market street. Hana put her hands on her head and thought hard about what had happened to her today. It made her feel heavy and uncomfortable. She didn't have the confidence to look after Ms. Kawanami's building by herself. She wasn't sure if she could pay off the mortgage. She didn't feel right taking over her building. The thought of such unexpected responsibilities made her afraid. Moreover, she wasn't Ms. Kawanami's family or even a proper friend. She was a stranger from hundreds of miles away who'd stayed with her for only six months. Ms. Kawanami might have no family members, but Hana wasn't sure if she had any right to take on Ms. Kawanami's legacy.

What if people thought she'd stayed with Ms. Kawanami only for the money? What if people judged her harshly at the meeting on Saturday? She decided to leave the house by the end of the following week, though she didn't know where to go next. She had no idea what would happen to her in the future. She felt confused and restless, and couldn't sleep at all that night. Over the next few days she kept thinking about it over and over, but she couldn't come up with a conclusion.

On Saturday the weather was cold but sunny, and the sky was perfectly blue with no sign of clouds. Around 2 pm, people started knocking on the door of the vegetable shop. Mr. Kato and Hikaru came first, then Ms. Oyama from the guest house, then a chubby middle-aged lady who was one of the regulars, then the owner chef of a local Japanese restaurant who was also a regular customer, and Hana.

Six people sat around the kitchen table. They greeted each other and had cups of tea together. Hana waited for another half hour, but no family members knocked on the door. Hana brought her fruitcake to the table, cut it carefully so as not to squash the marzipan, and placed the sliced pieces on each plate gently. She put a cake fork on each plate and laid them in front of each guest. The whole thing felt like a memorial ceremony, with everyone watching her quietly.

"Thank you for visiting when you're busy," Hana began. "Ms. Kawanami must be very happy now." She stopped and took a deep breath. "I'm sorry that I didn't tell you about her condition earlier. Ms. Kawanami didn't want life-prolonging treatment, so it happened rather quickly. She also wanted her funeral to be private. According to her will, her organs were donated to the hospital, and her ashes were buried with her family members in a small shrine in the suburbs of Tokyo. She prepared everything by herself in advance, so I didn't have to do anything. Everything happened smoothly and speedily." Hana's voice was calm.

"It's so her, isn't it?" Ms. Oyama said. When she moved her head, her round cabbage shaped hairdo bobbed sideways. "She was such an independent and proud lady. I'm not surprised."

"You've done a very good job, Hana," Mr. Kato said with a warm expression. "I know this must not have been easy to handle by yourself."

Hana thought carefully before proceeding. "I'm not sure what you'll think about this, but it seems Ms. Kawanami has left her building to me." She paused a moment, as if drawing strength from inside. "I had a meeting with her lawyer a couple of days ago and I brought the relevant papers with me. I've been thinking hard about it, but I don't feel I have the right to take her building. Also I'm not sure if can do a good job running it, so I'm thinking of renouncing the inheritance. If I write a memorandum of renunciation, the building will go to the bank which holds her mortgage. The rest of the paperwork will be done by her lawyer." She looked at the two members of the Kato farm. "Mr. Kato, Hikaru, I'm sorry that I can't keep the vegetable shop. Ms. Oyama and everyone else, thank you for being a loyal customer of the shop for a long time. I truly enjoyed living and working here. It was my pleasure to know you and learn from you. I will not forget a bit. Thank you for your help and support." Hana bowed deeply over the table, trying to show her appreciation to everyone.

Mr. Kato was first to speak, calmly and generously. "I'm very sorry to hear that, Hana, but I respect your opinion. I believe you've thought hard and you've made a difficult decision."

The chubby middle-aged lady dried her tears with a handkerchief. "She was such a lovely lady... I'm so sad but I'm happy that she met you in her last days."

There was a silence for a time, until Hikaru spoke up. He sounded a little nervous. "Are you going to stay in Japan?"

"Probably not," Hana said, then reconsidered. "I may go back, but I'm not sure. I haven't decided fully what to do next, but I do know I can't stay here on my own anymore." It made her feel sad to say it, and even sadder as Hikaru's face fell.

"You don't have to make the decision right now, do you?" Ms. Oyama said. "You still have some time to think. And it doesn't have to be in this vegetable shop. You can find a job you like and stay somewhere else in Tokyo, if it makes you happy.".

"That is true," the chef agreed. "You can think it over."

"Don't rush into something," Ms. Oyama said, more confidently now, enjoying a sip of Hoji tea. "Think carefully and make a decision for yourself so you don't regret it later."

Hana glanced at Hikaru. He seemed to be deep in thought.

Hana was left alone after the visitors were gone. She cleared the table, washed the plates and the sink, then sat down and tried to think clearly. Her head was like a big bowl of tangled threads. She wondered what Jin would say about all this. She still hadn't seen him, and it was over nine months now since she'd come. Time flies. She didn't want to go back to Korea yet, but she would have to leave Japan if she didn't make a plan to extend her visa in the next three months. She wasn't sure what her parents would think if she did. She didn't remember when she'd last spoken with them.

Hana picked up her phone and rang her mother for the first time in months.

"Hi, mom. How's things going?"

"Oh Hana," her mom answered, then gave a big sigh.

"What's going on?" Hana asked. "Your voice sounds terrible. How's Dad?"

There was silence for a moment, then her mom spoke fast, in a voice that seemed about to burst into tears. "Your dad has cancer."

It took Hana a second to comprehend. "What? What do you mean?"

"He asked me not to tell you many times, so I kept it secret," her mom went on, "but it is nasopharyngeal cancer. He's had it for months."

Hana's mouth opened and closed. Lots of thoughts ran through her head. An exhausted kind of guilt. A confused sense of responsibility. She'd run away from home, completely neglected her family, hardly called them at all, and now this?

"How bad is it?" she managed to ask.

"He collapsed recently," her mom went on, speaking now in a flat monotone. "They carried him to the hospital and took MRIs. They said there were several big tumors on his neck and nose. The doctor said it would be difficult to remove them through surgery, so we've decided to go for radiation therapy and chemotherapy at the same time." She paused for a long, heavy moment. "I've told him many times to stop drinking and smoking, but he never listened to me. He worried about you so much and kept nagging me not to tell you. But who's worrying who now? I'm so mad at him." The flat tone broke and Hana heard her mom start to cry.

She'd never heard her cry like that before. It flushed everything else out of her head.

"I'll come home immediately," Hana said. "Wait for me. It will be all right." She hung up the phone and booked a plane ticket straight away. The next morning she closed the shutters of the vegetable shop, attached a sign that it would be closed for the foreseeable future, then hurried to the airport.

18. Handmade soy milk and bean curd cookies with acacia honey

The flight passed in a flash, and all Hana could think about was her father. At Busan Airport she grabbed a taxi, not worried about the cost. In thirty minutes she was at the hospital. Her mom met her at the ward on the fifteenth floor. They hugged briefly, exchanged a few words only, then went to her dad's room together.

Lying in the hospital bed, her dad was thin and pale in his blue cotton patient's outfit. He looked almost like a skeleton, after losing over twenty pounds in the nine months since Hana had left. It made her feel emotional. It broke her heart.

"I'm sorry, Dad," she said, standing before him in the hospital room. "I didn't know until I talked to Mom yesterday."

Her dad seemed embarrassed and frowned, answering in a rough, husky voice. "I told her not to tell you. You shouldn't have come."

Tears welled in Hana's eyes.

"So why did you have to get cancer and make everyone worry about you?" Her mom said, raising her voice and glaring at him.

He blurted a little laugh, and Hana walked up to his bedside and took his thin, bony hands. "What happened, Dad?"

He squeezed her hands, but there wasn't much strength left in his grip. He hardly seemed to be the same man she'd left behind. "It started seven months ago, just after you left," he said. His voice was thick and sounded like something was blocking his throat, causing him to pause frequently and catch his breath. "In the beginning it was just difficult to breathe. I thought it was because I was tired, but pretty soon I almost had a heart attack. A few days later I collapsed. They took me to the hospital." He squeezed her hands again as he gathered his breath. "They ran some tests, and found tumors in my nose and neck. The cancer had spread so much by then that it was difficult to operate, so chemotherapy, radiation therapy and food therapy were the only options left." He took a long rattling breath. "I've been coming to hospital for various treatments for six months now. It seems it gets better then it gets worse, so it's difficult to know what's going to happen." He stopped and panted a little, out of breath from talking so much.

Her mom chimed in angrily. "I've told him to stop smoking and drinking. He didn't even listen to me, and here we are. What am I supposed to do now?" She shook her head. Hana took her parents hands and held them at the same time. She didn't remember when she'd last held their hands, but it made her sad how small and thin they both were.

"It's OK," she said, trying to soothe the argument she could feel building between them. "We're all here now. Dad's trying to get better."

"He's an idiot," her mom snapped. "He doesn't listen to me."

"Mom," Hana said gently, "he's sick."

"He's been sick for months! And where were you?"

Where had she been? That was a good question. Looking after Ms. Kawanami. Her eyes grew blurry with tears, and she didn't know what to say.

"It's not her fault, " her dad rasped, sounding miserable. "We've been neglecting her for years." He paused for breath. "You and me. We made lots of excuses about being busy at work and having no time, but it wasn't proper parenting, was it?" Her mom just snorted, so her dad turned his watery eyes to her. "Hana, how could I ask you to come see me when I got sick, when I wasn't there for you?"

Her mom spoke up angrily. "We made her into a healthy and pretty girl, didn't we? Isn't that enough?" Her dad said nothing, so her mom rounded on Hana. "We sent you to university, didn't we? We paid for everything. How is it our fault if you didn't want to finish in your final year? Instead you wanted to run off and go play in Japan!"

Now her mom was crying. Hana was crying too.

"Mom," she said.

"We didn't call you, you didn't call us, it's the same isn't it?"

"Mom."

Her mom looked as if she was about to shout some more, pumping herself up like a red-cheeked balloon, but then her dad put his hand on hers, and instead she just let go. The air and anger seemed to whoosh out of her in one breath, and she sagged a little.

"Well," she said, covering over so much. "Anyway, it's good to see you, Hana. It's good to all be together for now. Here, have a seat." She pulled a small plastic chair over.

Hana sat down. Her mom sat down. Her dad coughed.

Hana wiped her eyes. She'd imagined a moment like this coming so many times, and now it was here. "You're right, I should have called you sooner," she said, looking at her dad then at her mom. "I've been feeling bad that I didn't let you know I was leaving home. I should have told you that I was going to Japan, but I didn't think it was going to be for long. Then a lot of things happened to me, and I didn't really understand it. I don't really understand now. I don't think I can even explain why I kept on staying."

Her mom gave a big sigh. "Well, that's life. It just takes over." She rubbed her face hard like she might uncover some secret beneath the skin.

"But Dad's right, too," Hana went on. "Honestly, you weren't always the best parents. You used to fight so much. You're still fighting now. I hated it. It's definitely one of the reasons I didn't want to come home."

Her mom's eyes lit up then, the same way they used to whenever she was screaming and smashing plates. Hana could feel her pumping herself up again for another big fight, but again her dad gave a squeeze, and again the air just deflated out of her, and she slumped a little lower in her seat.

"Ah. Hana. I know that," she said sadly. "I know your dad and I didn't do a good job of looking after you. We were young and immature, I guess." She sighed again, then looked up at Hana. "It's true your dad and I argued a lot, much more than we laughed or had a good time. Life is funny, and sometimes meaningless." She took Hana's hand. "But you looked after yourself well. I'm not surprised you found your own way of living and protecting yourself. I suppose we forced you to grow up maybe a bit too early for your age." She looked over at Hana's dad in his hospital bed, then back at Hana.

An awkward silence filled the room. Her dad silently looked out of the window from his single patient bed. The three of them sat there in the room. Dim sunlight came through the half-opened window and made a long line on the shiny concrete floor.

Hana left the hospital after her father fell asleep. It was a weekday afternoon and the street was quiet, with few cars and pedestrians passing by. She walked slowly. White crosses stood in rows in the cemetery on a nearby hill. From the top of the hill Hana could see the blue of the ocean. Thick clouds drifted in the sky, and a dash of sunlight slid down to turn a patch of waves golden. Hana thought it wouldn't be surprising if an angel were to come down through that sunlight at any moment. It felt like death and life were connected by an invisible thread, always co-existing without her ever realizing it.

Hana stared at the peculiar light for a while. She sat down on the overgrown grass and leaned against an old pine tree, thinking about Ms. Kawanami's death, her dad's possible death, her mom's possible death as well as her death and Jin's death, which would both happen at some point. It was going to happen to everyone. There was no control over it. It could happen earlier or later. There was no point getting confused, sad, upset, miserable or desperate about it. Instead she wanted to be ready for her death when it came, to accept it calmly with an open mind.

Two birds were chirping on the branch of the pine tree over her head. A warm wind blew from the sea and gently rustled the tree's thin branches. Hana could smell the spring. It had been nearly a year since Jin went missing. She'd sat right in this spot with Jin on a sunny day, watching over the sea and the little island in the middle of nowhere. She somehow had a weird feeling that Jin was sitting right next to her.

A light rain fell on the grass and made a watery whispering sound. Hana stood up. The surface of the ocean shifted from patches of light gold to a uniform dark gray. Hana hurried along the small path out of the cemetery, past a little shrine where monks were singing sutras and striking wooden blocks together in prayer.

On the main street middle school kids in school uniforms were pouring out of their school gates like a big wave after the bell's chime. Hana passed the kids as they gathered in clumps and chatted loudly, walking to her old apartment block. At the door she turned and looked toward the horizon, mostly blocked by other tall apartment blocks. She put her palm out and covered the gray sky with her palm. All she could see were buildings.

She put the passcode in, took the elevator and opened the door of her apartment. It had been a long time since she'd come home, and it was much messier than usual. There were clothes piled up on the floor, a stack of flyers, letters and bills lay on the kitchen table, dirty clothes were squashed into the washing machine, and plates, cups, cutlery and leftover food were lying in and around the sink, making an awful smell.

Hana put her bag down on the floor and opened the windows. She opened the balcony door and stood outside at the railing. Black clouds loomed overhead now, threatening to pour down rain. She put her hand out and a raindrop splashed on her palm.

Hana picked the clothes off the floor and started the washing machine. She washed the plates one by one and set them on the drying rack. She put the food waste in the waste processor and turned the switch on. She wiped down the kitchen island and hoovered the house, then mopped the floor and scrubbed the sink basins and the toilet.

The house was finally sparkling clean and smelling nice. She sat down at the kitchen table and had a cup of tea. She realized she'd just followed Ms. Kawanami's cleaning regime. She thought about Ms. Kawanami's stubborn expression as she picked out the best fruits and vegetables, about her crooked back when she was out sweeping the market street, about the way she always blew on hot tea and the way her eyes wrinkled whenever she gave Hana firm directions.

Hana missed everything about her terribly.

She walked back out to the balcony and touched the raindrops on the railing. The black ocean swelled into a big parabola in the heavy rain and wind. She felt it would swallow her body in the blink of an eye if she fell. She closed the balcony door and called her mom, leaning against the glass balcony door.

"Mom, is Dad awake?"

"Yes, he just had dinner and a shower," her mom answered. Her voice sounded tired. "He has a painful throat, so he has no appetite and no energy. It's a vicious circle. He's going to sleep soon, so I'll check on him then come home."

"What about dinner?"

"I have no appetite either."

"I'll make something light then. See you soon, mom."

Hana hung up the phone and opened the fridge. She found eggs, soft tofu, some vegetables and kimchi. In the freezer she found a bag of dried anchovies. She poured water in a pot on the stove and set a stock of dried anchovies and shiitake mushrooms boiling. While it was bubbling nicely, she sliced carrots, onions, zucchini and fried them with a pinch of salt and pepper in sesame oil. She separated egg yolks and whites to be fried into thin rolls, then mixed soy sauce, red pepper flakes, sugar, sesame oil and finely diced green spring onions into a spicy sauce. She took the dried anchovies and shiitake mushrooms out of the stock pot and fed in dried noodles.

Just then there was the sound of the front door opening.

"Where's this great smell coming from?" her mom's voice came, sounding excited.

"I didn't have time to go to the supermarket so I made something out of the fridge," Hana answered. "How about some noodles?"

"Noodles with hot broth is a good idea when it's raining." Her mom came in and put her wet coat on the chair. "Gosh, you did all the cleaning as well. I haven't seen the house so clean for such a long time." She checked the living room then opened the bathroom door with a cluck of surprise.

"This is mostly done," Hana said. "If you have a shower, the food will be ready." She poured the egg mix into the frying pan with a hiss, and stirred the noodles at the same time. When her mom walked out of the bathroom, drying her hair, Hana poured the noodles with the hot broth into a deep bowl, set the vegetable garnish on top then drizzled it with the sauce. For a side dish, she sliced the egg rolls and laid them on a big plate.

Her mom looked stunned. "I didn't have an appetite before, but all this smells so good."

Hana smiled. "I hope it tastes OK. I haven't cooked for a while."

They sat down to eat, neither saying another word until they'd finished every last drop of the broth and every bit of the egg rolls and noodles.

"Oh, that was such a cozy and homey taste!" her mom said, putting her chopsticks down with a look of great satisfaction. "I feel I'm alive now. When did you become such a good cook? You've grown up a lot since you moved to Japan." Her mom sighed again. "I feel embarrassed that I haven't done much for you at all as a parent."

"You've been busy with work and looking after Dad," Hana said easily. It felt like she'd said enough already. The anger and confusion she'd once had now seemed to be just gone.

"But I don't even remember when was the last time I cooked for you," her mom protested. "I don't know what I've done with my life. I was just running forward like I was being chased by something, then I stopped and looked around but there was no one nearby." Her expression turned completely blank. "Once I noticed I was standing in the middle of desert all alone, I realized I didn't know what was important in life."

Hana just smiled.

"But look at me," her mom said. "Talking about myself, while you've been off on your adventures." She leaned over the table and took Hana's hands, her eyes twinkling now. "Tell me everything. Don't leave a thing out."

So Hana started talking about herself, and all the things that had happened to her so far in Japan: Jin's disappearance, his old apartment next to the shrine, the Sakura Japanese school, Mr. Abe and her new friends, the guest house and Ms. Oyama, the Kimura photo studio and Yoko, the vegetable shop, Ms. Kawanami and her death, the Kato farm and Hikaru. Sitting in her old apartment back in Busan, it felt almost like everything was a big dream.

Her mom seemed to be chewing on the story carefully, thinking. "It was sad Jin disappeared like that," she said eventually, "but what an experience you've had for a year! Why was I not interested in what you were doing at all? I just thought you were wasting time there, but that was my mistake."

Hana gave the slightest bow. "I did my best to move forward and not give up. I'm not sure it was successful eventually though."

"What do mean, not successful?" her mom protested. "It sounds like you've accomplished a lot, got a job, made friends, ran a marathon, even met a new guy."

It sounded better when her mom said it like that. Still, it seemed like too much to encapsulate in just a single sentence. It was too big, and all of a sudden she felt extremely tired. Her eyelids grew heavy and started drooping.

"Oh, I didn't realize it was so late," her mom said abruptly. "It's been a long day for you, and you've worked so much. Go to bed now and let's talk again tomorrow." She stood up from the chair.

"Sure." Hana felt her eyelids were as heavy as rocks. She sank into her old bed, and it was just like she hadn't been away at all.

She opened her eyes to the sound of seagulls and waves on the ocean.

It was a bright and sunny day, quite the opposite from the day before. Hana stretched her arms and yawned. Her body felt like a heavily soaked cotton duvet. She had a long warm shower and changed into a white cotton dress. When she went out to the kitchen, her mom was reading a newspaper while having a cup of coffee.

"Had a good sleep? It was pouring down last night but it's cleared up nicely today."

"Yes, it's lovely weather today."

Her mom poured her a cup of coffee, and Hana took it, holding it between her hands like Ms. Kawanami always used to hold her Hoji tea. "There's a carer today in the hospital," her mom said, "so shall we take a walk and have lunch before we go see Dad?"

Hana nodded. "Sounds good."

They headed out of the apartment block and strolled along the coastal road at the edge of the sea. They walked up some steep wooden steps and crossed a bridge up to the cliffs. The view of the sea stretched all the way to the horizon and was crystal clear. The sun was strong so they both started to sweat, but the wind from the sea was refreshing. They walked slowly along the clifftops without talking for a while. A couple of middle-aged people in colorful hiking clothes walked past them.

"I've been in the hospital and haven't done much exercise these days," her mom said. "I'm out of breath already. Shall we sit down for a bit?"

"Sure."

They sat down on the grass. Some people were fishing on the rocks under the cliff.

"Those rocks must be slippery," her mom said. "What if they lose control?"

Hana mumbled something about practice.

"I guess I'm getting old. When I see something a little bit dangerous, I feel extremely anxious about it." She wiped her face with a handkerchief, then looked at Hana. "Before your dad collapsed, I hadn't really thought about how important family was. I just took it for granted. After that, I started to feel guilty that I hadn't spent much quality time with you when you were growing up." She looked away, off to the sea. "And that just made me angrier. But there's no point feeling angry about what's already happened. Still, when I look back, I regret a lot of things. My life wasn't a big success." Her face went dark.

For a time Hana didn't know what to say, so she just sat quietly, looking out at the ocean. "Why are you talking like this?" she asked eventually. "You and Dad have plenty of life ahead of you. You can still make things better."

Her mom gave a little smile. "I suppose that's true. Even though I know it in my head, it'll still be hard to change. Things get repetitive."

"Because we're humans. We all have regrets. Nobody is perfect."

Her mom looked up at her then, with a new kind of twinkle in her eyes. "When did my own daughter get so wise?"

Hana didn't reply, instead they sat quietly, admiring the ocean together. Waves hit the sharp cliff rocks and frothed into white foam with a prickling sound, like fresh Coke poured into a clean glass.

"Shall we get going?" her mom asked after a while. She looked a little more resolved than before. "Are you hungry?"

Hana touched her belly. "A bit. We haven't had anything since the morning."

"There's an open air restaurant nearby. It's run by lady shellfish divers. Shall we have lunch there?"

Hana nodded.

The restaurant sat perched on a low cliff, with plastic tables and chairs laid out on a rickety-looking deck. An old lady sat out front by a steep path down to the rocks, fixing holes in her fishing nets. There were fresh looking shellfish in a big tub full of seawater.

Her mom went straight over to the old lady. "How are you doing? What's good today?"

The old lady answered with a deep, croaky voice. "Hello, it's been a while. Is that your daughter? Sea pineapple and squid are good today." A smile cut deep wrinkles in her face.

Hana's mom beamed proudly. "Yes, my daughter's come back from Japan. Could you give us one sea pineapple each along with a bottle of soju?

"Sure, have a seat."

They sat down and Hana looked at her mom curiously. "Since when do you drink in the middle of the day?"

Her mom leaned back in the plastic chair with a relaxed grin. "Well, it's a lovely day and I've been out with my daughter, so I can enjoy a little drink, can't I?" The old lady put down a plate of carrot, cucumber and bell pepper sticks as well as a bottle of soju. "But if you're worried we might get drunk, let's just have one drink each, to celebrate you being back." She poured the soju into two glasses, her eyes now sparkling mischievously.

"OK, one glass each," Hana agreed.

"To us!" Her mom raised the glass and downed it in one. Hana slowly sipped the soju too. It burned down her throat.

"Ah, it's sweet," her mom said, then dipped a carrot stick in the miso sauce and took a big bite. Hana munched on a cucumber stick. It was fresh and juicy.

Soon the old lady set down a big plate of cut raw sea pineapple and squid with salad leaves and red chili pepper sauce. "I cut the freshest and biggest ones. Enjoy it and let me know if you need anything else."

"They look tasty. Thank you." Her mom picked up a thinly cut slice of transparent squid with her chopsticks and dunked it in the spicy, sweet and sour red chili pepper sauce, then wrapped it in a big green salad leaf and ate the whole thing.

"Oh, it's melting in my mouth. Try it."

Hana picked up some raw sea pineapple and dipped it in sesame oil and salt sauce. It had a strong fresh sea smell.

"Have something to drink as well," her mom said, pouring more soju in the glass.

Hana watched. "We said one glass each, didn't we?"

"You said it, I didn't." Her mom grinned then knocked back the second glass, slapping the glass down on the table confidently.

They finished the whole plate and half the bottle while the waves beat on below like background music. Around noon more people started coming to the restaurant.

"Shall we get going?" her mom asked.

They walked back down from the cliff. Hana felt tired after the strong sun and exercise. When they came home, she slumped on her bed and fell straight asleep. She hadn't slept so much for a long time.

Hikaru opened his arms wide in her dreams. He gave her a big smile, but he was slowly fading out of sight. Hana felt confused. She didn't know what to do or where to go, and while she hesitated, he kept fading away little by little. When he was completely gone from sight, Hana became nervous. White petals fell down from the sky like raindrops.

When she opened her eyes, she found she was crying. She didn't know why, but she felt a deep pain in her chest.

"Are you sleeping still?"

It was her mom's voice from the other side of the door. Hana wiped her tears away. "I'm waking up now."

"I'm going to the hospital. Do you want to come?"

Hana rubbed her eyes. "Sure, I'll be there soon."

"You don't have to come if you're tired."

"No, it's OK. I'll see you in the hospital."

Hana got up after hearing the front door close. She looked at herself in the mirror. Her cotton dress was all wrinkled and her eyes were red and swollen from crying. She had a quick shower and changed into a plain white t-shirt and jeans.

In the kitchen she drank a whole pint of cold water with ice cubes, got brain freeze and felt extremely dizzy. She held onto the chair and put the glass down on the table. She sat on the chair, opened her laptop and started researching nasopharyngeal cancer.

It was a cancer which attacked the nose and throat. It caused shortness of breath, and if the tumor hit the brain, it led to neural paralysis. It happened mostly to males over fifty. Drinking and smoking were causes, particularly smoking made it worse. The surgical approach was difficult. Radiation treatment and chemotherapy were normally advised. The full cure rate was around 70 percent if it was treated in the early stages. Patients often had difficulty swallowing food due to the position of the tumors, so having a sensible diet plan was a crucial part of treatment.

Hana closed her laptop and opened the pantry door, thinking hard about what to make for her dad. There were bags of nuts, dried fruits, dried soybeans, rice, noodles and pasta sheets in the pantry. She thought soymilk would be easy to digest and healthy. She poured the dried yellow beans out of their bag and put them in a pan, picking out a few rotten black beans and washing the rest carefully. She poured a bottle of mineral water in the pan and started boiling the beans, scooping away the starch on top when it bubbled up. While the beans softened up, she fried some walnuts in a clean frying pan and peeled off the skins.

When the yellow beans were soft, she poured them with the water into the food processer, added a pinch of salt, some sesame seeds and the fried walnuts, then turned the blender on. It roared for a few seconds, releasing an earthy, sweet smell as the ingredients chopped into bits. She poured this thick mixture onto a sheet of clean cotton cloth, pinched the edges together then squeezed to separate out the soymilk.

It dripped out as a pure ivory colored milk, which she poured into a thermos bottle. Last she mixed honey, grapeseed oil, flour, eggs and black sesame seeds with the bean dregs, rolled this dough into small round cookie shapes then put them on a parchment paper tray and baked them until they were golden brown. She let the cookies cool then put them in a plastic tub, packed the soymilk in a bag beside them and headed out to the hospital.

When she opened the door, her dad was talking to the doctor.

"... lost a lot of weight suddenly," the doctor was saying. "You need to eat well and gain weight to fight the cancer, so the chemotherapy will work better."

"I lost my appetite, and it's difficult to swallow food." Her dad's voice sounded small and tired.

"Even so, you need to have a balanced diet to keep fighting back against the cancer cells. Try not to lose weight and instead focus on gaining weight by having good quality proteins, vitamins and minerals. Beans or nuts will be great." The doctor checked his chart and his pulse then left the room. Hana stood in the corner of the room quietly.

"Hi, Dad, how do you feel today?" she asked, putting on a cheerful face. "The weather's lovely outside."

"It's just another day," he said flatly. "Yesterday is like today, today is like yesterday. I'm tired of being in the hospital. I want to go home now."

Her mom frowned. "You heard what the doctor just said. You need to eat well to get better."

Hana interrupted before it could become another argument. "Dad, I made some soymilk and bean curd cookies. Why don't you try some of these?" She took a glass from the table and filled it with warm soymilk from the thermos.

"Did we have beans in the house?" her mom asked absently. "I haven't been in the kitchen for ages now, so I don't know what's in where anymore."

"I found them in the pantry." Hana handed him the soymilk. "I know it's hard to swallow, but this is soft. I hope it gives you some strength."

"Thank you, Hana." Her dad started to drink, stopping several times to cough, but each time he kept sipping and swallowing until finally he'd finished it completely.

"Can I have some more?" He handed her the empty glass.

"Sure, I've got lots more here and I can make more later." Hana poured more soymilk in the empty glass. This time he took longer, enjoying the taste like he was drinking whisky. He finished the whole second glass too.

"It's been a long time since I enjoyed such good food," he said, then gave a satisfied yawn. "It's so warm and smooth."

"That's great," Hana said. "You can lie down now." She helped him lie down and put the duvet over his chest. He was breathing evenly and fell asleep soon.

"He hates the hospital food," her mom said, lowering her voice. "He doesn't like takeaway food. I hired a cook to prepare him some dishes with the best ingredients but he didn't like them either. He said no to milk, soymilk, almond milk so I threw them all away. How did you do that?"

"I just made something out of simple ingredients at home." Hana whispered back.

Her mom wrinkled her lip. "He's just being rebellious to me, isn't he?"

"No, I don't think so," Hana said softly, still looking at her dad. "He must appreciate what you do."

"Do you think so?" Her mom didn't sound so sure.

"If you open your mind and listen to him, that will be helpful," Hana said, looking up. "Hold his hands and listen to him rather than always bustling around preparing big things. Do something small that won't cause a fuss. You'll be sad and confused if Dad disappears one day. When you're together, have some valuable time. So you don't regret it later."

Her mom stared at her for a long moment, like she didn't even recognize Hana, then blinked, as if she was breaking a spell. "You are wise. And yes, you're right. Small things." Her mom moved up to her dad's side and gently fussed with his blankets. "I don't want to regret things anymore. I don't want to feel so angry, either, and let it out on him, or on you." She looked up at Hana. "I'm trying to be better. When things get out of control, I'll just think of little things. Fix what I can fix, and don't worry so much about the rest."

Hana looked at her mom for a long moment. For so long she'd lived in fear of this woman; of her moods, her anger, of the sound of dishes breaking in the kitchen. Now the fight had all drained away. "You need some rest, Mom," she said. "You look exhausted." Hana took the plastic tub from her bag. "Here, I forgot about this. I made cookies out of the soybean dregs. Try some."

"Who's mother and who's daughter here..." her mom muttered, then gave a small laugh. They sat next to each other and ate the cookies in the dark hospital room.

"That smells sweet and nice," came her dad's sleepy voice. He opened his red and swollen eyes. "Where am I?"

"We had some soybean cookies while you were sleeping," Hana's mom said softly. "Get better and let's go home soon."

Her dad didn't go back to sleep though. It seemed like there was something he wanted to say, so he said it slowly and haltingly, squeezed by the tightness in his throat. "Hana, do you remember when we went to the beach for the first time?"

She nodded, but then realized he couldn't see her clearly in the dark. "Yes, Dad," she said quietly.

A smile spread across his drawn face. "You were holding onto my neck like a little monkey. You didn't want to let go. I tried to teach you how to swim in the shallows but I dropped you for a second by a mistake. Your mom got furious at me." His smile widened, and his voice drifted between rasping and even. "We came back to the beach and made sandcastles. We ate watermelons lying on the mat. You got tickled by the waves touching your feet. It was so sweet and I even cried a bit from happiness. I didn't expect that when you were all grown up, you would cook for me and look after me like this." He closed his eyes.

Hana held his hand. She was surprised at how thin it was. "Shall we go take a family trip once you're out of the hospital? Dad, you choose where to go and surprise us."

"Sure," he whispered. "I'll get better soon."

When he fell back to sleep, Hana and her mom went home together in the dark. Her mom went to bed, but Hana wasn't so sleepy. She sat in her room looking around at the walls, until she remembered something, then she opened her laptop and wrote out an email to Yoko.

'Yoko, I'm sorry to email you instead of talking to you in person. The other day I found out my dad has cancer, so I had to come home suddenly. I'll stay here and spend some time with him. I may not be able to go back to Tokyo anytime soon, and I'm sorry if this leaves you short-staffed. It was a great pleasure working with you and Mr. Kimura. Thank you for being so nice and kind to me. I will keep you updated once I'm back in Japan. Hana.'

She sat for a while longer, thinking about different things, and was about to close the laptop when a reply came in.

'Hana, thanks for the email. I'd guessed something must have happened to you, since you always looked quite concerned these days. Take good care of your father. I hope he feels better soon. And don't worry about the photo studio, we don't have many customers yet. Spend some good time with your family, and let me know when you come back. Yoko.'

In the days that followed, Hana's life fell into a simple routine, spending the daytime with her dad and coming home with her mom at night. She thought of Hikaru often, about how he was doing, how the new apples were growing, how Mr. Kato was getting along. In long, quiet afternoons spent by her father's side, she thought back on the day she'd visited the farm, when they'd eaten together and Mr. Kato had asked her about Hikaru.

She checked her phone and started writing out messages to him several times, but she didn't know what to say. She thought about calling him, but she didn't know what to say. And didn't want to add to his worries.

"The blood test result is very good," the doctor said one day to her father, looking confident. "You gained weight as well. Having a daughter nearby has definitely given you new motivation. I think you can go home soon."

Her mom looked down at her dad proudly. "Thank you. He eats well and he's keen on exercising these days." Hana felt mixed feelings to see them being so supportive of each other. She hoped they would be happier once they went home together.

Days became weeks, and as her father grew stronger, she thought more about her life back in Tokyo; not just Hikaru, but also the vegetable shop, Miyo and the other street cats. It had been over a month. She knew other people also fed the stray cats, but she missed Miyo. She had to go back and do the paperwork with the lawyer, and say a proper goodbye to her friends, to Miyo, and to Hikaru. The thought made her feel sad. Sometimes she thought about travelling to South America. She wanted to visit the places that Jin might have been to, and plan out her future step by step. Thinking about that made her feel calm. There were lot of things to do, and it helped to have a clear mind.

Hana took a walk with her dad in the small park with the pine trees next to the hospital. Seagulls were flying over their heads.

"Dad, once you're safely at home, I'll go back to Japan," she said. He listened quietly, leaning on her arm, waiting for her to go on. "There's some work I still have to do, so it may take some time." She paused and thought a little more. "Once I make a plan to come home, I will let you know. You just focus on getting better, so we can take a family holiday like you promised me."

"Sure," he said. He was breathy but sounding stronger every day. "Don't worry about me now, Hana. I'm so glad you came back, but now you should focus on your work. I support you. I know you'll do great."

"Do you think so?" Hana asked, turning to him. "I'm not so confident these days."

He smiled. "What are you afraid of? You don't have cancer, you don't have any debt, you don't have a family or kids to look after."

She gave a small laugh. "Well, maybe I'll have a mortgage."

Her dad laughed a little too. " But you're beautifully young, and you can still do whatever you want to do." They walked a little further, slowly and carefully, then her dad spoke up again. "I wanted to be a singer once. When I played guitar and sang the songs that I'd written, I felt so free. I was happy and I had no worries. I didn't care if I didn't even make money out of it. I was ready to be poor if I could follow my dream. But my parents wanted me to get a proper job and have a family. I couldn't disappoint them."

He paused and they walked in silence for a while longer. "Then I graduated university, got a job and married your mother. We had you immediately after the marriage, and I didn't have time to think about music. It was a luxury I had to sacrifice. I was too busy making money and looking after the family. I never even took my guitar out of the attic." He paused again, gathering his thoughts. "Sometimes I think about what might have happened if I hadn't listened to my parents and followed my own dream. Possessing nothing can be a blessing." He turned to her. "You're young and you've got nothing to lose yet. Don't be afraid to challenge yourself. Listen to your heart and follow your dreams. If you fail, you can always come home. It's not a big deal."

Hana stopped walking and looked at her feet. "I don't know what I want to do, Dad."

He smiled at her, and there was something of her old dad in his expression. Like he knew her better than she knew herself. "It seems you already know what you want, but you're hesitating. Isn't that true?"

She frowned. "Dad, how do you know when I don't even know yet?"

"Hana, you're my daughter. I've known you for twenty years, so I understand certain things. You check your phone a million times a day. Why don't you just call him? Don't lose him. You'll regret it later."

Hana was surprised. She hadn't even mentioned Hikaru. She couldn't believe her dad had even noticed. "Do you really think so?"

"I really do. Don't regret this moment thirty years later, while you're dying from cancer like a fool. Live for today, not tomorrow." He hugged Hana softly. His patient gown had a faint disinfectant smell.

Jin 2

Jin stood at the edge of the River Plate docks in Buenos Aires, watching over Ensenada Bay. He turned up his coat collar against the strong wind and pushed his long hair back with his fingers. It was about to rain. Thick and heavy clouds were moving sideways across the dark gray sky. Floating cranes were carrying container boxes from the port to the cargo ships rhythmically, like robots doing a slow motion breakdance.

A tough-looking middle-aged Asian guy walked over to Jin from the opposite side of the quay. He had short hair and a dark green waterproof jacket. In his mouth hung a slack cigarette, and his right hand was wrapped in a bloody bandage.

"Do you have a light? I lost my lighter." He spoke in fast Spanish, pointing at his cigarette and pretending to light it. Jin took a lighter out of his pocket and handed it over. The guy lit his cigarette, inhaled deeply then gave the lighter back.

Jin answered in English. "It's OK. You can keep it."

"Thanks." The guy finished his first cigarette quickly and lit a second one. "Do you want one?" He pulled a fresh cigarette from the red Marlboro box.

Jin smiled. "Thanks, but no thanks. I quit smoking."

"Where are you from? Are you traveling?" The guy spoke in strong Spanish-accented English, blowing out a cloud of cigarette smoke.

"I'm from South Korea. I lived in Japan for the last several years, but now I'm travel here and there without a plan."

The guy grunted. "I know that life. I'm Japanese, but I left home nearly twenty years ago. I'm a cargo shipman now, so I mostly just travel around the world randomly, like a stranger. I've been working with Spanish people for the whole time, so I suppose I'm mostly Spanish myself now." He blew out another big puff of smoke. "I haven't been back home once in all that time, but I expect Japan has changed a lot too."

Jin gave a subtle nod. "Well. I'm not sure about twenty years ago, but probably things have changed a lot. There are certainly things that haven't changed, though."

The guy dropped his cigarette butt on the floor and ground it under his foot. "Sure thing. Well, have a good trip."

Jin spoke before the guy could take a step away. "If you don't mind, could you tell me how you hurt your hand?" His tone was polite and calm. The guy looked back and stared.

"Sure. It's not a big deal. I was working on a container box this morning. It was raining last night and the metal was wet and slippery. I lost my balance and fell. I landed on my palm but I got a long cut from the sharp edge of the container. Ten stitches and the bandage, here we are." He raised his right hand. "It doesn't hurt now but I can't work until the cut is healed properly, so I'll stay in Buenos Aires for a while, until the surgery threads dissolve. The doctor said it will take a week or so." He shrugged.

"That sounds good," Jin said. "I've just arrived in Buenos Aires and I've been thinking about what to do. What about wandering around together until your cut is healed?"

The guy looked rather surprised.

Jin raised both his hands and smiled. "I'm not gay. Please don't think I'm coming on to you."

The guy laughed out loud. "I'm just surprised. It's the first time I've been offered something like this. Hmm." He sized up Jin. "A presentable young man like you can't be a thief or a con man. So, OK, sure. Let's hang around in the city, as I've got nothing else to do for a few days. My name is Kazuo. What's your name?"

"Jin."

"Nice to meet you, Jin." Kazuo held out his uninjured hand and Jin shook it. It was a thick, rough and warm hand.

"Kazuo, do you know any good restaurants nearby?" Jin asked. "Have you had dinner yet?"

"Not yet. If you're OK with street food, though, I know a good place for empanadas."

"That sounds good."

Kazuo and Jin left the docks and walked over to the market, stopping at a street restaurant with red parasols, where they sat at a wobbly plastic table.

"Beer?" Kazuo asked, and Jin nodded. He bought two chilled bottles of Patagonia beer and put them on the cheap plastic table. Kazuo drank right out of the bottle and gave a satisfied sigh. Jin poured his in a glass and had a good sip. It had a light and bright taste.

Soon, the waiter put a plate of two big empanadas on the table, each lightly charred with black grill marks. Jin took another sip of his beer and a bite of his empanada. Diced turkey, black beans, chopped onions, tomatoes and cheddar cheese were wrapped up in a light and soft dough.

"It looks like a Cornish pasty but it tastes totally different," Jin said. "The aroma from cumin and smoked paprika is well balanced. The dough is proved nicely so it's soft and fluffy. The texture is very good."

Kazuo almost swallowed his whole empanada in a few bites. "It's great, yeah. I often come here when I land in the harbor. It's a cheap place that fills you up quickly. But I guess you studied cooking?"

"No," said Jin, "I studied business and management. But my mother is a good cook and she runs a fruit orchard, so I've always been interested in cooking." He took another sip of his beer." When I was studying for my Master's degree in Japan, I had a part-time job in a French restaurant. I fell in love with cooking and baking from then on, and I started thinking of changing my career completely."

Kazuo raised one eyebrow. "So what's this, your gourmet travel? To look for new recipes and such?"

Jin thought about that for a moment. "I suppose, yes and no. I started this trip to find myself. I had a big problem to solve, but I kind of gave up; now I'm not sure there even is an answer or a reason I can find. Instead I started looking around at other people, rather than just looking at myself. I noticed that every time I filled up a stranger's glass, then my glass got filled up afterwards."

Kazuo made a puzzled face.

"I may have another chance to explain more details later," Jin said, and stood up. "Thanks for the dinner tonight. I'll see you tomorrow."

"Uh, what? I mean, where shall we meet tomorrow, and what time?" Kazuo fumbled.

Jin smiled. "You take it easy and do whatever you want to do, and I'll find you in the daytime. You must be tired today from the accident and losing a lot of blood. Have a good rest." He nodded then walked away into the middle of the crowded open square.

* * *

Later that evening, Kazuo laid on his bed in the inn and looked up at the cracked ceiling, thinking back over the things that had happened that day, one by one. He cut his hand by slipping on the wet container. One of the workers called emergency services and he was taken to the hospital by ambulance. He'd felt a bit dizzy from blood loss but the doctor stopped the bleeding and stitched the wound quickly in the emergency center. His original plan had been to be back on the cargo ship already, heading to Florida through Puerto Rico and Cuba, but the company were concerned about possible infection, so they wanted him to stay in the harbor until he recovered.

Then he'd met the young Asian guy by the docks. He hadn't looked like a crazy person, but there was something unusual about him. Like an interesting atmosphere. He hadn't asked for Kazuo's phone number or address, but he was somehow confident they'd meet again the next day.

It seemed like a weird day with a lot of peculiar incidents.

Kazuo took the stained bandage off his right hand, had a cold shower, washed his hand carefully then put antiseptic lotion on the wound along with a new bandage. He felt exhausted, so when he laid down on the bed, he fell asleep immediately.

The next morning, Kazuo opened his eyes to the sounds of people talking in the next room, and the maid pushing a trolley down the corridor outside. The weather was the opposite from the day before, beautiful and sunny with blue skies. His right hand throbbed. He got up and left the hotel. In a nearby park he watched people walking by for a while, then he went to a café and had Mate tea and ate a Medialuna, a half moon-shaped pastry.

He felt pessimistic about seeing Jin again in the big city. They hadn't set up a time or a place to meet; maybe Jin really was a crazy person. He put his hand in his jacket and touched the lighter Jin had given him. After breakfast he wandered around the streets, walking with no real purpose. When he saw a botanic garden full of green leaves, he went inside through the arch gate. There were yellow-orange flowers blooming on lush tropical Tipuana Tipu trees. He walked along the garden path until he came across a big greenhouse in an Art Nouveau style, then stopped to admire the black and gold gilding decorations.

"It's quite something, isn't it?"

Kazuo felt startled and spun around. There was Jin standing behind him, both his hands sunk comfortably in his camel color trench coat pockets.

"How did you know I was here?" Kazuo asked.

Jin smiled. "I guessed you would be here. Do you like nature and plants? I somehow felt that way when I first saw you."

It took Kazuo a moment to process that. Jin had guessed he like nature and plants, just by looking at him. It was a little unnerving. "That's a really good guess. I didn't even know I was coming here."

Jin tilted his head to the side. "But you do like nature, don't you?"

"Sure," Kazuo said. "I used to work as a gardener back in Japan. I grew up watching my grandparents maintaining their Japanese garden." He hadn't thought about those days for a long time, and found himself overwhelmed by a rush of memories. "They used to put a lot of care into it, placing rocks between the trees, building a bridge over the small pond, raking waves into the sand garden. I always admired the maple trees changing their colors in fall, and the cherry blossoms making buds in spring."

Kazuo stopped then. The memories suddenly felt so vivid, like he was caught up in a dream of the past. He wasn't sure he liked how it felt. "Anyway, all that was such a long time ago. Honestly, I completely forgot about it. It almost feels like it happened in a previous life."

Jin looked at him for a moment, then gestured to the path. "Shall we have a walk? It's great weather today."

They started walking slowly together. They walked without talking for a while, like they were both deep in thought. They stood in front of a big tall tree with long leaves and branches. Jin stroked the trunk of the tree with his palm.

"What a great looking tree this is," he said. "It looks like a proud medieval aristocrat."

"This is a Quebracho tree," Kazuo said. "It's nicknamed the 'iron tree'. It's slow to grow, so this tree must be at least a hundred years old. The timber is heavy, sturdy and durable, so it's very useful for building railways, ships, houses. It's also used for medical purposes; it's good for fever, emphysema or allergies. It's one of the ingredients to make wine or leather, too." Kazuo felt himself getting carried away again. When was the last time he'd even thought about a Quebracho tree? Still, he couldn't stop himself, and pointed at a nearby short tree with olive-green leaves.

"This is a Yerba Mate tree. Have you had Mate tea before?"

Jin shook his head.

"People here call the Mate tree the 'drinking god'. These long and shiny leaves are the ingredient for Mate tea. It has abundant iron and saponins, plus good nutrients so you feel full after you drink it. Normally dried leaves are used for the tea, but fresh leaves are also helpful to release fatigue." He plucked a leave and put it in his month, not chewing but just holding it there to release the flavors. He handed another leaf to Jin. It had a bitter green taste.

Jin and Kazuo sat on a bench looking at the Victorian style greenhouse, enjoying cold-brewed Mate tea.

"It's a wonderful botanic garden, isn't' it?" Jin said.

"I've been through Buenos Aires lots of times," Kazuo said. "I saw this garden often, but I never thought of coming inside." He didn't know what else to say, so he just watched the orange and white Koi fishes swimming lazily in the pond.

"Thank you for the tour of the garden," Jin said. "Also for the Mate tea. It was fun today. Where shall we go tomorrow? I'll have a think." He stood up from the bench.

"I guess you'll be able to find me tomorrow again?" Kazuo asked.

Jin smiled. "Sure. I'll see you soon, then."

Kazuo watched Jin walk away from him toward the entrance, haunted by strange feelings. Feelings that he'd squashed down for decades were now rising up slowly in his heart.

"Daddy, Daddy!" It was a little boy's voice. "Where are you Daddy?"

The boy was standing in a black space. It was raining and the floor and the walls of the space were cold and damp. The boy punched and kicked the walls, but there were no doors or windows so he couldn't get out, only a circular opening far above. He could see blue sky through the gap, but there was no way to get up there.

"Daddy, I'm here. I'm here. Help..." The little boy's voice got louder, full of tears and fear, and Kazuo tried to answer him but he couldn't make a sound. The only thing he could do was open and close his eyes. His eyelids felt as heavy as iron manhole covers.

'Please save my son. Please rescue my son.' He prayed for it over and over.

"Daddy... Daddy..." The little boy's voice faded slowly.

Kazuo woke up in the inn, panting and shivering badly. His whole body was soaked in sweat, and he'd bitten his lips so hard they were bleeding. Blood leaked out of the bandage too, as he was holding his fist so tight.

"Housekeeping."

It was the voice of the cleaning maid, in the corridor outside. Kazuo didn't feel like he could speak, so he just coughed loudly. The maid walked away down the corridor.

It was the same nightmare he'd been having for two decades. Exactly the same one, but this was more vivid than usual. He felt like a huge heavy stone was crushing his chest, drowning him in a bottomless black ocean. Desperation, depression and guilt pushed him down. He looked up at the cracked ceiling and wept.

When he finally composed himself, he left the inn and stumbled onto the street. The strong sharp sunlight hurt his eyes, so he looked down at the pavement. When he next looked up, he was standing in the middle of an open square. A shirtless guy was dancing to beatbox music. Young people were practicing on skateboards and other people were watching them. Kids were playing and running around. Business people were walking and talking on the phone, carrying briefcases. Cars were honking. Everything looked unreal to him. He wasn't sure if this was part of a dream, a scene out of a movie or real life. He felt dizzy and sat on the ground.

"Are you all right?" A young guy came over to Kazuo. "Can I help with anything?"

"No, I'm all right," Kazuo said, panting heavily. "I felt a bit dizzy, that's all."

"Your hand's bleeding. Shall I call an ambulance?"

Kazuo felt the hot damp in his right palm. "No, I'll be better soon. Please go ahead, I'll be fine, thank you." Kazuo waved his hands. The young guy hesitated but left. Kazuo watched him walking away, then laid down on the floor. The sky above was perfectly blue and clear.

"Hello there." A boy with no front teeth was looking down at Kazuo. "What are you doing there?"

"I'm looking at the sky," he mumbled.

"Why are you lying down on the floor?"

"I can see things better and the sky looks bigger when I lie down." The boy laid next to Kazuo and put his little head on his arm.

"That's true. The sky is huge and so blue! If I put my arms out then I can fly." The boy raised his arms and had a good laugh. It was a sweet, innocent smile.

"What are you doing, Riccardo?" A woman ran over from the other side of the square and yanked on the boy's arm, raising her voice. "Did I tell you to stay where I could see you or not?"

"You did." The boy's voice got smaller.

"Mama worried about you." She hugged the boy, kissed his forehead, lifted him high up then walked away through the square.

"Goodbye." The boy turned around in his mom's arms and waved his little arms at Kazuo over her shoulder. He was still lying on the floor and raised his unwounded left arm to say bye.

Once the boy was out of sight Kazuo stood up and started walking again. He didn't know what was happening to him or where he was going, but it felt like he should just keep walking. He was tired and thirsty and the sun was bright and hot. Bells were ringing in the air, and he followed the sound until he was standing in front of a huge cathedral. He looked up at the gleaming stained glass windows, then joined the throng of tourists walking through the ornate stone arch.

It was cool and dark inside. He took a deep breath, sat on an empty bench in the middle of the cathedral and closed his eyes slowly. It didn't take long. He didn't even really hear him come close, more it was something in the air.

"You found me again," Kazuo said, and opened his eyes. Now Jin was sitting next to him, wearing a black shirt. "Are you a priest?"

Jin regarded Kazuo with a calm expression. The side of his face caught the dim light through the stained glass and seemed to glow. "No, I'm just a stranger and a traveler."

Kazuo opened his mouth to say something more, but the service started at that moment.

"God bless you all for you sitting here in this cathedral," said the priest in a clear, resonant voice. "For strangers, for tourists, for seekers, for lost souls, for prayers. God will bless all." The choir started singing a hymn, accompanied by magnificent pipe organ music. It echoed throughout the entire cathedral.

Do not be sad. Do not regret things that already happened.
Do not get upset. It is not your fault. It is nobody's fault.

Forgive yourself. God is with you.
Forgive yourself. God already forgave you.
Love yourself. God always loves you.

Kazuo felt a deep agony in his chest. His shoulders shuddered up and down as he started to weep.
"Oh God, I can't forgive myself." He put his head on his knees. He hugged his chest with his shivering arms, feeling like he was about to burst.

It is not your fault. You deserve to be loved.
Love yourself. God is always with you.

The pure and clear singing voices filled the cathedral with warmth. Soon the service was finished and Kazuo opened his teary eyes. Jin was gone. Kazuo ran out of the cathedral and ran back and forth to find him, but there was no sign of Jin on the empty streets.

19. Kato farm and Hikaru

Hana packed up her dad's clothes and belongings in the hospital room, while her mom and dad had a meeting with the doctor and did some paperwork. It took a long time, but Hana didn't mind; strangely her mind was filled with thoughts of Hikaru. As she folded her dad's trousers and bundled his socks, she just kept thinking about him over and over, until finally she wrote him an email.

'Hi, Hikaru. How have you been doing? I'm sorry I disappeared so suddenly. Right after the wake for Ms. Kawanami, I got a phone call that my dad was in hospital with cancer. I just forgot about everything else and rushed home, so there was no time for a proper goodbye. I've been helping out with my dad since then. He's getting better now, so he can go home today. I'll come back to Japan soon to do the final paperwork on the vegetable shop.'

She paused for a moment, reading back on what she'd written. It wasn't bad, but it didn't seem to say what she really wanted to say.

'How's Mr. Kato doing? Is he getting better? How's your farm? I hope all is well with you and your father. Talk to you soon. Hana.'

It wasn't perfect, but she didn't know what was missing, so she clicked send. Soon after, her mom came back in with her dad hobbling beside her. With two weeks' worth of pills and the next appointment slip, they left the hospital and went home together.

They had a simple dinner of noodles, settled her dad down to sleep, then Hana and her mom sat in silence at the kitchen table. After a while, her mom squeezed Hana's hand and went back in to be with her husband.

Hana rubbed her eyes. She hadn't seen them sleep in the same bedroom together for years. Back in her own room, she opened her laptop and found a message from Hikaru.

'Hi Hana. My dad passed away two weeks ago. I opened his bedroom door in the morning but he was gone. It was a heart attack. He said several times he didn't want to be a burden, so it probably was the ending he was hoping for. He looked like he was sleeping comfortably, so I didn't feel too bad. It happened suddenly, and I didn't have a chance to talk to you. After the funeral, I went to the vegetable shop, but the door was closed so I thought you must've already left. I didn't expect to hear from you, so I'm glad you emailed me. Let me know when you come back. Hikaru.'

Hana didn't wait a second longer. She went into her parents' room quietly, whispered to her mom, hugged her and her dad, then grabbed her bag and left.

Due to heavy rain and an incoming storm, many flights had been cancelled in Busan airport. Hana waited impatiently in the lobby as the afternoon wore on. The weather forecast said over four inches of rain had fallen in the last twenty-four hours. Hana pulled on her fingertips. She counted to five in her mind slowly and carefully. 1. 2. 3. 4. 5. She took a deep breath then counted to five again.

'Please... make it happen.' She prayed she would be able to get on a plane to Tokyo that day. It was the first time she'd wanted something so badly since she'd stood outside the door to Jin's apartment, expecting him to open the door.

In the evening the rain grew weaker and the wind got milder. After waiting for eight hours in the airport, she finally got on a night flight to Tokyo. She sat in her seat and thanked Jesus, Buddha, Allah, and every single god she could name. Thick gray clouds dropped fat raindrops that splashed off the plane's windows as it lined up for takeoff. Hana gazed out at the dark sky as the engines roared to life and propelled her into the sky.

"What do you want for your dinner tonight, miss?"

Hana woke from a light doze. A member of the cabin crew was standing beside her, pushing a food cart.

"I don't have any appetite, thank you."

"Would you like a drink?"

"No, I'm all right. Thank you." Hana shook her head and closed her eyes to get back to sleep, and was just drifting off when the pilot's voice came over the PA system.

"We're going to be experiencing some mild turbulence. Please fasten your seat belts."

Abruptly the plane started shaking. People gasped and a baby started crying. Hana held the armrest tightly. The plane jostled side to side and up and down, and she began to feel airsick.

"Ladies and gentlemen, please remain seated with your seat belts fastened, we'll be through this in a moment."

It didn't feel like a moment; it felt like a long rollercoaster.

The plane made several attempts at a landing, swooping in then taking off again due to high winds, but finally landed at Narita Airport. People on the plane started to applaud, and Hana could at last release her tight grip on the armrest. Out of customs, she rushed over to the Limousine Bus helpdesk.

"One ticket to Chiba please."

"The next Limousine Bus to Chiba departs in half an hour." Hana paid and the guy handed her a ticket. She put the ticket in her pocket and bought a bottle of water in a convenience store. It was raining outside the building. Standing at the edge of the bus shelter, she drank the water with one hand and put the other hand out to feel the rain. Heavy raindrops fell on her palm and trickled down to the road. Soon the bus arrived at the platform and Hana got on, sat on the back seat just like before and leaned her head against the window.

"Please watch out for your belongings, we are departing now." Hana fastened her seatbelt and closed her eyes. When she opened them next, the driver was announcing they'd reached the last destination in Chiba. Hana rubbed her eyes and got off the bus. It was completely dark outside and a damp wind blew off the ocean. She took two local buses and arrived near Tateyama Castle, then walked up the steep and narrow unpaved road into the mountains. The rain stopped but the street was muddy underfoot.

Hana turned her phone flashlight on and used a tree branch as a walking stick. Soon she was panting like she was running a marathon, but she kept walking on the slippery roads until they got wider and flatter, and at last she saw the hand-carved sign for the Kato farm. She felt a burst of relief in her chest when she saw the warm orange light coming from the house, and right there illuminated by the light was Hikaru.

He was carrying firewood and seemed to be burying things in a big pit. For a second Hana was frozen, caught between two worlds, then she cleared her throat and called out.

"Hikaru."

He stopped and turned around slowly, peering into the darkness. When he spoke, it was with a kind of disbelief. "Is that Hana?"

"Yes. It's me."

He ran over to her and squeezed her freezing arms. "What are you doing here? What happened? You're soaking wet."

"I'm sorry I came so late. I should have come earlier. I didn't know Mr. Kato passed away. I'm so sorry, Hikaru."

"I, uh, where did you even come from?"

"I left home early this morning but there was a storm so the plane got delayed. I'm sorry I didn't come earlier."

His face cracked into a smile, and he hugged her gently. "Wow. Don't be sorry. I'm so glad to see you. I missed you." His arms were big and warm. "Let's go in. You'll catch a cold."

Hikaru made a fire for her in the tatami room, and they sat next to each other in front of the Irori firepit. The cozy sound of firewood burning and spitting lulled her gently.

"I was just organizing my father's belongings and burying some stuff," Hikaru said. It seemed like he'd lost some weight. He gave her a tiny grin. "I didn't expect to see you out there in the dark."

Hana held his hands. "I had to come. It must have been so hard."

Hikaru gave a small smile. "Right. But I think he already knew it was coming. He asked me many times to look after the farm. He also told me to say hello to you, but after I found you'd left the vegetable shop, it didn't feel right to contact you. I thought you'd left for good."

Hana's eyes prickled. She didn't like to think of Hikaru finding that hasty sign she'd left on the vegetable shop's shutters. "I'm sorry I left like that. I didn't know what to do. I was thinking of Korea when I was in Japan, and I was thinking of Japan when I was in Korea. I was so afraid of making a huge decision on my own. I was afraid of losing my dad. I was scared and wanted to run away from any big responsibilities. I didn't think I could handle them on my own."

Hikaru squeezed her hands. "Why do you think you're facing these big responsibilities alone? You have your family and friends. And you've got me too."

Her eyes filled up, looking at his handsome, kind face. "I guess that's true. I didn't realize it until just now, maybe." He reached out and stoked a strand of hair off her face. Her throat got choked up. "After Ms. Kawanami died, I just felt like I was completely alone."

"You're not alone," he said.

She put her head on Hikaru's shoulder, and he put his big arm around her, and together they watched the red flames burn the wood slowly down to ash.

Hana opened her eyes to a rooster crowing loudly. Warm dawn light glowed in through the paper doors. Hikaru's fluffy duvet was soft and cozy. She smelled subtle bonito flakes and heard the sound of vegetables being chopped in the distance. She opened the door and walked into the kitchen.

Hikaru smiled at her. "Did you have a good sleep?"

She rubbed her eyes. "When did I fall asleep?"

"Almost straight away. You were very tired. You talked in your sleep."

Her eyes went wide. "Really?"

"Yes, you snored as well."

"Seriously?" She felt her skin paling.

"No, I'm kidding." He laughed. "I fell asleep too so I didn't hear a thing. Anyway, breakfast is ready soon. Are you hungry?"

"I'm starving. I've had nothing since yesterday morning."

"Wow. OK, well it'll be done when you're ready. Maybe you'd like a nice hot shower, first?"

"That sounds wonderful!"

He smiled. "I thought it might. The bathroom's just on the other side of the bedroom. There are towels and shampoo and everything laid out. Take your time."

"I'll be back soon."

Hana had a quick shower and changed into a light linen navy dress from her bag. When she'd dried her hair and come back to the kitchen, there was rice, miso soup with tofu, chargrilled salmon, grilled sweet seaweed, and a tomato cucumber salad laid out on the kitchen table.

"When did you prepare all this?" Hana asked, impressed. "I feel like I'm on a fancy trip, staying in a five-star Japanese hotel."

Hikaru grinned. "Well, you travelled from far away yesterday, so it is a big trip. I hope it all tastes OK. Have a seat and help yourself."

"Thank you. It looks lovely." Hana sat down and had a sip of miso soup. The smoked bonito flake broth had a great taste. The rice was beautifully cooked, with just the right consistency. The salmon belly melted in her mouth without her needing to even chew. The fresh tomatoes and cucumbers from the farm had the flowery fragrance of the earth along with a great texture. The crunch of the dried seaweed just called for more rice.

"Hikaru, this is not a joke," Hana said between mouthfuls. "You should open a restaurant rather than running a farm. These are so tasty." She picked up a tomato with her chopsticks and munched on it. "These tomatoes could be used for cakes, they're so soft and sweet. They taste like fruit."

Hikaru smiled. "I'm glad you're enjoying it."

"May I have another bowl of rice, please?" She pointed at her empty rice bowl.

"Of course." He brought a new bowl of white shiny rice and put it in front of her. When she finished all that, he brought out a big plate filled with strawberries.

Hana gawped at the big red and shiny strawberries. "Wow, you don't mean to feed me up and sell me in the market, do you?"

He laughed. "Absolutely not. I picked the ripest ones this morning. They're in season now." The strawberries were a deep and even red all the way up to their green tips, even redder and sweeter-smelling than David Austin roses. Hana picked one and took a big bite.

"I can't describe the taste well enough," she gushed. "It's juicy, fragrant, sweet and sour. It's just perfect." She stared at the half-bitten strawberry with wide open eyes. "Strawberry and whipped cream sponge cakes! Reduce the sweetness on the whipped cream to emphasize the fragrance and taste of the strawberries." She looked up. "Hikaru, can you show me all the fruits and vegetables you're growing now?"

Hikaru grinned and nodded. They went outside and walked over to the farm together. Red poppies were blooming in the wild garden. Hana stroked their fragile papery petals and walked on. Hikaru opened the greenhouse door and Hana was struck dizzy by the overwhelming strawberry fragrance. Fresh strawberries plump with juice shone like rubies against the rich black soil.

They walked out of the greenhouse and Hikaru showed her tomatoes, cucumbers, eggplants, spinach, carrots, onions, corn and sweet potatoes. There were three types of tomatoes growing; red, yellow and orange. Hana imagined how wonderful the different colors would look on cakes. On the other side of the farm there were blueberries and fig trees, and beyond that were apple and pear trees. Hikaru stood in front of the peach trees; each swelling fruit had been hand-wrapped in a paper bag, to protect it from insects.

"The peaches are ripening well now," he said, touching one of the hanging paper bags. The peach inside seemed round and heavy. "They'll be in season soon. This is called a Madoka. It's a white peach with a good fragrance and sweetness. It's still hard when you first pick it, but it gets softer if you leave it for a week, so you can enjoy two textures."

"It sounds perfect for a peach tart."

Hikaru flashed that grin again and moved on. "This apple is another experiment, a mixture of Japanese Fuji and Pink Lady. I'm looking for the right sourness and texture. We'll find out this fall."

Hana smiled. "I'm sure it'll be a success. The Kato farm apples are always popular. This'll be perfect for apple pie."

"And come over here," he said, beckoning her on. "These fig trees were planted by my grandfather. The figs are bigger than normal, with a perfectly round shape. I'll harvest them in the fall, once they're fully ripe. They're sweeter than honey."

Hana's eyes widened further. "These figs can be used for mousse cakes. Use the whole fig and once the cake's cut, the figs will show up in cross-section. They'll look beautiful, like modern art."

Hana looked out across the farm. Everywhere flowers and plants were shining in the bright sunlight and swaying in the breeze like dancing waves. The endless possibilities thrilled her. For a long time she hadn't known what the future held for her, or even what she wanted, but standing there on Hikaru's farm, she suddenly saw it all.

"Hikaru." Her voice trembled slightly. "I know what I want to do now. I'm going to make cakes and desserts using your fruits and vegetables. I feel like I can do it. I may fail but I will not run away and I will do my best. I'm not going to regret this moment in thirty year's time. I want to live right now." Hana held her hand out toward him. "Are you with me?"

Hikaru's eyes gleamed with happiness and excitement. "Of course I'm with you. My dad would love it too." He took her hand and held it tight.

Hana went back to the vegetable shop, put her bag down, and set to work. First up, she reverently took down the old half-ripped sunscreen that read 'Kawanami Vegetable Shop' in faded white letters. Next she started scrubbing away years of dust on the dirty walls with sugar soap, until the water in the bucket looked like strong black coffee. She washed and scraped the walls back to bare concrete. Where there were cracks and gaps, Hana filled them with silicon filler from a hardware store, making a perfectly smooth surface. She painted the walls and the ceiling white using rollers and paint brushes, then she painted the outside of the building white too, while the inside was drying. She washed the door and the windows so they were sparkling clean. She got covered in white paint and dirt, her arms and shoulders were stiff and painful, but she felt extremely fulfilled.

Altogether it took two days and nights. Afterward she sat on the street in the afternoon and watched people walking past on the market street while having an ice cream. A chubby round-faced lady, one of Ms. Kawanami's many customers, saw Hana covered in white paint and walked over.

"Oh my my. The vegetable shop was closed so I thought it was gone forever, but you've come back. Are you going to start it again?" She sounded cheerful.

"Yes, it has been a while," Hana said with a respectful bow. "Now I'm going to open a bakery shop with Hikaru, using the Kato farm's fruits and vegetables to make all kinds of cakes. I'll still sell his fruits and vegetables on a separate stand as well. What do you think?"

The woman's eyes popped wide. "All kinds of cakes? That's a great idea. You've made a great decision. I always thought your desserts were special. I'll share the news with everyone I know, and I'll drop by when you open the shop. Good luck."

"Thank you." Hana felt her energy renewed. She went back into the shop. The walls were all nice and clean but the concrete floor was dirty and bare still. She mopped the floor with sugar soap and wiped it dry, then painted it a glossy epoxy white. She turned the lights off at midnight and went upstairs with exhausted arms and legs, feeling like she'd run another marathon.

The next day she checked the delivery dates of all her new furniture; pre-fabricated shelves, showcases, glasses and lamps. Once the schedules were set, she posted the photos of the bare shop on her bakery blog.

'I'm planning to open a bakery shop with lovely organic fruits and vegetables. It will take some time until it's ready, but I will update the progress regularly on my blog. If you come to my shop after reading my blog, you'll get a small present. Stay tuned.'

She uploaded the post and checked her email box. There was an email from Hikaru.

'Hi Hana, how are things going? Any good progress on the shop? Let me know if there is anything I can help you with. Hikaru.'

She swiftly wrote a reply. 'Hello, partner. Yes, everything is going well here. Thank you for checking in. How are your strawberries and peaches doing? I painted the outside and inside of the shop today. I'll finish them off tomorrow. Once the wooden pieces arrive, I'll put shelves up, make a showcase and a stand up signboard. I've decided on the menu, and I'll also display your vegetables and fruits for sale. Don't worry about me, and good luck with the farm. See you soon, Hana.'

She made flyers and name cards for the shop, using the graphics skills she'd learned at the Kimura photo studio, planning to print them at a printing company the next day. When that was done, she closed her laptop and opened her thick recipe book. A postcard dropped from the recipe book, showing a half-cut avocado on a golden beach against the blue sky.

'A rich chocolate cake with good quality liquor would be perfect. It will suit you.'

Jin had written that. She'd completely forgotten about the postcard. She wondered if Jin had somehow known she would open a bakery shop. On a whim, she called Hikaru. It was late, but he didn't seem to mind.

"I have a quick question. What kind of liquor would go well with a rich chocolate cake?"

He thought for a second. "What about bourbon? I've got handmade bourbon from my Uncle Jack in America. I was saving it to drink with my father, but unfortunately we didn't get a chance. I can't drink it on my own, so I've been saving it still, but you can make chocolate cake with it, if you like."

"Bourbon... I never thought about that. It's a great idea. Thanks, Hikaru. Would you mind bringing it to the shop the day after tomorrow? I'd also like to order strawberries, tomatoes and spinach, one box each."

"Sure, I'll be there before noon."

"Wonderful, I'll be waiting for you."

It was late and she was already tired, but the thought of bourbon chocolate cake reinvigorated her, and she spent another hour or so hunting across the Internet for the perfect recipe, listing up ingredients in her head.

The next morning she checked the walls, ceiling and floor then double-painted them. She had a quick lunch of a ham and cheese sandwich while the paint dried, then received delivery of a big secondhand baking oven, right on time. The guy maneuvered the oven into the back of the shop for her, behind the storage space. Already it looked more like a bakery shop than a vegetable shop.

In the afternoon she had professional looking flyers and name cards printed. She wrapped them in a silk cloth and put them in a box of handmade Korean seaweed, along with some homemade Earl Grey cookies, then put the box in the basket of her orange bicycle. When she was about to leave, Miyo popped his head out of the cat house.

"Miyo, my dear boy," she said cheerfully. "You look prettier and your fur looks shinier." She tickled his chin with two fingers. Miyo stretched his arms and yawned. "I'm going to open a bakery shop here. Do you think I can do a good job?"

Miyo pushed his little head against her hand.

"That means yes, right? You too do your job, stay well and be a good boy, OK?" Hana stroked his forehead. After Miyo went back into his cat house for an afternoon nap, she took the bicycle and cycled to the Kimura photo studio. The air smelled like summer was coming.

Mr. Kimura and Yoko were doing photo editing work at the big table when she opened the door. They looked up from the table at the same time.

"Hello," she said brightly.

"Who is this?" Yoko opened her arms wide open and pulled her into a hug. "Hana, it's been such a long time! I was about to email you. You read my mind."

"You look so tanned and healthy," Mr. Kimura said with a warm smile. "How are your parents doing? Please, have a seat."

Hana sat down. "My dad came home from the hospital last week. The chemo went well and he's getting better now. Thank you for asking. Ah, I brought some handmade Korean seaweed from my mom, and Earl

Grey cookies that I made. My mom and dad said thank you to you both for looking after me so well."

Yoko smiled and took the box. "Oh, you didn't have to do this, but thank you! By the way, this cloth is beautiful." Yoko touched the smooth and colorful silk wrapping cloth. "We've actually just had a long holiday and only came back to work today. And I also have some good news." Yoko beamed with a secret-looking smile. "I'm pregnant! It's three months now."

Hana's jaw dropped. "Wow, that's wonderful! Congratulations!" Hana held Yoko's hands, beaming right back at her. Mr. Kimura grinned too, then popped up to make them some oolong tea. Hana and Yoko sat down and munched Earl Grey cookies while gossiping about the coming baby. Mr. Kimura came back and they chatted a little longer; whether the baby would be a boy or a girl, what they might call it, who it was going to look most like.

"I've also got a little more good news too," Hana said, when they were all smiling and filled up with baby talk. "I'm going to open a bakery shop soon!"

Both Yoko and Mr. Kimura seemed stunned. "Wow, that's sudden," Yoko said. "But you do make excellent cakes. How did that come about?"

Hana gave a quick summary of everything that had happened to her so far, and the Kato farm and Hikaru.

"I had no idea you went through all that," Yoko said. "It's great that you'll stay in Japan, though. It's such a wonderful idea. I'm so happy for you." Her eyes got teary.

"Congratulations, good luck with it." Kimura put his hand out and Hana shook it.

"I probably can't work in the photo studio anymore, and I'm sorry about that. I know you'll get busier soon."

Yoko waved a hand. "What are you talking about? We thought you wouldn't come back at all. I'm so glad I can see you again. Don't worry about us, and good luck with your own business now. I'll definitely drop by once you open it. And come visit us anytime you want."

"Let us know when you open up," Mr. Kimura said. "I'd like to take a photo as a present."

Hana bowed. "Thank you. I've been so lucky to work with you. I'll come back to you as soon as I have more news." She put her new bakery shop flyer and name card on the table, then left the Kimura photo shop. It felt strange, but she was glad she could hold onto and cherish such great people, even as she moved on.

Back on her orange bike, she pushed the pedals hard up the steep hill to the Oyama guest house. It was still an outstanding hot pink building that nobody could possibly miss.

"Hello?" Hana opened the door, and walked into the dark lobby with its bubbling fish tank. Ms. Oyama was standing behind the reception desk, her cabbage hairdo in perfect position, talking to a tall and tough-looking guy.

"Oh, hi, Ms. Oyama. How are you doing?"

Ms. Oyama seemed surprised to see Hana. "Oh, Hana! It's good to see you again."

Hana smiled. "You too. How have you been doing?"

"So well." She turned to the man to introduce them. "Honey, this is Hana. I mentioned she stayed here for a while and helped me a lot."

"Yes, I've heard all about you," the man said with a deep voice, then put his big, thick hand out. "I'm Kazuo Oyama."

"Hana, my husband came back home!"

Hana stared for a second. Ms. Oyama's husband? She remembered a windy winter evening, when Ms. Oyama had shared her tragic story; the day her son had fallen down a construction hole while she'd been out buying a birthday treat for her husband. Their son had died, and her husband had never come back.

Now he was here. He was looking right at her. "That's great news," she blurted.

"It's been twenty years," Ms. Oyama said with dreamy eyes. "I was waiting for him in the beginning, but I never really expected him to come back."

Kazuo gave a small bow. "I heard you helped my wife a lot. Thank you."

"No, not at all," Hana said. She felt flustered, though she didn't know why. Twenty years was such a long time; like a character from ancient history had popped into existence before her. "I came to Japan and had nowhere to go. Ms. Oyama was very kind to me, so I should say thank you."

He bowed again, and came up smiling. "By the way, I heard you're from South Korea."

Hana blinked, then nodded. "Uh, yes, I am."

A faraway look came into Mr. Oyama's eyes. "What a coincidence. In Buenos Aires I met a young Korean guy who'd studied in Japan. He had a calm atmosphere and gave me some important advice, but I never got to say thank you. He just disappeared without a proper goodbye."

Hana felt her eyes get big. Buenos Aires was in South America. A calm atmosphere. "Excuse me?"

"I actually came back home because of him." He lifted Ms. Oyama's hand and kissed it. "He gave me a whole new perspective."

"Oh, I see." Hana's mouth was dry. She didn't know what to think. "Do you, uh..." she paused. "Do you happen to remember what his name was?"

"His name?" asked Mr. Oyama. "Yes, of course. I could never forget. It was Jin."

Hana stared. Jin. Her Jin?

Mr. Oyama just went on. "Without him, I'd still be working on container ships all around the world. Even when I came back, I never expected my wife would still be here. It's been decades since I left. When I saw this building from a distance, you can't imagine how shocked I was."

"And it's hot pink," Ms. Oyama reminded him.

Hana listened but struggled to think, so the words just washed over her.

"Yes, that's how I knew it was you," Mr. Oyama said cheerfully, then grew serious. "Really, I can't say how happy I am to be with her again. If I think about it too much, it breaks my heart."

"Now we've decided to close the guest house and open an orphanage!" Ms. Oyama said, and her face lit up with some newfound joy. Hana blinked, pulled back into the moment. Ms. Oyama's were wide and bright, and Hana had never seen her so excited, like a light had been switched on inside.

She felt her own eyes prickle with tears. First Jin, then this? "That's so beautiful."

"Thank you. Now, what about you Hana? Don't leave a bit out."

Hana didn't know what to say. Suddenly there was so much to think about, and she didn't know where to begin, but both of the Oyama's were watching her expectantly. She cleared her throat.

"I came here to see my boyfriend, but he wasn't here. I feel like I've been waiting for nearly a year to see him again, but I think..." Hana paused for a few second. If Jin had truly helped Mr. Oyama, that was beautiful, but it wouldn't change her life now. "No, I'm sure, I want to move on. I'm going to restart my life here, and open a bakery shop with the help of Hikaru and his farm."

Ms. Oyama smiled. She'd hardly ever smiled before. "You finally found what you wanted."

Hana nodded. "Yes, I think so."

Ms. Oyama reached out and held Hana's hands softly. "I hope you're happy."

"I hope you are too. Mr. Oyama, I'm so glad you came back." They all looked at each other for a long moment, with the fish watching on.

20. The Tokyo Bicycle Bakery

Hana worked diligently to prepare her bakery shop for opening day. The delivery of her pre-fabricated furniture came, and she put the shelves up on the walls. She made the showcase from flatpack wooden panels and glass, then varnished it so it shone. She hung the big blackboard on the wall behind the showcase, for the menu and prices, then hung the cozy wooden lightshades from the ceiling, with low-light bulbs to make the cakes look tastier.

She put a standing blackboard outside the shop and wrote 'The Tokyo Bicycle Bakery' on it, with sketches of Miyo's face in the corners and the Kato farm at the bottom. She placed a large plant pot by the big window and transferred her favorite peppermint plant into it, so it could grow strong and green in the bright sun. Kneeling by its side, she touched the beautiful green leaves and they released a lovely soothing aroma. She prayed that Ms. Kawanami and her son would look down on this shop and feel happy and pain-free together, on the other side of life.

Soon enough it looked like a proper bakery shop, and Hana was pleased with it. She chose the menu items and recipes for opening day. As soon as Hikaru came with the ingredients, she would bake the cakes and they'd taste them together. She prepared two types of cookies in advance, soybean dough and Earl Gray, and two types of jam, strawberry and peach in glass jars, for display on the shelves. Last of all she cleaned the floor, the shelves and the showcase once more, watered the plant and hung a light blue glass bead windchime over the shop's sliding door.

Hana spent two weeks preparing for opening day. That night she was tired but she couldn't sleep easily for the excitement. A new chapter of her life was about to begin. 1. 2. 3. 4. 5. She counted to five again and again until she finally fell asleep. She promised herself she would enjoy the days to come, follow her heart and not regret a thing.

The next day, Hikaru opened the shop door carrying a huge box of freshly picked strawberries, three types of tomatoes and many bunches of spinach still trailing white roots dappled with fresh soil.

"This is a complete transformation," he said, looking around at the shop with wide eyes. "How have you done all this? I almost walked past the place; it's completely different from before!"

Hana smiled. "I've been working hard and enjoying myself doing it."

"Well, it's amazing. It has such a cozy and soft feeling, just like you."

Hana felt herself blush. "It's nice of you to say so."

"It's how I feel. Now, where shall I put this box down?"

"Could you come into the kitchen?"

"Sure." He followed her in. "Oh, you've got a big professional oven as well."

Hana patted the oven. "Yes, one of Ms. Kawanami's regular customers introduced me to a bakery owner who was closing his shop, so I got it almost for free. Like a sayonara sale."

"Ah," said Hikaru.

"It's old but it's sturdy, so it should last for at least a few more years. Now." She clapped her hands together. "I'm planning to make some cakes with your ingredients today, and I need a taste tester. Do you think you're up for it?"

He grinned. "I think I can handle that. I finished up at the farm early today, so I've got plenty of time."

Hana nodded sharply. "Good. Then have a seat out there in the shop, read a book and take a rest while you wait. When the time comes, please judge the cakes just as a customer would. I want to get your true feedback today."

Hikaru tried to make a serious expression, but struggled not to smile. "Sure, I'll judge very harshly, just like Paul Hollywood."

"Great, I'll start baking then." Hana fastened her apron and tied back her hair, took a deep breath, then got to work.

First, she separated and whipped two batches of egg yolks and whites to make two genoise cakes, adding fresh Hokkaido double cream to the first batch and spinach juice to the second. She put the two batches in the pre-heated oven, and soon a soft and sweet smell filled the kitchen. Next she opened Hikaru's brown glass bottle of bourbon; it had a smoked-oak scent with vanilla, caramel, cinnamon and a hint of cherry fragrance. Hana dried her hands on her apron and walked back to the shop holding the bottle. Hikaru was still staring around at the re-decorated shop.

"I can see this is very special bourbon," she said. "Are you sure it's OK for me to use it?"

He smiled. "Definitely. My grandfather would be happy too."

Hana nodded, went back into the kitchen, then poured the bourbon into two small brandy glasses. She turned the FM classic radio on. Claire de Lune by Debussy was playing, and it gave her the confidence to go back into the shop, holding one glass out to Hikaru.

"Shall we toast first?"

He grinned broadly and held his glass up. "To the Tokyo Bicycle Bakery!"

Hana raised her glass too. "To the Kato farm!"

They clinked glasses then knocked the bourbon back. The strong smoky and woody fragrance hit Hana's throat first, followed by the sweet scent of flowers in her nose. It left her with a lingering image of tall green cornstalks rippling in a warm wind on an endless farm at sunset. Her eyes began to water and she didn't know if it was the bourbon or something else.

"I'll be back in a moment," she said sharply, and hurried to the kitchen accompanied by a funny sound; she wasn't sure if that was Hikaru chuckling softly or just the rustle of her feet on the kitchen tiles. Regardless, she threw herself into making the chocolate cake.

She beat more egg whites and yolks separately until they were stiff, adding icing sugar and vanilla extract. She melted a dark swiss chocolate mix in a water bath, poured in the honey-colored bourbon, then folded the mix gently into the flourless batter, so as not to lose any air bubbles. She felt drunk off the heady scents of bourbon and chocolate.

While the chocolate bourbon cake was baking in the oven, she took the two genoise out of the oven and left them to cool on an airing rack. She mixed two fresh batches of double cream, and added spinach essence to the second, so it took on a subtle, elegant pea green color, then she set both to chill in the fridge. After that she prepared a plate of sliced strawberries and tomatoes in three different colors.

"Hikaru, they're mostly done!" she called. "Just cooling down and only the decorations left. Was it boring to wait?" She brought the plate out to Hikaru. He was looking out through the window, but turned when she came in.

"No, it was fun to look at people walking past." He gave a shy smile. "I had a peek at you while you were baking too. You looked like an orchestra conductor, making so many different things at the same time. It was cool."

Hana laughed. "You're the cool one, not me. You have so many talents; whiskey, specially-bred apples, and grilled oranges! I'd never heard of that before you showed me." Her eyebrows squeezed together as she had an idea. "I'll have to make a grilled orange cake."

"Sounds good," said Hikaru, though his gaze was drifting back out through the window.

"What's out there?" Hana asked. She sat down by his side and leaned close to Hikaru to peer out at the street, but she couldn't see anything.

Hikaru smiled, and turned to her. They were sitting pretty close, but his eyes had a strange faraway look. "I was just wondering. What do you normally think about when you're walking on the street?"

Hana thought for a second. "Well... sometimes I think about stuff, but mostly I think about nothing. At least I think so. Why?"

"No reason. I was just watching these people, and wondering what kind of worries or concerns they had." He itched his cheek. "What if the inside of this shop and the outside of this shop are different worlds? I read a book like that, once. What if a sixty-year-old version of me was looking at me right now. What would happen? What would he say to me? I'm just curious."

Hana smiled. "I think you're doing great. Everything's going well. Sixty-year-old gray-haired Hikaru would say that too, I think."

His big black eyes sparkled. "Do you think so?"

She nodded firmly. "I definitely think so."

"And where would you be at that time?" he asked, eyes so wide it seemed she might fall into them. "Do you think we'll still be sitting next to each other like this?"

Her heart fluttered. She didn't know what to say, and felt her cheeks starting to burn. "Well, let me finish the cakes first. I'll think about sixty-year-old me when we taste them. Now," she pointed, trying to avoid getting flustered, "what kind of strawberries are these?"

Hikaru's eyes danced with amusement, but he turned to the strawberries. "They're called Aiberries. 'Ai' means love, you know? They're bigger and juicier than normal strawberries. They have a good shape and the taste is a perfect balance between sweetness and sourness."

Hana ignored the talk about 'Ai' and took a big bite; the sweet and sour juices burst in her mouth. "You're right, they're absolutely sweet and juicy. I feel sorry putting them inside the cake. They should be the star of any dish."

Hikaru shrugged. "Well, they're freshly picked this morning, and I chose the biggest and best-looking ones for you."

That look was back in his eyes even stronger now. Hana hurried on. "Well, thank you. What about these tomatoes?" She picked up a sliced yellow plum tomato.

"These are sun sugar tomatoes," Hikaru said smoothly. "They're sweeter and less sour than normal tomatoes, as you can imagine from their name." He took the tomato slice from her hand, letting his fingers linger over hers. "I planted three colors this time. I don't pick them early or let them after-ripen. I pick them once they're properly ripe. It takes longer to grow that way but it tastes much deeper and the texture is much better too."

Abruptly he took a bite. Hana felt startled.

"I see," she managed. "Well, they have lovely colors and they do taste great. You go ahead, have some of these and wait just a little bit longer. I'll put icing on, then it's all done."

He took another big bite, looking her right in the eyes. She hurried back into the kitchen, heart skittering madly. It took her a second to re-focus on the task at hand, breathing deeply. She turned the oven off and left the chocolate cake to cool down inside. She sliced the genoise cakes into three layers each, then spread whipped vanilla cream and sliced Aiberries into one, with the best-looking whole Aiberries and piped whipped cream on top, dusted over with icing sugar that looked like snowflakes falling on red snowmen. She spread and piped the pea-colored whipped cream into the spinach genoise, along with sliced sun sugar tomatoes instead of strawberries. She decorated the top with more green cream, three different tomato slices and a garnish of peppermint leaves.

Last of all she took the cooling bourbon chocolate cake out of the warm oven. The top was slightly sunken and cracked, but it looked natural and rich, so she only sprinkled it with a light coat of icing sugar. She put the three cakes on cake stands and brought them out to the shop.

"Hikaru, they're all finished now."

He jumped up to help her get them situated in the showcase, side by side behind the counter. Hana started talking fast as they twisted one cake this way, nudged that cake that way. "After this I'll add the information and price to the blackboard," she sped on. "I'll change the menu regularly based on seasonal fruits and vegetables from your farm, and tell customers through my blog so they can pre-order other cakes in advance."

By now she'd found the perfect position for all three cakes, but still she kept turning them slightly, her hands occasionally touching Hikaru's. "Once you harvest your new apples, I'll make apple pies and add them to the menu. I'll also bake peach and fig tarts when the season comes." She pulled away from the showcase, and Hikaru followed. They were standing very close together now, looking right at each other.

"What do you think?" she asked.

"I think they look splendid," Hikaru said, without looking at the cakes. "Your customers are going to love them. It's also a good idea to change the menu regularly, then customers will be excited to see what comes next." He paused, looking deep into her eyes. "It can be a good marketing tool too."

"Great," Hana said, too fast and too loud, then ducked back into the showcase to cut the cakes and put a piece of each one on a plate. "Shall we taste these now?"

She bustled away from behind the counter, laying the cakes out by the window. Hikaru came to sit beside her. The surface of each cake shone in the morning light, perfectly clean and smooth.

"Please tell me the truth," Hana said. "You can be brutal."

Hikaru put the cakes in his mouth one by one, and Hana felt her nerves fraying while he slowly chewed and tasted. He also didn't forget to drink water after tasting each cake to clear his palate. Every second was agony for Hana.

"Can I be honest with you?" he said, after thinking for a while.

"Of course." Hana nodded eagerly. She suddenly felt extremely thirsty.

He closed his eyes then opened them again. "This is not a lie. This is my true feeling. I'd be delighted to have these cakes every day for the rest of my life. The genoise are fluffy and airy. The icing is not too heavy or greasy and elegantly sweet, so the strawberries and tomatoes become the star. Their textures and the cakes are well balanced. I can imagine the elderly would prefer the tomato cake and young people would like the strawberry cake. And this bourbon chocolate cake?" he paused for a moment, maybe trying to find the right words. "What can I say. I'm speechless. It smells so gorgeous. Such a lovely fragrance from the chocolate and the bourbon. It tastes spot on, too."

Hana let out a breath. Her heart was hammering in her chest. "Oh, that's a big relief. Your ingredients did everything, so I didn't have to do much at all."

After that Hana and Hikaru displayed jams and cookies on the shelves, then put price tags on all the items as well as listing them on the blackboard. Hana added some drawings of heart-shaped Aiberries and fat sun sugar plum tomatoes too. At the bottom Hana wrote the message: 'All Tokyo Bicycle Bakery items are made with organic fruits and vegetables from the Kato farm in Chiba.' She also added a sketch of Miyo's face.

"I think it's ready to go," Hana said, putting her chalk down.

"It's perfect."

"Would Ms. Kawanami be happy?"

Hikaru beamed. "Absolutely, she'd be so proud of you."

Hana beamed too. They were standing close together again now, next to the blackboard in the back of the shop. It had grown dark outside and she hadn't even noticed. A shiver ran up her spine. She thought about what he'd asked her earlier that day, about where they'd be at sixty years old. It seemed so very far away, but maybe...

"If I didn't have you, I would never have come this far," she said. "I don't know how to thank you."

Hikaru reached out to gently touch her shoulders. His touch felt electric even through her thin orange cotton dress. "If you hadn't come to see me on that rainy night, I think I would have been lost." He was so close now; she felt the heat coming off his skin. "What are you... thinking now?" he whispered.

"Perhaps... the same thing as you?" Hana whispered back. His eyes were so large and dark, and loomed larger as he leaned closer. She leaned in too, and their lips met in the middle. The kiss was as warm, sweet and soft as a perfectly baked genoise.

Epilogue

The Tokyo Bicycle Bakery was a big success. Hana's blog followers, Ms. Kawanami's regular customers and word of mouth made her shop popular quickly. Amy from the blog came with her boyfriend, and wrote a great review on her blog too. Hikaru's vegetables and fruits grew popular alongside her cakes. Hana was kept busy thinking of new recipes every day. The bourbon chocolate cake became the signature cake of her shop, and was featured in various magazines as 'Tokyo's Best Kentucky Bourbon Flourless Chocolate Cake'. A photo of Hikaru's Uncle Jack, Kentucky bourbon distiller, was added to many of the articles.

Jack himself came to visit Japan, half a century since his first visit when he'd spent time with Hikaru's grandfather. He joined in on press interviews with Hana and Hikaru, laughing happily each time. He'd never expected his handmade bourbon would become so popular in Japan, and said he felt he was reborn, becoming like a young guy again.

Mr. Kimura took the photos for the articles in the magazines. Hana hung an enlarged photo of Jack wearing his cowboy hat in a field of grain on the wall of her bakery, next to a photo of Hikaru on the Kato farm, standing under an apple tree surrounded by white and pink apple petals, holding a bushel of his own experimental apples. In between those photographs hung a black-and-white picture of Ms. Kawanami's old vegetable shop. It always seemed to Hana that Ms. Kawanami would walk out through the shop and start sweeping the street any minute.

Hana opened baking classes twice a month after the shop was closed, on Nok's recommendation.

"Hana, don't worry," she said cheerfully on the phone. "I'll organize everything. You just focus on teaching." Nok was happy to manage the cooking classes. She also helped with newsletters, emails and social media marketing. She even recommended the Tokyo Bicycle Bakery to her friends, so Hana had lots of international customers as well as locals. Sometimes Hikaru joined special classes on organic fruits and vegetables, always bringing the ingredients for the cakes himself, along with a sample of earthworm soil from his farm.

Watching him stand in the shop and talk about his passion for farming always brought a fresh surge of excitement in Hana's chest.

"Your food waste is the perfect ingredients for compost," he'd say, standing in front of an audience of old ladies, students and a few businessmen. "Earthworms love to eat it and make eco-friendly organic soil. All the fruits and vegetables in the Bicycle Bakery were grown with organic farming techniques. You can grow delicious tomatoes and strawberries even on your balcony, with just a little of this quality compost."

The students always paid attention to every single word that Hikaru said, taking notes vigorously. One time Hana's other Sakura Japanese school friends joined the class, and afterward they shared pancakes with sweet potato purée and caramel filling.

"This is a perfect collaboration between female and male energy!" Mr. Abe exclaimed enthusiastically after tasting the pancake. Nok brought her signature vegetable spring rolls and milk puddings too, so everyone shared them as well. Leo sat on Nok's knees and smiled happily while enjoying the soft milk pudding.

It was almost too good to be true for Hana. Everything was like a dream, but it was real. She'd made it happen and she appreciated and enjoyed every bit of it. She donated ten percent of her profits to Ms. Oyama family's orphanage, as a small return for the people who'd supported her. Hikaru planted flower and tomato seeds with the kids in the back garden of the bright pink orphanage. Soon beautiful flowers would bloom in the fall.

Back in Korea, Hana's dad made such a good recovery that both he and her mom came to visit her in Japan and check on her. After seeing the shop and tasting the cakes, her mom gave a huge, warm hug.

"Hana, I'm so proud! I can't believe you've done all this by yourself."

Hana smiled. "I'm not alone. I've got so many great friends to support me, and Hikaru too. I could never have done it without their help."

Her dad's eyes shone with proud tears. "Hana. I'm so glad you listened to your heart and followed your dreams. I can see you're living today and tomorrow to the full."

The days flew by. Every day most of the cakes sold out. Every day Hana closed up the shop and went upstairs, where Hikaru was sometimes waiting for her, some delicious dinner on the table, ready to enjoy it together. Most days they held hands and talked and kissed late into the night.

One day was different. It was 7 o'clock, time to close the shop. It had been another busy but great day. It was quiet outside in the market street, growing dark as the spring sun sank. Hana checked the invoices of the items she'd sold that day, cleaned the showcase and swept the floor, watered the plants and wiped the peppermint's leaves with a damp cloth. She fetched the Martin vintage guitar, sat on the small chair in the corner and started to play Priscilla Ahn's 'Lullaby' slowly. The guitar had a pure, resonant sound. When she was about to sing along, the wind chime under the glass door rang musically.

"Excuse me." It was a young guy's calm and low voice. It had grown dark in the shop, and Hana couldn't see his face clearly, but he was a tall and thin guy with long hair.

She stood up and placed the guitar down on the chair. "Sorry, the shop is closed for today. Please come back tomorrow."

"I'm here to try the best chocolate bourbon cake in the world."

There was something familiar about his voice, and Hana's heart skipped a beat. He felt like a wind blown from the other side of the world. No matter what had happened between them, he would always remain her best friend. They stood there looking at each other for a long moment, until Hana's face cracked into a warm smile. Out through the window, white cherry blossom petals fell like fluffy snowflakes from the dark sky.

THE END

EXTRAS

Thank you for reading The Tokyo Bicycle Bakery. I hope you enjoyed it. If you'd like to know when Su Young's next sweet, slightly surreal book is out, please check the website below.

https://suyoungleesblog.wordpress.com

-    Su Young Lee

ACKNOWLEDGEMENTS

Thanks to Mike for supporting me all the way through, Jess and Matt for reviewing and sharing feedback, and Linc and Church for being cute and lovely.

- Su Young Lee

ABOUT THE AUTHOR

Su Young Lee is a Korean romance author who lived in Tokyo, Japan for 10 years and now lives in London, England with her husband and two lovely cats.

Su works in academic publishing and loves baking, playing piano and working on her calligraphy.

FICTION

The Tokyo Bicycle Bakery

NON-FICTION

Korean Story Box

Printed in Great Britain
by Amazon